# ARC OF LIGHT

## LINDA JANE ROBERTS

1977

MYSTICAL RABBITS
CRYSTAL LIGHT PRESS

Printed in Victoria, Canada

Published in Association with Mystical Rabbits Crystal Light Press

Illustrations by Linda Jane Roberts and Heather Fisher

National Library of Canada Cataloguing in Publication Data

A cataloguing record for this book that includes the U.S. Library of Congress Classification number, the Library of Congress Call number and the Dewey Decimal cataloguing code is available from the National Library of Canada. The complete cataloguing record can be obtained from the National Library's online database at: www.nlc-bnc.ca/amicus/index-e.html

ISBN 1-4120-2520-6

This book was published on-demand in cooperation with Trafford Publishing. On-demand publishing is a unique process and service of making a book available for retail sale to the public taking advantage of on-demand manufacturing and Internet marketing. On-demand publishing includes promotions, retail sales, manufacturing, order fulfilment, accounting and collecting royalties on behalf of the author.

Suite 6E, 2333 Government St., Victoria, B.C. V8T 4P4, CANADA

| | | | |
|---|---|---|---|
| Phone | 250-383-6864 | Toll-free | 1-888-232-4444 (Canada & US) |
| Fax | 250-383-6804 | E-mail | sales@trafford.com |
| Web site | www.trafford.com | TRAFFORD PUBLISHING IS A DIVISION OF TRAFFORD HOLDINGS LTD. |
| Trafford Catalogue #04-0348 | | www.trafford.com/robots/04-0348.html |

10        9        8        7        6        5        4        3        2

The Kingfisher waits
For the return of his Lord

My son, Pendaran, encouraged me to complete this book. I am thankful he was determined that I should. This book is dedicated to him, as without him I would not have completed it in an edited form. Our Creation inspired me and a wild Raccoon, Opossum and Groundhog, who befriended me years ago and gave me the idea of a mysterious adventure including them.

Linda Jane Roberts
October 2002

# Table of Contents

# Chapter ONE

## Moonbeam

*It was possible* in the moonlight to see the tops of the trees beyond Deer Meadow and, yet again beyond those the rippling silver of the Potomac River or Silversheen as the Garden Animals called it. Few from The Garden wandered that way anymore. By day men came and went that way hauling timber and corn to the head of the canal. There they loaded them on flat-boats and poled or pulled them to the wharf at River Cove where they were loaded on large sailing vessels that filled the sky with billowing, white sails and the loud shouts of workmen, or so the Garden Creatures had been told; they had never been there. And then by night it was difficult to follow the trails along the Wood's edge unless you were used to traveling in darkness like the Raccoon or Opossum. But the Garden Raccoons never traveled to Silversheen on account of a fierce battle with the Bridge Raccoons of the Great Dark Forest Bridge many, many Winters ago. "Brigands!" Father Bright-Eye had called them then and the name had stuck in The Garden, and dark tales had grown and grown until even the Red Field Fox was scared to wander that way either by day or by night.

Nevertheless, Moonbeam always looked that way with longing. It was not that he was a restless sort of Raccoon, anxious for danger and excitement as his cousin Swiftpaws had been. It was not even that he was particularly curious about what was beyond The Garden where he was born and raised. It was instead that he was fascinated by stories of The King of The River who lived on the banks of Silversheen and who traveled, it was rumored, as far inland as the Great Forest Bridge.

"How courageous he must be!" remarked Moonbeam for the fourth time turning in the walnut tree to get a better view of the back door of the Great House.

"The King of The River you mean I suppose?" said Ringtail solemnly lifting his tail gracefully out of his way and staring at the door.

"Yes, how brave to face the Bridge Family all alone in the darkness of the Great Dark Forest!" exclaimed Moonbeam excitedly. "Tell me again how The King looks." He added softly, his eyes glistening again with expectation. How often he had heard the description, and how little it tired him, how much it thrilled him!

Ringtail sighed. "I have told you so often Moonbeam," he said a little chidingly. But he looked at Moonbeam's dreamy and excited eyes and had not the heart to refuse. "He wears, or so the legends say, flowing robes of brilliant blue, bound up at the neck with a collar of silver-white gems like smooth crystals in a stream-bed. His crown is studded with sapphire and jet that glisten in the moonlight; and he is more fleet-footed than the Deer and swifter than the Swallow; and his call can be heard throughout all the Five Worlds."

Moonbeam gripped the branches beneath his feet more tightly and stared towards Silversheen with longing eyes that shone in the darkness like fire.

Ringtail was alarmed by that fire; "You know what happened to Swiftpaws!" he chided touching Moonbeam's shoulder sternly.

Moonbeam nodded. But he did not know. In fact, no one in The Garden did, but it had become traditional to say "You know what happened to Swiftpaws!" when anyone showed that restless flame in their eyes and talked about traveling. Moonbeam, to his own annoyance, had found himself saying it once or twice to the younger animals along Boxwood Way whose view of the world was even narrower than his own. He, at least, wandered in the woods and had crossed Deer Meadow to Cedar Dip and Whiteoaks.

"Hush! Her she comes!" whispered Sniffer excitedly turning a full circle on the branch of the Walnut Tree.

Moonbeam turned again to stare at the back door of the Great House. Outlined in the light he saw The Girl. "How beautiful she is!" he said dreamily. Her dark auburn hair hung in cascades to her waist like trailing dark blossom. Her green robes flowed out behind like billowing Willow branches in the breeze. Her eyes, as blue as Summer day-sky, were full of comfort and quiet friendship, and she smelt as always of fresh baked cookies and creamy chocolate. He could hear her calling softly as she came, as she always did; and as she placed the cookies beneath the Walnut Tree she looked at them and smiled.

"How like a princess! How like a queen!" Moonbeam exclaimed to himself with joy as he began to climb down the tree. He would go down to her. He was not afraid of her – the Golden One - as the Garden Creatures called her. Did she not come to them as a messenger from the world of the Great House bearing gifts for his own world? Had she, he wondered, staring deeply into her dark blue eyes, seen The King of The River in his sapphire and jet crown? Somehow he thought she had for in her eyes were both contentment and adventure, and he had heard stories that told she traveled by day alone along the Old Wharf Road and that she even had crossed the Great Dark Forest Bridge. "My Moon-Eyes!" she called to him softly.

～⒭

"It is a long way to Silversheen," Uncle Sharp-Ears said with concern, "and a goodly portion of the way is dangerous unless you have pacts with the Bridge Family and the Red Fox. Besides, there are men too along the canal, even by night. They sleep along the banks in Spring and Summer. They have dogs. I have heard too that the Great Dark Forest Bridge is mysterious, even magical. The water below is as black as poisonous Nightshade juice."

Moonbeam shifted his weight irritably. He wanted so much to go to Silversheen, and everyone was so against it! "Perhaps that is all tales!" he cried cheerily; "We have heard nothing from the Bridge Family in a long time. Perhaps they are gone!"

"I doubt it!" exclaimed Ringtail impatiently. He was growing more and more alarmed each moment by all this talk about the Great Dark Forest, Silversheen and the Bridge. "Besides, the way is unmarked now. There are no winding tracks along the ground, not even in Autumn."

"Isn't there a map?" asked Moonbeam a little surprised. "Our family used to go to Silversheen in Great-Grandfather Climber's day to look for fish and to wander along the river's edge. I have heard that they even went as far down as Moonlight Inlet where the first sliver of dawn could be seen.

"How long ago! How long ago!" sighed Uncle Sharp-Ears; "There are no maps now! You know what happened to Swiftpaws!"

Moonbeam sighed impatiently. "What did happen?" he exclaimed swinging round swiftly and lashing his long, thick tail.

Everyone in the Den fell silent. Eyes met eyes and quickly darted away. Paw moved anxiously against the earth floor. No one had ever asked that question before. No one had ever dared.

"Well?" cried Moonbeam irritably looking around at each of them.

"It is not for me to tell you." Remarked Sharp-Ears solemnly, dipping his head as if in sorrow, "He never returned that's all."

Those words filled everyone with fear. Their eyes widened in horror. Moonbeam frowned deeply.

But when Dawn came, flushing the sky with brilliant silver so bright that Moonbeam had to close his eyes, he was filled again with the same longing. Perhaps Swiftpaws did not return because he did not want to. Perhaps he supped now every night at the court of The King of The River and wore blue robes and a golden crown. Or perhaps he lived by the white sands of Moonlight Inlet and rose each day to watch the sun flood the woods with glorious red and orange and then fell asleep in the first silver glow of Dawn's light. How easy to live there, right at the water's edge, where fish and crayfish were aplenty, and nuts and berries and roots thrived along the banks in the warm sunlight. Moonbeam licked his lips.

"Perhaps Old Grandfather The Fisher would know the way." He said to himself touching his forehead with a pointed finger, "He knows everything there is to know about fish and fishing. Surely he know about Siversheen and The Old Wharf Road."

It was not too far to Old Grandfather The Fisher's. One left The Garden on the west side and skirted the woods on the east until one came to the Deer Meadow. And then, if it was daylight or bright moonlight, one raced breathlessly across the open spaces to Cedar Dip and Whiteoaks. From there one followed a covered trail to a narrow creek that ran down into the woods.

Old Grandfather The Fisher sat as usual on the green bank staring down into the shallow water. The water glistened faintly in the moonlight, and, as a sort of greeting, Moonbeam bathed his hands in it lovingly. Nothing felt better than the smooth coolness of the water as it dripped through his fingers to make small circles in the creek below. The circles widened outwards around him as he watched. He felt as if he stood on the silver surface of the moon.

"I cannot fish as I used to," said the Grandfather with a melancholy sigh, "My hands are not as strong; my feet are less sure on the rocks; my eyesight is dim. But I can still hear the fish, nonetheless, skimming by me, skirting the rocks and circling the reeds, and, if I am very patient and very quiet, I do well enough."

Moonbeam continued to stare at the water and to stroke it with his hands. The pebbles felt delightfully smooth under his feet, and they glistened in the moonlight like the shiny backs of swift moving trout in clear water. "My father took fishing lessons from you when he was young." Whispered Moonbeam excitedly without looking up.

"Ah, yes!" replied the Old Grandfather dreamily, remembering the days of his own youth and the small Fishing School he had started at the creek head not far from there. "Your father was a lively fisher!" he exclaimed somewhat reproachfully, "Too restless, much too restless, to fish really well. Now me, I can stand for moons and moons, Spring after Spring, watching and watching." He stared into the water cherishingly as if his whole world was there on those gently ripples for all to see.

"You love the water?" questioned Moonbeam sensing a good opening for questions about Silversheen.

"Who of our kind does not?" Old Grandfather The Fisher answered softly, "What more in life could anyone want than to feel that coolness and smoothness, than to hear that gurgling voice calling across Deer Meadow and The Gardens?" He moved to the water's edge again and paddled in with a thrill that time could never lessen.

"And have you fished in other places?" Moonbeam asked hesitantly, drawing himself up to his full height and tilting his ears so he would not miss a word, "Have you journeyed far beyond Cedar Dip and Whiteoaks? Have you past Chestnut Ridge say or Poplar Grove?"

Old Grandfather The Fisher turned and smiled knowingly. He had not lived this long not to sense when a youngster was thinking of journeys to far off exotic places with wonderful names that rolled off the tongue and filled the heart with restless longing; "Of what do you think, young Moonbeam?" he asked swiftly with a touch of humour in his voice.

"I?" questioned Moonbeam lazily while he paddled about nonchalantly and tried to act as if he did not care, "Nothing; nothing at all. I just wondered. That's all."

"Do you think of swift streams in emerald forests or of wide rivers that shine like polished sea shells in the moonlight? Do you dream of clear, bubbling springs surrounded by wild Moccasin flower and fluffy laurel flowers or of dark seas pounding the shore like your own heartbeat?" Old Grandfather The Fisher asked solemnly.

The call of a Whip-o-will filled the night like a longing sigh, and Moonbeam's eyes widened in wonder. He imagined the river The Grandfather described pulsing brightly before him, journeying on and on until it met the deep, green sea, swirling on bright, white sands like transparent dragonfly wings. He was overcome again with his desire to see The King of the River, and, although he had not intended to tell his dream, he said quietly, hauntingly, "I think of The King of the River."

Old Grandfather The Fisher sighed, "In my youth I did the same. It is a wonderful idea, and far better than any other, for The King of the River, legend tells, is the greatest of fishermen, uncompared in all the Five Worlds from The Garden to Silversheen itself."

Moonbeam gasped. "He fished too?" he asked with surprise and delight. "He fished like us, like an ordinary Raccoon?"

"So stories tell," whispered The Grandfather as if he feared to talk too loudly of their ideas; as if he feared they would destroy it. "He is the King of all fishers. The Martens call him the Fisher-King. Why! When I am unable to catch as I used to do, I imagine him there before me and the mere thought inspires me!" He sat back and lifted his hands to his face and stared into them. "It is remarkable how much I have caught while imagining him!"

"But how does he come before you?" whispered Moonbeam, looking at Old Grandfather The Fisher in wonder. "Is he dressed in blue? Does he wear a crown?"

The Old Grandfather looked at Moonbeam with a puzzled expression on his face. His eyes widened and his whiskers twitched. "It is hard to say," he said seriously, and he placed a finger to his mouth in thoughtfulness. His eyes shifted from side to side as if he was searching through all his experiences and memories for the right description but could find none that would really do. But then, suddenly he brightened and smiled: "He comes and goes in a flash of blue and white and midnight blue like the sight of periwinkles when the moon dips in and out of drifting clouds."

Moonbeam stared. "Oh!" he exclaimed breathlessly.

"Yes, it is quite beautiful." Said The Grandfather slowly, realizing again how much his idea had meant to him through all the long, cold winters spent mostly sleeping in his den.

"But how does one get to Silversheen?" asked Moonbeam suddenly, rather loudly. He was not content to just sit and think. He wanted to see this King of all the fishers. He wanted to greet him and tell him about The Garden and all the creatures there who talked of him.

Old Grandfather The Fisher looked alarmed. Dreams, after all, were one thing, and in their way quite alright, but pointed questions about how to travel to Silversheen, the farthest point in the Five Worlds, was quite another. "Too far! Too far!" he cried anxiously, "Too far for Garden Creatures or Deer Creatures or even for those of Poplar Grove and Chestnut Ridge. It does not bear thinking of."

"But I do!" cried Moonbeam impatiently, "I think about it every evening – all the time!"

Old Grandfather The Fisher turned away from him and paddled back into the cool water as if he did not want to talk about such dangerous and difficult matters. The world at the Creek was pleasant, familiar. Here there was no Bridge Family, no foxes, no dogs and very, very few men. Even the winter was calm and safe once he was cuddled down in his snow-covered den which no one, not even his many fisher-students, had ever found.

"It is a very large world out there Moonbeam," The Grandfather said solemnly as if warning Moonbeam against even the thought of traveling, "Silversheen is part of a dark, deep sea that goes on forever and ever. It may begin a pretty, shallow blue, but it soon turns to dark greens and greys that crest in huge waves." He stressed each word as he spoke as if no one could go to Silversheen without ending up far out to sea, never to be heard of again. "You know what happened to Swiftpaws!" he added with a chiding nod.

Moonbeam shrugged his shoulders, signed and turned to leave. Perhaps, he thought, he should forget all idea of seeing The King of the River. Perhaps it really was too far, too unknown, too dangerous. He padded back up hill to The Garden unhappily. The Garden felt somehow small and confining now. The Boxwoods, the flowers, the deep grasses, the Cherry trees, which had all always brought him such joy, seemed plain now like cut-out from winter leaves, drifting in muddy water or held up against a grey sky.

He sat down at the top of the hill, at the bottom of The Garden and stared out across the treetops in the moonlight. As he did so, he heard a scurrying among the leaves and a lot of sniffing. Moonbeam looked about sharply and hunched his body ready to run if need be. Something bright white, shining in the moonlight like a new duck's egg, ran out from the undergrowth, trying as it ran to lift pink feet one at a time to its mouth. Moonbeam saw fresh, red berry-juice trickling between pink fingers and a small pink tongue licking round them. The creature moved forward to the edge of a clearing where moonlight flooded the ground, and Moonbeam saw a Opossum, rather plump but still quite young.

"Berries is it?" Moonbeam enquired gingerly still hunched ready to leave. He was not afraid of Opossums, but he was in no mood for quarrels this night. It would ruin his silvery river-dreams of the Fisher-King.

The Opossum looked at him gruffly and pursed his mouth. Now, the Opossum thought irritably, if I admit to the berries, the Raccoon will search them out and eat them, and if I do not, how shall I explain all this rich, bright berry-juice on my fingers. He scratched his head puzzledly and stared at Moonbeam without answering.

Moonbeam smiled at the puzzled, unfriendly expression on the young Opossum's face. "Don't worry," he said cheerily, "I was just a little lonely – only trying to make conversation you know. I've eaten already. Anyway, I much prefer fish." He lifted a front foot and patted his stomach reassuringly while nodding his head.

The Opossum frowned and ducked to the side as though he was not sure whether this might not be a clever trick. Raccoons were know for higher spirits and sharper wits than any other creature in all the Five Worlds whether of The Garden, The Wood, The Creek, The Forest or The River. He stared into Moonbeam's eyes as if trying to catch him out in his cunningness and still said nothing.

"Well, if you don't want to talk, there is no need. Continue on your way! I shan't trouble you!" Moonbeam said a little irritably. He turned away to look again at the tree-tops with wide dreaming eyes.

The Opossum shrugged and lifted his front feet. "Well, its just that I usually don't," whispered the Opossum anxiously, looking about fearfully.

"Don't what?" asked Moonbeam a little exasperated. Was everyone going to be so difficult to talk to? Was there no on who would talk about the way to Silversheen and The King of The River? Suddenly Moonbeam remembered Ringtail, and he jumped up. Ringtail at least would describe those glorious blues and whites to him again and retell all the legends he knew that surrounded The River World. Ringtail could at least tell a good story even if it was just a story.

"Talk, talk much," muttered the Opossum with frightened eyes, pricking up his ears to catch each sound. The very sound of his own voice seemed to startle him.

"Well, perhaps that's wise," answered Moonbeam comfortingly. He suddenly felt rather sorry for the Opossum who always seemed to be on the move and who always seemed to be alone and never really secure. "We Raccoons talk too much anyway."

"Do you?" inquired the Opossum chidingly.

"Yes! Well, as a rule, but I tend to imagine more than the others, too much I suppose, but, then, its so hard not to." Moonbeam spoke now as if he was trying to understand himself and his feelings rather than answer the Opossum whose eyes, by the way, had grown large and round and limpid and quite impressed.

"Do you?" he exclaimed in quite a different tone than before. He started again at the sound of his own voice and swished his thin, pink tail.

Moonbeam felt sorry for him again now. How glad he was to have his own beautiful tail, circled with lovely, dark rings, that he could wrap around himself for warmth. He would not have liked to have a tail like Opossum's.

Opossum saw the critical stare and moved his tail behind himself self-consciously. How could he ever explain how useful his tail was in every way although quite lacking in beauty and grandeur. Raccoon's tail might have lushness and drama, but is was not useful like his tail. He could hang by his tail from tree branches, well out of the reach of his enemies, will all four legs free to ward off attack! What Raccoon's tail could do that?

"What do you think?" asked Opossum suddenly after several nervous moments of silence.

"Of the River, of Silversheen," answered Moonbeam without looking at him.

"Oh!" cried Opossum breathlessly, lifting his hands to his face.

Moonbeam turned to him; "Do you? Do you too—?" he muttered excitedly.

"Yes! Yes! Often!" exclaimed Opossum, "When I walk on warm summer nights along the Creek, I imagine – I imagine The River, and I pretend…" his voice trailed off suddenly as if he was embarrassed to say anymore. He looked at the ground.

"You pretend what?" asked Moonbeam encouragingly.

"I pretend – well, it's really rather silly," he said fidgeting and swaying from side to side.

"Yes?" said Moonbeam drawing nearer.

"Well, I pretend that I've seen pirates on The River, the rich, red, luscious berries the Fairies are said to have planted at Moonlight Inlet and, and – well – and – The King of the River!" Opossum said these last few words very hastily as if he didn't want Moonbeam to hear them. It was as if he had had a secret for many, many winters that he would rather have always kept to himself. He turned suddenly, and Moonbeam was afraid he was going to dart into the undergrowth and disappear.

"How lovely!" cried Moonbeam leaping forward to block his path. The Opossum was startled, even frightened, and he looked over his shoulder at Moonbeam with dark, sharp eyes and a drawn face. How he wished he had not fallen into this trap of telling ideas! How embarrassed he was now!

"The Fisher-King wears flowing robes of brilliant blue," Moonbeam cried out passionately. "At his neck he wears a collar of silver-white gems as smooth as crystals in a stream-bed. His crown is studded with sapphire and jet that glisten in the moonlight," Ringtail's words came pouring out like a bubbling spring. He had not realized how well he knew them before!

Opossum stared, "Have you seen him?" he asked enthusiastically but still in a whisper.

"Oh, no!" cried Moonbeam, "but I long to. I plan to travel to Silversheen and search for him. I plan to tell him about The Garden." Moonbeam had never before felt so sure that he would go – perhaps even tomorrow. There was something in the Opossum's manner that spurred him on. Perhaps it was knowing Opossum's secret thought and at the same time seeing his shyness, his fear, his reluctance to ever go to Silversheen. It made The Garden and the Deer meadow seem very small, and his familiar world suddenly seemed to close in around him and press on him. He longed to be free, to travel and adventure, see new places, smell new smells, see all the miraculous wonders of the world. He was restless now as Swiftpaws had always been; and perhaps, he thought shaking his head, he was really restless all the time!

Then in a sudden moment of inspiration and generosity, he flung an arm around the Opossum's shoulders and, pointing out across The Wood, sang out enthusiastically,

"Come, let's go, you and I,
Across the meadows green.
Come, let's go, you and I,
To bright, sparkling Silversheen."

Opossum flinched and looked quite frightened and, to escape Moonbeam's squeeze, flattened himself to the ground in a peculiar way. The grass was wet and cold underneath his stomach, and he began to shiver.

"Well, really! Can't a body get any sleep?" cried a voice with an exasperated sigh; "Do you have to sing at my door? Couldn't you move farther off?"

Moonbeam and Opossum searched the darkness with startled eyes. Then, just above them, a little towards The Wood, they saw a Flicker Woodpecker staring at them irritably from a hole in a large oak tree. His dark-black mustaches were twitching in annoyance, and he was turning his head from side to side, flashing the brilliant red at the nap of his neck in the moonlight. Moonbeam thought that his sharp face, black mustache and dramatic bib would make him look angry and serious at any time, and at that moment he looked so determined and ill tempered that young Moonbeam actually hunched a little and held onto Opossum tightly in anxiety.

Opossum squealed and flattened himself even further to the ground. He was dreadfully upset to be caught in such an embarrassing situation - being hugged by a Raccoon and talking about Kings. Nevertheless, he felt some comradeship with the Raccoon in their plight. The Flicker's indignant expression annoyed him. Did he think that he owned The Wood?

"We are planning a journey!" Moonbeam said defiantly, proudly, "All the way to Silversheen!"

"Well, and is there any need to be so noisy?" inquired the Flicker testily, drawing himself up until almost all his body could be seen in the moonlight. He was covered with spots, Moonbeam noticed, and not nice rings like himself.

"We are sorry and all that, of course," murmured Moonbeam reluctantly, "We got carried away. We got excited!"

"Well, well," muttered the Flicker, "but really it is a very improbable time to be talking of journeys. It is not yet quite Spring. I have no eggs. The weather is quite unreliable. The tracks are muddy. Now if only you could fly…" he rattled on vainly.

Opossum pulled himself up tightly. "We prefer to walk," he said quietly, but not in a whisper as usual. He stressed each word.

"Yes," said Moonbeam proudly, "the feel of the earth and pebbles and water beneath our feet is wonderful, and we like to see the flowers and grasses around us. We love it!"

"Well, well," exclaimed the Flicker in mock surprise, "You won't journey now in any case!"

Opossum was getting quite cross. Like all his kind he had a habit of losing his temper in short, sharp bursts, totally unexpected. "But we will!" he cried defiantly, and almost at once he regretted the words. He hoped that the Raccoon didn't really think he meant it. He really didn't want to travel, and in his heart of hearts he knew the Flicker was right.

"Well, in that case, you should visit Old Owl," the Flicker said quickly in a resigned tone, "Perhaps he will knock some sense into you or at least give you good directions."

"Does he know the way?" asked Moonbeam excitedly rushing forward and leaving poor Opossum to slink behind a log.

"Well, I don't hold with the idea he really knows," exclaimed Flicker in an annoyed voice, "I don't hold with the idea he is wiser than the other birds, but everyone will think that, and everyone will go to him all the time with this and that question, and this and that idea, and, in the course of things, of course, he finds out everything! I shouldn't like it at all. All those creatures forever at one's door gossiping and questioning. How exhausting!"

Moonbeam smiled to himself and touched his forehead in a friendly farewell, "Well, thanks for the tip anyway," he said cheerily.

"Well, well!" muttered the Flicker sounding both surprised and forlorn, "Well, well!"

# Chapter TWO

# South of the Sun

**O**possum didn't know how it happened. It may be that he could feel the piercing eyes of Flicker at his back and hear that, "Well, well!" every now and then; but he now found himself traveling to the Wise Old Owl's with Moonbeam. He promised himself he wouldn't go further than that, and he promised himself that, once out of Flicker's sight, he would turn back and go Home.

It was rather a long way to Owl's. They traveled in the direction where they usually saw the last shreds of evening light when they walked through forest. They crossed The Garden and then followed The Meadow Fence to the narrow woods just beyond the white and wooden work-cottages. Everywhere was very silent, and The Meadow glowed strangely in the moonlight. Damp with rain, it glistened like a shallow lake around which dark trees stood stark and bare in their winter nakedness. Here some holly leaves shone out like wet, mossy rocks in morning sunlight, and there pines bristled in the night breeze and shimmered with silver when the moonlight touched raindrops caught among their needles.

The winding trail to Owl's was well marked as it always was, whether Summer or Winter, sunlight or snowfall. Moonbeam and Opossum could clearly see and feel it beneath their feet. For as Flicker had rightly remarked every creature went to Owl's at one time of another for advice or out of curiosity.

Familiar and strange smells welled up around them as they scurried along.

Moonbeam smelt Weasel, Mouse and even Strew on the trail beneath him, and Opossum shivered and whined in recognition at the smell of a Fox. Here and there, where the earth was soft or muddy, they saw tracks, neat, dark impressions that told them more than smells every could.

"Here goes a Grouse in a hurry and not long after a Bobwhite who is unsure of his way," said Moonbeam softly trying to take Opossum's mind off the smell of the Fox.

"But didn't you see the tail mark of the bird landing in that mud over there and the wing marks where he took off again? He landed for barely five hops!" whined Opossum in a frightened voice, crouching as near to the ground as possible, "Something must have frightened him! Something big!"

"Why should it have been big Pos?" asked Moonbeam a little exasperated, "Don't let your imagination run away with you! Besides, all birds are asleep now but a few. He must have been here before our Rising-Time."

Opossum grunted, "But some hunt by night," he whispered anxiously, looking about sharply and slipping in some mud.

"Well, and here goes another of your kind Pos! Don't you see the tail-drag and the hind-foot beside the smaller front-foot as he ran?" Moonbeam said reassuringly, touching Opossum's shoulder.

"Yes! But he does run you see!" Said Opossum in a hurt voice. He did not like to appear less brave than another of his own kind.

A breeze shook raindrops from the trees on their backs and across the track in front. Moonbeam sniffed contentedly. He loved the fresh, cool smell that always seemed to perfume the air when rain gathered on growing things. It was as if the water itself was a silver key that unlocked the sweetness within things like a pirate opening a treasure chest full of gold and jewels. For Moonbeam the smells tumbled out around him in the depth of those woods as if that pirate had turned the chest upside down and let all the treasures fall around his feet.

Moonbeam smelt the still sap that lay deep down in living things waiting and waiting to surge upwards like a fountain in the Spring. He smelt the lushness of the grasses, not as a separate thing from their beautiful greenness but as part of the greenness itself. He could have closed his eyes and told anyone from smell alone whether what he held in his had was green or not, newly sprung from the earth or mature and full after many warm summers. Even deep in these woods he could still smell The Garden behind him and The Creek beyond that at the bottom of the hill.

"Well!" said Opossum in an irritated voice, "I do wish Porcupines would keep to their own tracks! They make such large, deep troughs in the ground. I have tripped up more than once!"

Moonbeam looked down at the round prints, alternating as usual, covered with a strange winding pattern that had been made by the Porcupine's tail. Each print was half full of rainwater, and Opossum's feet made a splashing sound when he accidentally stepped into one. He sighed loudly in an annoyed but resigned way as if to say "what we Opossums do have to put up with from others!"

Moonbeam laughed, "Couldn't you look where you are going and avoid Porcupine's tracks?"

"And not see what's going on about me!" wailed Opossum indignantly, "wouldn't that be a sure way to end up as Fox's dinner!"

Moonbeam smiled, "Well, Pos, I could keep a look-out and alert you, so to speak. I don't seem to have trouble with Porcupine's foot-prints. Aren't you rather exaggerating how large and deep they are?"

Opossum refused to answer, and Moonbeam began to wonder why he had ever encouraged Opossum to come with him to Owl's or why in the world Opossum had ever consented to it. Yet, like a miner spotting glistening diamonds in drab bedrock, Moonbeam sensed Opossum's excitement under all the irritation and reluctance. By now Opossum was covered with raindrops that sparkled when touched by moonlight. He looked as though he was bespangled with jewels and going to a feast.

Moonbeam thought that he looked very different, much more mysterious, magical and princely in this garment of raindrop gems. There was also something determined and positive about the quick way Opossum moved forward despite all the slips into foot-print holes.

"You know Pos," Moonbeam said in a dreamy voice but as though he was beginning to see things in a new light. "We may really do rather well in the end. We may really see The King of The River."

Again Opossum did not answer. He still had not decided to go journeying at all, but he did think he would rather like to see Owl. He had never seen him, and he had heard so much about him.

They walked on in silence, each lost in their own thoughts, when suddenly they heard a small but pompous voice exclaim, "Well! And if it isn't quite a procession!"

"Where? Where?" squeaked an even smaller voice, "Where? Where?"

Moonbeam and Opossum stopped still, listened, looked around and sniffed, but they could see nothing. A light pattering of rain combined with a fresh breeze mingled all the woodland smells together in a confusing way. They could smell Rabbits, Weasels, Mice and Mink all at the same time, and Moonbeam could even smell a Pheasant down by the Meadow fence.

"And would you be going to The Wise Old Owl by any chance?" questioned the first voice in a tone that implied the speaker knew rather a lot about the Owl, more than he was willing to tell.

"Are you? Are you?" asked the second voice sounding quite excited and awed.

Moonbeam sniffed and searched the shadows for what there could be no mistake about now, "It's only Moles who constantly ask questions like that," whispered Moonbeam to Opossum in a confiding way, "Usually impertinent ones too!" he added with a disdainful nod.

Opossum immediately felt very close to the Raccoon for he liked to think that he had a great deal more in common with a Raccoon than a Mole, despite his pink, furless tail and ears. Moles were so chattery, so frivolous, so unreliable, here one minute and gone the next! This talking from hiding places was a good example. Opossum was suddenly very proud to be on such an important quest. Going to Owl with questions about a journey to a King! He lifted his feel highly and walked down the woodland train with a newfound dignity and grandness which hid his growing tiredness so well that Moonbeam had no idea that Opossum was having difficulty keeping up. When opossum foraged at night, he usually did so in short, sharp bursts, stopping often to eat and rest and look around. He didn't have the energy of Raccoon or his ease of movement, and he especially didn't like being so wet underneath.

They were, however, quite near to Wise Old Owl's now. Animal scents were coming from all directions because creatures from every corner of the Five Worlds always joined the trail there to cover the last part of the journey to Owl's door. Ahead, Moonbeam saw a clearing. The wet grass looked like a small silver pond surrounded by shadowy banks and tall, dark trees in the moonlight. Above, the night sky was smoothly, bespangled with bright stars and streaked here and there with grey and silver clouds that looked to them like Thistledown or Willow branches in the wind and which haloed the moon with beautiful pastel shades.

Moonbeam looked up. "The halo!" he said pointing above them to the delicate colours glistening around the silver moon. "There must be snow there.

I remember there are always halos around the moon before cold snows, heavy falling snows, hard beneath my feet."

"Yes," murmured Opossum, "it is not a good sign although very lovely to look at." He stared up in wonder, refreshed a little by the beauty. "But I have never much minded the other kinds of snow, soft snow that lay in fluffy fullness over the earth, over my den doors. They protect me from the dry, chill wind and cover my tracks from the keen eyes of fox or hawk," Opossum sighed as he remembered a past less fraught with dangers and more full of the gentle comforts of home.

"Well, Pos," whispered Moonbeam as they stepped out into the grassy clearing, "You are not so far from any of your dens. You could easily be home by sunrise."

Opossum sighed again. He longed for home, and yet the idea somehow seemed boring too. He longed to cuddle down in his deepest, darkest, warmest den and tuck his nose under his paws and fall asleep, and yet he liked to see new places like this one, and he really rather liked the company of Raccoon. His own kind tended to be so solitary, so possessive of their dens and independence, so quarrelsome, especially in winter. He shivered as a gust of wind blew through the clearing, swaying the trees.

"You know," Opossum whispered, "I don't do well in the cold, I mean the coldest cold. There's no hair on my ears or tail or feet." He said all this in a hurt but confiding tone of voice as though he had been put together all wrong or cheated in some way. He eyed the Raccoon's thick coat and bushy tail with self-consciousness and a little envy.

Moonbeam did not know what to say, and it was some minutes before he could think of anything particularly comforting or helpful. "Well, you have good eyes Pos, and ears and nose, better than any Raccoon I shouldn't doubt, and you manage well on hot, summer nights when I am sweating and lazy from the heat."

Opossum nodded and smiled weakly. "Perhaps," he murmured unsurely still looking longingly at Moonbeam's soft, long fur as it shimmered in the moonlight.

Suddenly the clouds completely cleared and bright moonlight flooded the clearing. "Who, who?" came a voice from the other side of the clearing. "Who are you, you?" it called across to them. Neither Moonbeam or Opossum had ever visited an Owl before, but they knew the sound of his inquisitive voice, repeating the same questions in a demanding, somewhat superior tone, and they remembered having seen his silent, ghostly outline against the moon as he flew across The Gardens and The Deer Meadow towards Chestnut Grove on wide, still wings.

Opossum froze in fear. "Oh dear!" he whispered anxiously, "Has he seen us?"

Moonbeam stopped. He thought he could see a dark shape high up on a branch on the other side of the clearing. He suddenly felt uncomfortable and not a little afraid, but he swallowed hard and reminded himself that he had an important question that only Owl could completely answer. For Owls have stored up knowledge about the Five Worlds for winters and winters like squirrels hoarding nuts. Owl would surely know all about Silversheen and The King of the River. Moonbeam moved forward again uneasily.

"Who, who, who are you?" came the voice again, this time a little louder than before.

"Perhaps, we should call out our names from here," said Moonbeam to Opossum touching his shoulder firmly. "Perhaps that's only polite. Owl expects it I shouldn't doubt. Even now we may be in his territory."

Opossum flinched. How dreadful, he thought, to have to tell the whole of the Five Worlds that he was there, there in the center of a clearing for all to see! "I couldn't possibly do that," Opossum muttered in fright.

"Well, you stay here, and I'll go on ahead alone," said Moonbeam sounding very practical and grown-up.

"I couldn't possibly do that either," whined Opossum, remembering that Raccoon was his newfound friend and very special to him.

"Oh dear!" moaned Moonbeam sitting down with a bump and lifting his paws in disbelief, "Why ever not? You are difficult!"

"Oh, I know, I know." Wailed opossum but under his breath, "I'm such a problem. Oh, go ahead! Call out your name!" Opossum turned around and hid his face in his hands and tried not to squeal.

"Well not if it's going to upset you so much," said Moonbeam with irritation.

"Oh go on! Do!" Wailed Opossum tearfully. It was entirely against his nature to even contemplate yelling across open spaces, especially moonlit ones. He felt as if his whole world was about to fall apart.

Moonbeam ran forward. His eyes and nose shone with excitement. His whole body twitched as he sniffed in anticipation. "I am Moonbeam of the Garden Raccoons," he called out proudly standing on his back legs and opening his front paws wide as if imploring welcome from whoever watched him. "I have a question."

"Well, well, but who, who travels with you?" asked the Owl hauntingly.

"Oh dear!" said the Opossum, "Dear, dear, he has seen me!"

"It is just an Opossum," called Moonbeam hastily, "A friend who travels with me now for company."

"Come! Come! Both of you!" replied the Owl encouragingly. Moonbeam and Opossum moved forward cautiously, one step at a time. They did not like to be so far out in the open, lit up by moonlight, which sparkled on their noses and in their eyes and along the wet fur on their backs. Gradually, as they drew nearer, they were able to see the powerful and large shape of the Wise Old Owl among the branches of a gnarled oak tree. He stood squarely, his black eyes as still and round as two dark pebbles were circled by a gold as startling as buttercups in sunshine or yellow daisy centers in dark woods. His long ears jutted sharply and fiercely from above a wise oval face outlined dramatically by both white and black.

Moonbeam stared. Opossum started, "Oh dear!" he said again but this time with amazement and admiration.

"What can I do for you-ou-ou?" asked the Owl gravely, tilting his head to look down at them without moving any other part of his body.

"Well," said Moonbeam looking up and lifting his paws. He was startled to be talking to the wisest creature in all the Five Worlds.

Everything he had planned to say swam in confusion before him like tadpoles in a pond. "Well," he said again as he fished for the right beginning to explain his thoughts, "Well."

The Owl's ears twitched in anticipation, and his eyes grew rounder and rounder as he took on the usually quizzical and surprised expression he assumed when visited by other creatures. The dark bands of feathers above his eyes looked for all the world like two raised eyebrows, and the way his beak now tilted in towards his chin made him look both serious and short-tempered. Moonbeam was not sure that he liked that, but he tried to begin his sentence again for the forth time. Opossum was prodding him from behind and tilting his head encouragingly.

"Well, Pos and I have been thinking of The King of The River." Began

Moonbeam very hesitantly, stopping between almost every word to catch his breath and raise his courage.

"And you wish to see him," replied the Owl slowly and casually as if considering something very ordinary like a wish for fresh berries or a new, deep den.

"Well, yes," said Moonbeam, a little offended by the Owl's casualness. "We have heard he is…", Moonbeam was going to say, the most beautiful in all the Five Worlds, but he stopped himself suddenly, a little worried that Owl might not like to be considered less beautiful than The King of The River. He didn't think it would be wise to offend Owl when he wanted to ask him the way to sparkling Silversheen. "We have heard he lives in Silversheen," said Moonbeam clumsily, biting a finger.

Owl rolled his eyes. "You meant to say that you have heard he is the most beautiful creature in all the Five Worlds and that is true of course. My kind have not lived so long and gathered so much wisdom by denying what is true. The King of The River sparkles in Day's bright colours and his soul is cheerful and light like sunbeams that dapple our trees in these woods and gild the dew-decked spider's web of Spring's morning."

"Oh!" Moonbeam exclaimed in enthusiasm.

"But it is a dangerous undertaking," remarked the Owl mysteriously while looking searchingly into Moonbeam eyes, "It is not so much that the journey is a difficult one although it is indeed difficult. It is that what you will see will change your world for you, will change reality. You will not be the same Raccoon as you are now, and there are those who would find that uncomfortable, unpleasant. It is easier to remain in The Garden, to sleep in the same warm, familiar dens, to eat berries from the same trees, to dream the same dream night after night."

"But I shall always imagine the Fisher-King," exclaimed Moonbeam.

"No" said Owl with certainty, "once you have been to Silversheen, you will have a new idea, a greater one. One that grown naturally out of this one like a bright butterfly from a dry cocoon. There are many layers in you Moonbeam. This is just the first one, the simplest one. You do not yet know yourself, nor Opossum either."

Moonbeam was stunned. How could Owl know is name! Yet it seemed natural that he should for did not Owl continually glide over his world, searching out knowledge with piercing eyes and a curious mind, to carry and store it in some mysterious way only his kind knew. No doubt Owl had seen him in The

Meadow by The Creek and in the Walnut Tree. No doubt Owl always knew one day he would come here to him with this question.

"How do we go to Silversheen?" Moonbeam asked quickly, not wanting to hear anything more about danger and change.

"Follow the path of the morning sun from The Garden," said Owl seriously staring beyond them through the trees to The House, The Garden and Deer Meadow. Every detail of which, whether shape or colour, sound or smell, he knew by heart. "Keep to the high side of the water and cross any bridge before dusk, especially the Great Dark Forest Bridge which is high and dangerous and guarded by the Bridge Raccoons."

"But we cannot travel by day!" cried Moonbeam with alarm. Day's light is too bright and turned everything to a dazzling gold in which all shapes and colours are difficult to see.

"There will be another," said Owl mysteriously still staring beyond Moonbeam into the darkness, "Another shall go with you. He is almost awake."

"Who is he?" asked Moonbeam surprised and feeling peculiarly uncomfortable.

"I cannot say," said Owl oddly, "but he goes by Day's light, and he thinks as you do."

"How odd," muttered Opossum who had so far remained entirely silent. He did not particularly like any of the creatures who went by Day's light although it was true he actually had never seen very many of them. Anyway, he certainly had no intention of traveling by Day even if he went with Raccoon to Silversheen at all, which he doubted more and more every time the Owl spoke.

The Owl did not answer Opossum but turned his head one way and then the other as if he could hear something in the distance that bothered him. He gradually stretched his wings ready to fly.

"But where shall we find The King of The River?" cried Moonbeam afraid Owl would leave before he found out all he wanted to know.

"Where there is water and silence and sunlight. South of The Sun!" said Owl spreading his wings as wide as possible and tilting them upwards. Moonlight caught on the tips and traveled down each shaft until Owl looked as if he was wearing shining silver robes, graciously trimmed with glass raindrops. Opossum's eyes widened in wonder. "Go to The Garden! Wait for morning!" Owl said, and he lifted off the branch silently and rose and rose and rose into the air until he was nothing more than a dark speck against the silver moon. "Who! Who! Who are you?" he called down as he glided high in the night sky across the woods towards The Garden and The Deer Meadow.

# Chapter THREE
## In the Morning Light

**M**oonbeam and Opossum decided to wait for dawn before settling down to sleep in one of Moonbeam's Garden dens not far from the Walnut Tree where The Girl came. They planned to memorize the exact direction of the first tip of the sunrise and the way the sun's rays traced across the treetops, and then travel that way by night. It was not the first dawn sky Moonbeam had ever seen. Sometimes, too excited to sleep, he watched the night sky turn slowly silver, then white, then blue as the sun rose, and he knew well that when that dawn sky flamed red and orange with such brilliance that he was forced to close his eyes and go to his den. It usually meant that it would rain while he slept, perhaps even storm, and that when he woke puddles of water might trickle into his sleeping area and logs and branches cover his den entrance.

In contrast, this was almost the first dawn that Opossum had ever seen. Usually, when the faintest sliver of silver appeared on the horizon, he scurried home in an agitated flurry, muttering to himself about the frightening creatures of Daylight's World, all of which had grown and grown in terror and strangeness in his mind over the long Winters, until the mere mention of them sent him shaking. What he actually imagined would be hard to describe. It was anyway everything that Opossums do not care for, jumbled up in a nightmare in which the Fox walked stealthily and bright light hid everything from view. In fact, during the day, Opossum imagined that part of the world that pleased, berries, nuts, juicy roots, savory herbs, all disappeared.

It was therefore not without a great deal of anxiety that Opossum considered the journey that Moonbeam was now enthusiastically planning. The Raccoon was running this way and that, moving this and that thing, denning things up, digging out stores, hiding precious nick-nacks that he feared to leave unguarded and crying out "Ah-ah!" in a practical way every time he entered on another feverish burst of activity. Opossum was getting quite dizzy from watching, and he also felt rather sad when he realized that he couldn't remember having any such objects in his own dens. He didn't exactly have the Raccoon's inclination to collect smooth trinkets and colourful baubles, and now, for some reason, he wished he had a few to worry about and fuss over. He might even have used his fear of losing them as an excuse to remain behind. He was still thinking very seriously about excuses, but for some reason, he never finished explaining them to the Raccoon and ended by looking wide-eyed and rather odd. He did, he thought ruefully, feel very odd.

"I can't imagine why you keep all this junk!" he remarked petulantly, swishing his tail. He was growing more and more irritated with himself that he had ever got into this nuisance of journeying.

"Junk! Junk!" cried Moonbeam, "Where is there junk? Have you no appreciation of Beauty, of works of Art?"

Opossum looked at a collection of bright buttons of all different sizes that lay in disarray along an earthen shelf.

"Well, those for example," said Opossum pointing at them. "What good are those?"

"Good!" exclaimed Moonbeam running to the shelf. "Feel their smooth sides," he chimed clutching a yellow button in his paws lovingly. "They are smoother than sea shells in water! See the bright buttercup yellow, round like owl eyes!" Moonbeam thrust the button towards Opossum, but Opossum did not take it. He sighed and waved it away casually.

"Well, you can't eat them," he said at last in a dissatisfied voice, "and what room all this stuff take up!"

"Can you only think of eating!" wailed the Raccoon, "Must everything be thought of in terms of food?"

Opossum felt quite defeated. He felt as if he really did lack something, some lively appreciation of his world that the Raccoon had. "Well, anyway," he said fretfully, "I'm good at finding food. We have to eat you know."

Moonbeam felt rather sorry that he had lost his temper. There was, after all, no point in being angry with Opossum for being an Opossum in every way. "That will be a big help," he said cheerily squeezing Opossum's shoulder.

"But I still don't understand about all these things!" Opossum said softly, wishing, perhaps, to have that last word.

"Well, it doesn't matter," said Moonbeam quickly trying to change the subject, "What do you think we should carry along?"

"Oh dear, oh dear!" said Opossum getting upset all over again, "you are not going to carry some of all this about are you?" Opossum spun round on his heels and opened his front paws wide to point out the whole room, every canny of which was filled with something. Dizzily, his eyes finally rested on a large, blue ball almost as big as he was himself. "What is that?" he asked in surprise as if confronting a strange animal or fruit.

*Moonbeam*

"I don't exactly know," said Moonbeam seriously touching it with gentle hands and sliding his fingers along its smooth sides. "Once it jumped with The Girl in The Garden, but it is very silent and still here. I had hoped it would jump about for me as it did for her, but it seems to have no energy without her and to be quite sad and lost. Do you think I should take it back?"

Opossum raised his shoulders and stared anxiously at it as if he was afraid the ball would bounce towards him and bite, "It might be wise," he said solemnly. "You never know." He circled around it slowly, keeping a good distance from it, staring at it quizzically. "Does it never ever move?" he asked, more than a little surprised that it ever had at all.

"No, never," said Moonbeam slowly, "I thought it would be jolly fun and that we might race together over the meadows, but without her it is nothing. It refused to move."

"Oh, you have tried then," said Opossum with alarm, frowning deeply.

"Yes, I have prodded it from behind and pinched it from underneath. It doesn't care."

"Well," said Opossum raising his eyebrows, "best forgotten I suppose. You can't take that along on our journey anyway, or for that matter, anything else."

Moonbeam didn't like the way Opossum emphasized those sharp words, "anything else". They sprang at him sharply and seemed to echo along the passageways. But it was true that, try as he might, he would have to either completely leave his den or completely stay. It would be impossible to carry all he loved along to Silversheen with him. And so it seemed that, in exchange for this excitement and adventure, he would have to shoulder this worry of leaving all his things behind. Owl must have foreseen that, of course, Moonbeam thought to himself. This must be the first skin of that mysterious layer Owl had talked about so mysteriously. It did feel as if he was peeling reality down in some way.

"Well, I shall block the doors and hide them behind logs and grasses and leaves," muttered Moonbeam to himself forlornly, "Perhaps, I'll ask Ringtail to keep watch. But I will not tell the others."

"Well, you know, we may not really be that long!" exclaimed Opossum encouragingly. "I dare say we shall be back by Nest-Time." Opossum was a little surprised to find that he took courage when the Raccoon needed him to. He felt himself swing from courage to fear and back again like wildflowers in the breeze.

Moonbeam shrugged his shoulders. Long was for him loneliness, hunger, getting caught in a storm, hiding from a Fox, not being able to find any fish. Short was eating chocolate cookies under the Walnut Tree in The Garden, seeing The Girl come from The Great House, hearing Ringtail's description of The King of The River and trying to imagine his glorious blue robes, his glistening crown. Who could say which of these the journey to Silversheen would be? It could be one day's dream to Nest-Time or a whole Life-Time, and Moonbeam began to sense that something would depend on those layers, like this one he was now peeling off in leaving his den and all his precious things. Owl's words, "You do not yet know yourself, nor Opossum, either", came back to him rustling softly in and out of his memory like rushes in the breeze down by The Creek. He suddenly felt very cold and he hugged the blue ball tightly.

*Groundhog*

"I don't know whether I want to stay here with all I have always loved, or travel and find what I have always dreamed of," said Moonbeam slowly, in deep thought. " I really don't know exactly what I want. Somehow I have imagined I could stay and go too if you see what I mean?"

Opossum frowned and bit his lips. "Well, I'm not much different than that myself although I don't have so many colourful possessions to worry about. But I have always loved The Garden and The Meadows and The Woods, and I have always dreamed of Silversheen and The King of The River, too."

"Life is rather more complicated than I had supposed." Said Moonbeam looking up suddenly and staring at Opossum.

"What you mean," said Opossum hesitantly, afraid to butt in on thoughts that were not his own, "is that we are rather more complicated than you had ever supposed."

Perhaps Moonbeam would have denied that or, perhaps, he would have admitted that that was what he meant if it hadn't been for a series of bouncing thumps overhead that shook the whole den and caused earth to fall around them, dusting everything. They ran to the doorway and saw red-brown fur rolling over it in a peculiar fashion and then a face with bright eyes and large front teeth, which appeared and disappeared suddenly.

"A rabbit?" questioned Opossum looking puzzled.

"No, I think not," said Moonbeam crisply, "Its ears were too short."

"Were they?" exclaimed Opossum. "I didn't see, he rolled by so quickly."

Then the thumping began again, and they heard a voice exclaim, "Wonders of wonders!" In an amazed tone.

"On no, not again!" cried Moonbeam running outside just as his den began to shake. He looked up behind him, above his den and saw a red-brown creature rolling towards him at a great speed in a rather clumsy, if enthusiastic, somersault. Moonbeam tried to jump aside, but as he did so the creature whirled up into the air, landed on top of him and knocked him flat to the ground. Arm and legs went everywhere. Teeth gnashed.

"Good gracious!" exclaimed the somersaulting animal trying to untangle himself from the Raccoon. "I say! I am sorry, but must you appear out of no-where at the bottom of a slope? Gave me quite a fright!"

"You a fright!" cried Moonbeam indignantly standing and brushing himself off furiously as if he had on his very best clothes and had no others, which for a

Raccoon is always the case. "This is my slope! You are in fact at this very moment in my front garden!"

The animal looked quite upset. "Well, I am sorry, but there's no sign you know. You might have put up a sign."

Moonbeam looked at him questioningly. "I don't know what you mean," he answered angrily, "I don't need a sign! What is a sign?"

"They are here abouts!" said the animal waving a paw in all directions in a superior way. "I always avoid them. They are always where people are, people and dogs. Now, if you had put up a sign, I would have thought you were people, people or dogs, and I wouldn't have rolled here. I would have rolled somewhere else, further off."

Moonbeam rolled his eyes in irritation. He didn't understand a word the creature was saying, but then, he didn't encounter people or dogs that often because he didn't often go about by day. He closed his eyes and tried hard to imagine The Girl. Was there a sign by the Walnut Tree in The Garden? Unable to remember anything he couldn't name easily by another name, Moonbeam became suspicious that all this talk about signs was a trick. He squinted his eyes and looked at the creature from under brooding brows.

Opossum had stuck his snowy head outside the den door and was sniffing anxiously. He recognized the smell, but couldn't place the animal at all who seemed rather large and rather rust-coloured against the first silver of dawn stretched in a thin ribbon along the horizon. The grass in The Meadow glistened with dew, and birds were singing noisily overhead.

"All this about signs doesn't excuse anything," said Moonbeam At last in a final way as thought the creature couldn't escape his anger or do anything to smooth things over.

Opossum nodded approvingly. He was, after all, a den-dweller too, and he had no friendship for these den-shakers whoever they were.

The creature didn't answer but smiled oddly and seemed to be watching the horizon rather than listening to the Raccoon's words. "Wonder of wonders!" he exclaimed under his breath with eyes as large as two Wren eggs in a nest.

"Well, I don't know what there is to wonder about!" cried Moonbeam quite beside himself. "Everything in there, all my precious things, are covered with dust! It will take all night to clean things up!"

"No, I mean, look, look at the sun!" the animal answered in a daze staring out and pointing to the horizon.

Moonbeam turned and saw a sliver of red sun peep over the horizon like the edge of an orchard apple. Delicate pink flushed the sky and caught in the mists over Deer Meadow until the whole view down below them glistened warmly in the morning light.

Moonbeam yawned unexpectedly and found that he now had to force himself to keep his eyes open. Sunlight always made him sleepy, and besides he had been very busy all night arranging the journey, and then the day before that he had slept fitfully, trying to remember the exact tracing of sunlight across The Wood. If they were to ever leave for Silversheen, he would need some sleep. And so he continued to yawn widely but noticed out of the corner of his eye that the creature's eyes were getting bigger and bigger, and his smile wider and wider, and that his whole body was starting to bounce up and down.

"Oh no! cried Moonbeam, grabbing the creature's shoulders, "Please, not again!"

"But, but!" cried the creature pulling free from Moonbeam's hand and spinning on his toes, "The morning is so beautiful! Wonder of wonders! How long I have waited to see this!"

Opossum was dumbfounded. He showed his teeth in displeasure and pulled back into the den. "You do have strange tastes!" he said sarcastically, scratching the ground.

The animal whirled 'round. "I didn't see you there in the darkness," he said in a practical tone. "An Opossum hey!" he said cheerily, looking Opossum up and down with dark, beady eyes.

Opossum was more than a little offended, and he felt very disadvantaged because he didn't know who or what the creature was. He would like to have said "A Whatever hey, dear me!" in return. But he just bit his lips nervously instead. "And what are you?" he said haughtily as if the animal was too insignificant to really need a name and certainly quite unworthy of being in the Raccoon's front garden.

"Groundhog," muttered the creature looking down. "But you can't imagine how excited I am! Everything is just the same but different! Wonder of wonders!" He began to tap his foot again and to hum loudly.

Raccoon looked at Opossum and raised his eyebrows and signed to him that the creature appeared quite crazy.

"Quite, I should think!" muttered Opossum with a sigh.

"Yes, you understand!" exclaimed the Groundhog misunderstanding and springing towards Opossum smiling widely and showing large front teeth and a bright pink tongue.

Opossum ducked back into the den in alarm. He was not sure what to make of this friendliness, this excitement, or this "wonder of wonders!" the creature kept repeating. Raccoon's blue ball seemed now to be a much more steady and certain companion, and Opossum hid behind it and clutched it tightly with is two pink hands. It didn't move.

"Strange!" muttered the Groundhog scratching his head. "Did I say something?" he asked turning to the Raccoon and looking suddenly crestfallen.

"No", said Moonbeam seriously, "It's just, well, it's just, well, you know, you are rather odd. I mean different." Moonbeam uttered this very gingerly watching the Groundhog at each new word with apprehension. He didn't want to cause any more somersaulting, dancing or whirling. He was worried about all his precious things.

"Well, you can't please everyone!" lamented the Groundhog in an offended tone scraping the ground with his feet. "I was just excited."

"Yes, but that's just it," said Moonbeam sheepishly, really rather afraid to continue with this conversation. "What exactly are you excited about?" The sunlight was getting brighter and Moonbeam moved into the shade of some shrubbery. He yawned again and rubbed his eyes.

"The morning!" exclaimed Groundhog mystified by the Raccoon's obvious inability to understand anything. "This morning!" he added with another wide grin, "especially this morning!"

"But, if you don't mind me asking, "hesitated Moonbeam sitting, "why this morning especially? It is hard enough to understand your enthusiasm for any morning, but why this one?" He stared at the Groundhog and sighed as if he expected a rather long and involved explanation.

The Groundhog's eyes widened in horror. "Why," he exclaimed with such force that Opossum came scurrying back to the den entrance to save Moonbeam if need be. "I only just woke up! I have been asleep all Winter! In fact, I have been asleep so long that I can hardly remember this world at all, except as a shadowy dream bathed in sunlight and smelling of fresh greenness."

Moonbeam and Opossum looked at him and at each other with surprise for, although they stayed in their dens most of the Winter, pottering about and snoozing, they didn't sleep all the time, to wake to a world that they hardly remembered. Opossum shivered, "I shouldn't like that, "he said in a frightened voice. He didn't like the unfamiliar.

The Groundhog looked offended. "But really it is quite fun", he said softly, fearful that he would never be able to explain what he meant. "It is fun to escape the Winter cold and to wake to all the deliciousness of early Spring. I really would hate to trudge about endlessly looking for green grasses and roots when they would be almost impossible to find. Friends, not as lucky as I, have described Winter to me. I do not know whether everything they tell me is true though. It sounds rather exaggerated". He smoothed his hands through the grass and became very thoughtful.

"What have they told you?" asked Moonbeam wondering about this creature who had never seen what he knew so well and dreaded so much.

"I have heard that everything I treasure, green grass, deep thickets, shady trees and gentle breezes, mysteriously disappear," said the Groundhog sadly with a deep sigh.

"But not as in Daylight's world, "cried Opossum, proud that he knew more about life than the Groundhog and had seen what the Groundhog never had and never would.

"What do you mean?" asked the Groundhog jumping in surprise and stressing the word "do" in a peculiarly harsh way.

"Well," said Opossum in a dignified voice as if he were about to explain the nature of the Five Worlds, "in a short while, when the sun is higher, all this will disappear," he moved his hand along the horizon and stared out ahead. "The sun melts everything!" he exclaimed with sudden inspiration, well satisfied with his own clever explanation.

"Well, there I have to disagree," said the Groundhog cheerfully, "I may know nothing much about Winter, but I know a lot about the day. Nothing changes I assure you. Nothing disappears, and the sun doesn't melt anything." Opossum looked a bit cross.

"Pos" said Moonbeam chidingly, "I told you everything is here all day. It's just that it's too bright to look at.

Opossum pursed his lips defiantly. "Speak for yourself! There is absolutely nothing wrong with my eyes," he said peering at the Raccoon in irritation. The light doesn't bother me."

Moonbeam sighed loudly. The Groundhog laughed.

"Do you believe there are creatures who go by Day, Pos?" said Moonbeam in a practical voice.

"Yes, I do," muttered Opossum firmly. "Frightening creatures with long teeth and deep jaws. "He drew into himself and curled his tail around his body.

"Then, if the world has disappeared, if the sun has melted everything, where do they walk? Where do they go?" Moonbeam asked with a smile.

Opossum looked cornered for the moment. He dipped his head and ran his eyes along the ground nervously. Then suddenly he looked up and laughed a small self-satisfied laugh. "They run and fly through white-gold air!" he chanted, "Gnashing teeth and looking for Night-creatures to prey upon!"

"And, where are you then?" said Moonbeam exasperated, "are you there? Have you disappeared, too?"

Opossum was now really offended. All these questions were a real nuisance. How had this discussion started anyway? "The dens don't disappear!" he exclaimed, greatly infuriated, "The Earth and all those underneath don't melt!"

"Well, good gracious!" laughed the Groundhog, "And what about me then? I know full well I walk around on top of the Earth all day long!"

Opossum had never been so angry. "You imagine it," he cried wildly, "You are in a den asleep, and you dream you are walking around up here!"

"Oh, Pos, you know full well that is rubbish!" cried Moonbeam annoyed with his newfound friend.

But Opossum just stuck his chin out stubbornly. He couldn't bare the truth to be any other way. Day's world frightened him, and it was much, much easier to believe it didn't really exist.

"You know Pos," continued Moonbeam gently, realizing it was Opossum's fear of the Day that caused him to refuse to believe it really existed, "Ringtail has always said that The King of The River is a Day creature, and he is very real as well as of astonishing beauty, all blue and jet and moonlight silver. A distant look had entered Moonbeam's eyes, and he began to forget where he was or the silly quarrel he was involved in. The Groundhog smiled and nodded happily. He preferred this praise of a Day creature to Opossum's furious denial of Day's existence, and he had heard many tales about The King of the River. The wild Deer in The Wood knew wonderful stories, and the old brown Otter who lived down by The Creek claimed to have seen him in his youth.

"Otter has seen The King of The River," cried the Groundhog with excitement leaping about again and then rolling over, "and what's more," he said winking at Opossum, "the Otter is a Day creature and lives in dens!" The Groundhog was really pleased with this, and he said it with complete enthusiasm.

Opossum frowned and slowly withdrew into Moonbeam's den to sulk. He really didn't think he liked the Groundhog at all. The Raccoon and he were doing so well, had so much in common, and then along came "that Groundhog", and now "that Groundhog" was talking about their dream, The King of The River, in a glib, cheerful tone as if he was no more than an ordinary bunch of berries or patch of mushrooms. "Oh dear," cried Opossum, "Oh dear!"

On the other hand, Moonbeam was rather intrigued by the Groundhog. He liked his cheerfulness and excitement, and he liked his interest in The King of The River which had surfaced so unexpectedly and which now showed in his glinting, brown eyes. Moonbeam couldn't resist boasting a little about their intended journey to Silversheen, and so he threw out his chest and tilted his tail proudly while he said, "Pos and I are planning a journey to The King. In fact, we were preparing things when you rolled by. I dare say I had best get back to work and then take a nap, too. It is a long journey you know." Moonbeam said, "you know" in a way that gave the impression he had detailed knowledge of all the paths and bridges through The Forest and would be surprised if any creature in all the Five Worlds had not.

Groundhog looked startled and his nose twitched excitedly. "Have you been there before then?" he asked softly, well expecting the Raccoon to nod firmly in reply.

"Well, not exactly," hesitated Moonbeam rolling his eyes, "but the Wise Old Owl gave us detailed directions, secret ones." He added rather clumsily.

The Groundhog smiled knowingly. He knew full well that the Owl did not give away secret knowledge to any of the creatures, whether of Day's World or of Night's. He was, however, too kind and too generous to catch Moonbeam out. "How wonderful!" he said trying to appear really impressed.

"Yes," said Moonbeam lifting his paws, "if all goes well, we leave tonight from Whiteoaks. I'm not exactly certain because Opossum is rather slow getting ready. I dare say he will hold me up in the end."

Opossum may have left them both outside, but with such keen hearing, the Raccoon's words didn't escape him. "I say!" he called out of the den, sounding both shocked and hurt, "it is you who have held us up so far by insisting on sorting out all those useless things!" Groundhog heard a loud dramatic sigh and a lot of irritated scratching.

"As I was saying, we have been held up, but that is all part of the problem of journeying I suppose," said Moonbeam, ignoring Opossum and sounding as if he knew everything about the Art of Journeying.

"I suppose so," said the Groundhog without understanding, "You must know. I haven't been on too many journeys myself. Only changed a meadow for a field, a field for a meadow now and then. But then these Long Sleeps do reduce my time."

"Quite," said Moonbeam sounding very knowledgeable and very mature. He was glad to see that the Groundhog wasn't going to argue over everything like Opossum.

"I do think it's unfair!" whined Opossum from the den with another dramatic sigh.

"Do you think the journey will go well?" asked the Groundhog eyeing the Raccoon carefully, "I mean, well, the two of you don't exactly…" he nodded towards the den.

Moonbeam quickly didn't allow the Groundhog to finish the sentence, "We get along splendidly! We are tired at present. We are Night-Creatures you know!" He said loudly.

"Yes, I know," said Groundhog gently. "Don't you think you are going to need a Day-Creature with you on this journey of yours. The King of The River lives by day anyhow".

Moonbeam grunted and then remembered the Owl's words, "The Owl told us as much, not exactly in those words, you understand, but something of the sort."

"I expect so," said Groundhog raising his eyebrows and flicking his tail. There was an odd excitement about him again now, and the Raccoon took hold of his arm.

"You're not going to?" he said quietly.

"Somersault, you mean?" said the Groundhog cheerily, "Oh, no! I was just thinking that I might go a little of the way with you, just to Chestnut Grove or something, if you don't mind that is? I have always wanted to explore the other side of The Creek and visit Otter again. I might stay a few suns over there and then walk back."

Groundhog said all this casually, not wanting the Raccoon to think he was especially excited to go along or that he might go as far as Silversheen. He sensed, rightly, that Opossum would object rather strongly. His heart, however, was pounding within him and ideas full of the blue and silver of The King of The River flashed through his mind with every word he spoke. How often, settled cozily in his Long Winter Sleep, he had dreamed that dream, and how often he had woken in Spring to run out and search for some shred of it, some suggestion that it was more than a dream, some suggestion that he might relive it in Day's World.

"I wouldn't mind," answered Moonbeam in a friendly way, "It might even be a good idea. I have always wanted to meet an Otter. Ringtail tells me they are silver underneath, as silver as Silversheen itself!" Moonbeam was excited by this thought, and he sat up quickly and raised his front feet to his chin.

"Good gracious, yes!" exclaimed the Groundhog, happy to find there was no objection on the Raccoon's part to his joining them. He looked anxiously towards the den where Opossum was still listening carefully. He was surprised Opossum had said nothing and presumed he must be sulking. "He is a superb swimmer too, can flip and float and dive without any effort at all. I rather envy that. He appears to have such fun and to be so at home in the water. Think what somersaults I could do if I could swim as well as that!"

Moonbeam was not sure he wanted to think about that. His den had suffered enough from somersaults to have turned him quite off the subject, but he loved water passionately and was delighted to be thinking about it again. He was thrilled with the idea he might meet another water-lover, even if a somersaulting one.

"Well, we shall leave tonight at sunset," he said seriously, pointing a finger at the rising sun. "Meet us here if you wish to go too." He turned and began to walk back to his den. He was yawning. "I presume you can see by moonlight?" he asked suddenly swinging 'round and frowning. He was still puzzled by this new creature he had just met.

"Oh, yes!" cried Groundhog happily, "I see quite well although it all rather gives me the creeps!"

"What do you mean – the creeps?" asked Moonbeam in surprise.

"Well, strange things wander around at night. Strange beasts with long teeth and great jutting jaws. They hide in the darkness and pounce on Day-Creatures when they are unaware," Groundhog answered shivering and shrinking to the ground.

Opossum stuck his head out of the den and stared in anger. "No, there are not!" he exclaimed, ready to defend his world with all his strength. "Those belong to Day's World not mine!"

Moonbeam sighed, "Between the two of you, we would never go anywhere, by day or night! What imaginations you both do have!" But perhaps in that similarity was the seed of a deep and enduring friendship.

# Chapter FOUR
## Beyond Whiteoaks

*It was a glorious* evening. The crescent moon shone brightly in the clear night sky. It drifted silently over the woods and meadows like a strange and magic ship full of silver treasure, from which, perhaps, Moonbeam thought, fell those sparking stars that twinkled among the tree branches like thousands of fairy lanterns.

The air was crisp and full of wonderful smells. The strong smells of cedar and pine mixed with the delicate smells of woodland wildflowers and vines in a way that excited Moonbeam. White-tailed Deer with forward-curving antlers and dark winter coats were still browsing in the Deer Meadow savoring their favored pine and cedar needles. They jumped with a snort when disturbed by scurrying Moonbeam, Opossum and Groundhog. Some turned and sprang towards the woods with their long, bushy tails upwards behind like white flags. Moonbeam thought he heard their leader cry, "Hurry! Hurry!" At the edge of the Deer Wood he could also hear a vole who had surfaced suddenly from his network of tunnels, usual to his kind, to gnaw the base of a tree.

Whiteoaks, the ancient gathering ground for Woodland Creatures, appeared ghostly, bathed in bright moonlight that shone along white-grey branches and caught around the blackness of hollows and holes. Moonbeam remembered the scrumptious acorn meals he had had there, and the chattering squirrels quarreling over which acorns they would take to their winter stores. He remembered too, before that, in the Summer-Time, wavy leaves, whitish underneath, rounding out the trees like a cloud or mossy hill. Underneath the branches grew Moccasin Flower, nodding like fairy shoes with white, curling ribbons.

The three creatures stood silently for some time staring above them at the filigree of branches against the moon-bright sky. They could hear the gentle rippling of The Creek in the distance, and they saw, now and then, other glistening, anxious eyes fixed on them from the undergrowth. They were almost near enough to touch.

"I will have to admit," whispered the Groundhog, "the night is full of busyness," He could hear animals coming and going all the time.

Moonbeam had often been this far from The Garden to collect the delicious thin-shelled Pecan nuts, even before they fell from among the spear-shaped Pecan leaves. He had licked the glistening rich sap that ran down the trunks like wild honey from holes bored by the Yellow-bellied Sapsucker, that furtive woodpecker with a dull yellow stomach and off-white and black stripped jacket. He remembered having seen his bright red cap and throat, splendid in the last rays of the setting sun among the Pecan branches. He had of course come this way not so long ago to see Old Grandfather, The Fisher. He hoped somehow that he would not see him tonight. He remembered well the Old Grandfather's words about how Silversheen became a dark, green sea that went on forever and ever.

"Have you ever seen a sea?" Moonbeam asked Groundhog trying to sound conversational and not at all anxious about it.

"Can't say that I have," said Groundhog casually. He was not in fact sure what a sea was although he suspected it had something to do with water because he remembered Otter had talked about it a good deal in an excited way with his whiskers twitching constantly.

"Otter said a sea was one of the most marvelous things on this earth, full of adventure and treasures galore," said Groundhog waving a paw in a large circle.

"I heard rather the opposite," muttered Moonbeam pursing his lips.

"Well, tastes differ," said the Groundhog cheerily, "We are a good example of that."

"Yes, I know," said Moonbeam thoughtfully. "What adventures and treasures do you think Otter means?" he added, keeping well to the side of the trail that was in the shade of the spreading branches of the Chestnut Oak and Yellow Poplar.

"I'm not sure. He seemed to like fish better than anything. I shouldn't doubt it has something to do with fish," the Groundhog laughed remembering Otter's frolicsome fish-chases.

"Then it may really have something to do with Silversheen after all," murmured Moonbeam. "A sea I mean. There are fish in Silversheen I have been told." He looked anxiously at Opossum and Groundhog but neither understood what he meant.

"The bird-bath in The Garden at The Great House has something to do with Silversheen, too," muttered Opossum. "Both hold water, but they are nothing alike!" He looked at Moonbeam carefully. He sensed that the Raccoon was thinking about something worrisome, but he couldn't guess what it might be. Raccoon's after all, unlike his own kind, relish water, love its touch and different sounds, like to paddle and fish. "I should think you might have a lot in common with this creature called Otter," Opossum said more loudly, swishing his tail.

"You never can tell," said Moonbeam sounding quite disinterested because he was still trying to imagine a sea and couldn't for the life of him really understand it except as a vast sky crested with clouds. Yet, he knew full well that the sky was not water and really nothing like a sea at all. But it was the only thing he knew that seemed to actually go on forever and ever, getting deeper and deeper.

"Do you suppose a sea is like the sky?" he asked at last staring up in wonder and running his eyes across the heavens until they came to rest on the moon.

"Well, there aren't any fish in the sky!" answered Opossum very seriously.

As they rounded the trail, they saw The Creek glistening softly in the moonlight. It began several miles upstream at a gurgling natural spring. Ringtail had visited there once and returned with charming tales about jewel-like waters, swirling on amber pebbles, surrounded by mossy banks where white Queen Anne's Lace and golden Buttercups mingled with Bluebells.

The Creek water smelt sweet, and Moonbeam was now quite thirsty. He had left his den on an empty stomach which was, perhaps, not such a good way to start a journey unless you planned to stop and eat and drink here and there as those travelers did.

There were many tracks going down the banks and across the mud to the waters' edge, and Moonbeam could smell each of the different animals who had come there recently. Opossum was sniffing excitedly as he cautiously crossed the mud. He recognized the smell of another Opossum and soon saw quite clearly the five thin-toed track in the mud. Staring at the tracks around him, he was glad to see no four-toed ones such as belonged to the Fox and the Dog. Those he feared with a deep fear that set his body quivering.

In the darkness the Groundhog could not see as well as the other two, and he slipped and slithered in the mud and tripped in holes. He waved a paw at his side every now and then, patting the air in search of his companions. He was, however, despite all his difficulties, extremely happy. He loved the smell of earth at any time, and earth, when wet, smelled more heady and refreshing than the richest wildflower perfume.

"Wonder of wonders! What tunnels I could build here!" Groundhog exclaimed to himself, sifting the earth of the banks through his fingers with a tunnel builders' instinct. "I could have a back door right by The Creek like any muskrat or mink!" The idea was enchanting!

Moonlight caught on the gentle ripples of The Creek, and flooded the water to light the muddy streambed and all its nooks and crannies, twigs and reeds. Small, shining fish skimmed by casting tiny shadows below them. Moonbeam touched the water with loving hands and then waded on in up to his knees. A breeze wafted past, following the curves of The Creek as it wound through The Woods, and on the breeze were delightful smells that seemed to expand around him in a rich layer, both spicy and telling. He smelt the red tinted bark of the Water Oak, the fresh green of Frogs and the moist pungency of damp mosses. He also smelt Mallards, squirrels, Quail and other Raccoons. "How delicious!" he whispered savoring the air with a connoisseur's nose while he paddled about and squelched his feet in the mud, as he loved to do.

Opossum trod nimbly to the water's edge and drank daintily without even wetting his front toes. He really disliked getting wet! He always got too cold when he did and ended up shivering and quivering – all so unpleasant to think of.

They were all very quiet, resting and enjoying The Creek, each his own way, when all of a sudden something leapt from the opposite bank straight into the center of the water, spraying everyone, and soaking even poor Opossum who couldn't believe his misfortune and began to shake. The "something" then began to gurgle piteously and flay its arms and legs about in an attempt, none to expert, to swim across to the small mud flat.

"Oh, how unbecoming!" cried a whining voice, "What will the others say!"

Moonbeam stared about, but although he saw flashes of what looked like white and black stripes in the moonlight, he couldn't for the life of him make out what creature this was that had so suddenly disturbed their quiet rest. It didn't move gracefully and couldn't swim well, and it seemed to be uncommonly long, thin and oddly pointed at both ends.

"Don't just stand there!" cried the creature in terror and irritation, "Can't you see I'm drowning!"

"It's not deep enough for drowning," said Moonbeam moving a little nearer, but cautiously. All this pathetic flapping might, after all, be a clever trick. He couldn't imagine any creature so terrified of water, except perhaps an Opossum.

"Must be related to you!" Moonbeam call to Opossum nodding his head.

"Not me!" cried Opossum indignantly with a hurt whine. He would have hated to look so ungainly and was rather afraid that he often did.

Moonbeam moved a little nearer then a little nearer and finally grabbed the creature and tried to wade with him to the opposite bank. He kept whining and flapping all the time, which made it difficult to be especially helpful. "Can't you keep still?" asked Moonbeam exasperated.

"But I shall drown!" came the gurgling reply.

"It's not very bright of you to jump in so extravagantly if you can't swim!" cried Opossum. At least he, he thought, would never do anything that silly! Why! He was standing at The Creek side very sensibly! Not even his trailing pink tail was wet!

"Well, its all very well for you!" whined the creature flopping on the muddy bank in a bedraggled mess of long fur, "You weren't being chased by a Fox!"

"Fox!" cried the Groundhog in terror turning in a circle.

"Where is the Fox now?" whispered Moonbeam looking up and down the banks with piercing eyes that saw each blade of grass, each twig, each dark hollow. Beside him Opossum sniffed anxiously, but Opossum couldn't smell a Fox.

"How should I know where he is now!" whined the creature raising a bedraggled head, which looked almost as small as a vole's now that its wet fur clung to it so unbecomingly. Opossum stared at him with a puzzled expression and then smiled brightly and tapped his forehead with a sharp, pink finger.

"Wouldn't you be a Skunk if you weren't so wet and odd looking?" he asked just a little scornfully.

The creature looked up at him with mournful eyes full of tears. "I am a

Skunk whether wet or not. The water makes no difference you know!" He tried to lift his nose into the air proudly but water trickled off the end making a puddle in the mud at his feet.

"I suppose not," said Opossum in an unfriendly voice. Once a Skunk, always a Skunk! He thought with a nod. He remembered some rather nasty encounters with Skunks, including a fight over a cozy den that had once belonged to a Badger on Hickory Hill. A fight he remembered he had lost! But then Skunks were so restless, always changing their dens, several times in just one Winter to be exact! That meant, if you happened to be a den-dweller too, you could hardly avoid fighting with one sooner or later. "It was all so inevitable!" Opossum sighed loudly and shook his head.

"I don't know what that comment is meant to mean!" whined the Skunk, sitting up and trying to shake the water out of its fur. The three creatures ran to the cover of the bank. Even the Raccoon didn't like water sprayed on him like that!

"They're always the same," muttered Opossum under his breath to the Groundhog, nodding as if to say "you know what I mean!" And this is what comes, he thought, from constantly living in over-crowded dens and going about in groups. No sense, no independence, no real politeness!

"But what about the Fox?" asked Moonbeam, concerned to know what danger they might be in.

"I think I gave him the slip," the Skunk answered furtively, looking around with eyes as bright and dark as two small beetles. "I thought anyway to finally lose him at The Creek, but I did misjudge the depth, and my swimming is not up to snuff. I've been denned-up most of the Winter! Are there any insects about now? I'm rather tired of nuts and berries and seeds."

"Hard to believe that you are related to the Otter in a distant sort of way," said the Groundhog, very puzzled by the Skunk's clumsy dive into The Creek.

"Well, and it is really very, very distant," muttered the Skunk quite embarrassed, "I know I don't have his speed or good humor, but then who wouldn't be jolly to be made so perfectly for one's Own–World. Otter moves in water as though he is water, and I walk on land slowly, oddly, as though I don't quite belong here. I have dreams sometimes about moving with the swiftness of falling water. But what becomes of dreams!"

"You think the Fox isn't nearby then?" asked Moonbeam still anxious. He couldn't smell or see a Fox and there was no wind now. Opossum wasn't sniffing either which as a good sign as he was always so sniffy at the mere hint of Fox.

"I think he is a long way off now", said Skunk with a grateful sign, "I wasn't the only one running, and I crossed tracks several times. Once with a Mink, another time with a Weasel, and several times with Deer.

"Well, I still think that jumping into the middle of The Creek was rather foolish!" said Opossum thrusting out his chin, "Couldn't you see the Raccoon?"

"Not really, not in the moonlight shadows," answered the Skunk. "Those black marking of yours do hide a lot!" He added turning to Moonbeam with admiration, "Especially your eyes! Now Opossum here I saw a good distance off. White coats really show you know. They really catch the moonlight.

Opossum looked quite put out though he had to admit that Opossums were rather obvious. "I look better in snow," he said testily waving a paw.

"But you hate the cold Pos!" said Moonbeam.

The Groundhog, not wishing to sit through another quarrel, butted in suddenly. "Don't you think we should move on our way now? We have a deal of traveling to do before sun-up." He patted Moonbeam's shoulder and began to climb up the bank.

"Good thinking!" nodded Moonbeam following quickly. He liked the Groundhog more every moment. "But we should travel in the shadows I think. We are better hidden up there in the woods than down here by The Creek where moonlight floods through the tree-tops and reflects on the water," he said thoughtfully.

"A –journeying are you?" asked the Skunk without any real interest, "Going from one place to another?"

"Yes, a very great place," answered Moonbeam with enthusiasm. "Well. I'll be moving along if you don't mind," said Skunk with a yawn, "I don't like journeying. I have no talent for it. I don't care for straight lines to distant places, but like to meander about slowly. Sometimes I visit the same place two or three times a night." Here he nodded at each of them as if to see how impressed they were with his thoroughness. "Indeed, I often end up just where I started. I may change dens a lot, but usually they're fairly near together."

Opossum grunted at the word "dens" and his eyes hardened into a glassy stare that might have bothered the Skunk if he had noticed, but he had already turned towards Whiteoaks. His fur was drier now, and he looked fuller and less pitiful; his face no longer had the pinched and scared look they had seen in The Creek. He meandered off casually, winding from one side of the path to the other. Behind, imprinted on the soft earth, he left a trail of small, round prints. When he came to the curve in the path, he turned and smiled back at them and called "Sorry about all the commotion," and he was gone!

"Do you think he really was chased by a Fox?" asked Opossum as they walked along.

"I'm not at all sure," answered Moonbeam carefully. "Foxes, I've heard, have no taste for Skunks, and besides they generally keep to a trail and don't wander about all over the place."

"Shouldn't wonder about that lack of taste!" cried Opossum irritably. "It was more likely to have been a farm Dog. They often hunt in haphazard fashion, forgetting where they started and what they're after. Foxes never do that!"

"Good gracious! But don't you think Skunk would know which it was? He has keen eyes after all! Foxes smell absolutely nothing like farm dogs – nothing like!" exclaimed Groundhog, tripping over some roots and then some twigs in the darkness.

"Oh, his eyes weren't that keen!" cried Opossum, stressing the word "his" very strongly, as though what naturally belonged to Night-Creatures couldn't possible apply in the Skunk's case.

"He was perhaps rather too excited and young for good judgment," whispered Moonbeam.

"I should say!" chimed Opossum, "Jumping into creeks on top of other folks! Oh dear! Oh dear!"

Moonbeam sighed. He felt sorry for the Skunk. He was still young too, and he knew how difficult it was to do the right thing in an emergency unless you happened to have an adult Raccoon nearby. Besides, as he had never really seen a Fox, he felt he couldn't really judge the Skunk's behavior. The Garden Raccoons had fantastic stories about foxes, stories of great danger and daring. Uncle Long-Ears claimed to have once chased a Fox all the way down Hickory Hill, which may have been quite true for Long-Ears had been large and fierce in his day. But Moonbeam remembered his own reflection in the silver Creek water and thought that he was perhaps still rather small for fighting with foxes or chasing them down-hill, especially Hickory Hill, which was steep, rugged, and covered with thick, tangled roots that tripped you up and sent you flying head-over-heels. Sharp-Ears had given running lessons there last Autumn, and had lectured long on the danger of roots and vines when he got caught in a mass of tendrils of hanging vines that had trailed across his path.

"Good gracious!" whimpered Groundhog sorrowfully, "I just can't see well enough up here. Now I have hit my chin on a root!"

"Well I don't know where else to walk," said moonbeam slowly. "It is much less safe down by The Creek, where it is lighter and all the creatures of the Five Worlds go to drink and bathe. Not all may be as friendly as the Skunk!"

"Oh, but you really can't judge anything by that Skunk!" said Opossum, starting to whisper again as usual.

# Chapter FIVE

## Soft Footsteps Falling

*The trail wound* upwards towards a ridge that looked out over The Creek. A chill breeze came through the dark woods, rustling all the vines and bracken. The large, spreading branches of the Southern Red Oak swayed and glimmered silver in the moonlight. Mountain Laurel grew up here thickly. Its beautiful, dark green leaves provided shelter for many of the woodland creatures. Moonbeam remembered that this was the shrub that would be massed with pink and white flowers in the Spring; Flowers that looked like tiny bells or fairy cups, and in which the rainwater collected like sweet nectar in delicate, swinging goblets. Sometimes, here, high above, a mere speck in the bright sky, the Bald Eagle could be seen as he winged his solitary way towards Silversheen. There, his squeaky cackling pierced the river dawn. Ringtail, that teller of wonderful stories, had told Moonbeam about the kingly Eagle with snowy white head and fanning tail and blackish suit tinged in the evening light with reddish glow. His massive nest of sticks was said to be just beyond Moonlight Inlet on a spit of land the Garden Creatures called Eagle Bridge.

Moonbeam stared up at the mass of branches above him and, beyond that at the star-studded sky. He saw an old round Wood Thrush nest in the notch of a branch. He knew from all his tree climbing that it would be lined with rootlets and fine grasses and have leaves and mud woven into its sides. He knew also that in Spring it might contain four greenish-blue eggs as shiny and beautiful as dewy Periwinkles. How lovely was the Wood Thrush with her rusty head and dramatic spots and large, round eyes as soft and gentle as any Deer's. In the evenings moonbeam had liked to wake to her song, welling across Deer meadow to The Gardens. She would call a sharp pit-pit-pit-pit followed by rich, melodious songs that sounded like the flute Moonbeam had heard in The Great House and sometimes in The School House. In mid-winter he liked to wander through the snow to the windows and sit and watch the lively people singing and laughing to the tune of fiddle and flute. Sometimes a pert Mockingbird in a cage on the windowsill would stare back at him with glowering eyes, bowing his head and lifting his tail menacingly.

Moonbeam felt as though he was a long way from The Great House and that Mockingbird now. It was not that they had traveled very far yet, but that with his mind so set on the way ahead—the world ahead—everything, even his old den full of precious things, seemed far, far away in another more cozy, less adventurous, world, which was mellow around its edges like the last shreds of sunset.

They heard Night-Creatures scurrying along the bank below, and they thought that they heard deer, startled, then running in The Wood. The trail rolled before them like a dark, meandering stream until it suddenly curved and disappeared among the bushy Laurels in distant darkness. But that darkness was not for Moonbeam the pitch black that made poor Groundhog gasp. For Moonbeam, it was full of shapes and shadows, lines of fine light and spots of colour. All of which seemed to revolve around a dark, distant center, as dark and distant as the bottom of a well.

"It must be a sudden drop or a dense wood or even a mud flat where there is nothing to catch the light," thought Moonbeam. He began to wonder if they were entering the territory of The Bridge Raccoons. There was something frightening about that darkness and the way it seemed to whirl about and change shape at its edges, like dark water lapping a jagged shore. Old Grandfather The Fisher's words returned to him again. But no, it could not be a sea, for the sea was at the end of The River, not before it.

The Groundhog sighed unhappily. "I believe," he said tiredly, "that it is getting even darker. I fear I will have to remain behind and wait for Day's Light. I can't see where I'm going, and strange faces with long teeth peer at me from among the laurels."

"They do not!" snapped Opossum, shaking his head. "I see absolutely no creature anywhere but you and Raccoon. I hear them, I smell them, but I can't see them, and your eyes are a good deal worse than mine because you can't see in the dark very well.

"I'm glad that you at least can see me!" whined the Groundhog, "for I can see nothing of myself—not one paw! I might have well have disappeared for all I know!"

Opossum looked at him sideways and rolled his eyes. "Yes, you're still there all right—a little on the plump side, too. Anyway, how do you see all those creatures with long teeth when you can't see your own paws?" he asked chidingly.

Moonbeam couldn't help laughing, and he patted the Groundhog on the back encouragingly. "Don't mind Pos," he said cheerily. "He means no harm. Opossums are by nature a little sharp and unfriendly. Take it as a compliment he walks with us at all! You are usually quite alone aren't you Pos?"

"Yes, that I am. Can't think how I got into this idea of traveling about in threes," Opossum answered, clicking his tongue.

"Well, really, I don't take the comments amiss," answered Groundhog softly, "but I do feel I can't walk much further in this pitch black." He tripped up again, let out a scream, and sat down with a bump.

"I'm really hurt now. A huge root has torn my paw, or it may have been a stone. Sharp it was—painful!" Groundhog began to lick the wound, whining and mumbling to himself all the time in a resigned tone as though there was no escape now from the perils of adventuring with Night-Creatures.

"It was a stone," said Moonbeam, studying the ground carefully and rolling the stone over in his sensitive hands. "Its edges are really sharp! Strange it should be in the middle of the trail. Stones on the trail usually get quite worn down." Moonbeam gently turned the Groundhog's foot up and looked at the black sole. "It is only a small cut," he said comfortingly, "very small."

"I am glad to hear it!" exclaimed the Groundhog. "I can't see it myself."

"A short rest and it ought to heal well enough," comforted Moonbeam, squeezing the Groundhog's shoulder. "You can rest under the Laurel branches if you like. Pos and I might climb a tree and take a look about, perhaps even a short nap."

The Groundhog sat up again and leaned over to lick his back paw. Moonbeam and Opossum saw the rich red-brown of his stomach and the pure white of his two front teeth in the moonlight. "I'm sorry to hold up the adventure in this way," he said mournfully, stretching out and then waddling towards the spreading Laurel branches. A sun-lover and a day-lover, he did not like to be above ground over night, and so he scratched about under some roots to make a hollow in which to curl.

Moonbeam and Opossum waited until he was quite settled down before climbing the tree above. And the further they climbed, the more hidden Groundhog seemed in the deep shade of the branches and roots. For his brown fur mingled marvelously with the brown earth until all Moonbeam could see was one black paw and a thin line of dark tail fur.

From the top of the tree, Moonbeam saw a pit-like opening in the trees ahead. "Is that a hollow, a water inlet, or mud flats do you think? There are no trees there to catch the light," he asked Opossum, pointing out across the tree-tops.

Opossum looked and blinked. "I don't know," he whispered, drawing his tail around his feet. He twisted his head over each shoulder as if looking for hidden enemies among the branches.

Moonbeam also noticed that the trees before that dark pit were thick and tall, making a mighty forest wall that swelled upwards following the steep curve of a hill. "It can only be The Great Dark Forest," he thought, with a shudder. He looked at Opossum, but said nothing. Turning on his heels, he saw, in the North, a narrow break in the trees following the Creek's course. Bright silver moonlight flooded in, shining on Holly leaves on the opposite bank, and on the new brilliant red of leaf shoots. With his eyes dazzled by this beauty, and his mind so full of The Forest, Moonbeam could not sleep although he relaxed his back in a hollow and wound his tail carefully around his feet for warmth.

"What is that?" whispered Opossum, leaning forward and seeing the tail of an animal slink past below.

Moonbeam peered down and saw a strange creature appear from behind a tree. He was stunned by its bright ginger fur and full tail, both of which stood out startlingly against a snow-white bib and white tail tip.

"It's a Fox!" whispered Opossum, gripping Moonbeam's paw.

They watched the Fox move cautiously down the trail, skirting the trees on its darkest side where he could not be easily seen. He looked nervous and shy, and glanced behind each tree trunk as he passed, turning his head from side to side. Sometimes he looked up and blinked in the light of the stars, and Moonbeam saw clever ginger-brown eyes, as intelligent and deep as any Raccoon's, in a thin, sharp face. It was the first Fox that Moonbeam had ever seen, and he couldn't take his eyes away. He felt too a growing surge of energy such as he had never known before. His limbs stretched out. His back began to arch, in defense, in case the Fox was unfriendly.

"What about Groundhog?" whispered Opossum, his whole body tensing with anxiety. He sensed that Groundhog would be no match for a Fox in a fight.

But before Moonbeam had time to answer, the Fox smelt Groundhog and sprang to the base of their tree in one high leap. Poor Groundhog gave a loud, sharp whistle and ran from under the Laurel on the opposite side. He ran into the woods, chattering his teeth, hissing, squealing and growling in alarm. Without even thinking, Moonbeam climbed and then jumped down from his tree in front of Fox. He lowered his head, bared his teeth, flattened his ears and growled. The dark fur along the back of his neck and shoulders stood on end. He swiped out in front furiously, with sharp claws, while lifting his tail to show he was ready to fight. Energy surged through his body. Every muscle was tense. Speedily his eyes traced the Fox's body with a care he had never known he had. He saw each hair, each angle, and, beyond that, each rippling muscle.

The Fox was young and frightened. He had heard much about the dangerous Raccoons of The Bridge, and The Bridge was not far from there—just down an incline and around a bend.

Opossum, not to be left out, scrambled down the tree and hissed at the Fox while opening his mouth as wide as possible to show all his fifty sharp teeth.

"Forgive me," said the young Fox, shifting his eyes from side to side, looking first at Moonbeam's claws and then at Opossum's teeth. "I was merely curious, I meant no harm!"

Moonbeam did not relax one muscle. His eyes stared fiercely at the Fox. "Go on your way!" he exclaimed firmly, lashing the air with one dark paw. Opossum hissed. Both were afraid.

"Yes, well, I see I am quite unwanted here," he said softly, lifting his feet stealthily towards the trail with every word. His feet were dark and silent. They touched the ground like feathers falling on snow.

Moonbeam moved forward carefully, one step at a time. He lifted a clawed paw and showed his teeth at every move.

"I do not think," said the Fox shyly, dipping his head and crouching forward slightly, "that we have met before. Do you travel now or are you of The Bridge?"

His ginger tail stroked the ground softly. The white tip gleamed in the moonlight. He seemed to be smiling.

Without answering, Moonbeam ran forward as if to fight. "Go on your way!" he cried, even more loudly than before. He had quickly seen that they would be safer if the Fox though he was one of the menacing brigands of The Bridge that all the Five Worlds talked about and feared.

"There is no need for such unfriendliness," the Fox whispered, pulling back across the trail. "I mean no harm." But there was a strange glow in the Fox's eyes; a glow they all feared, fierceness despite the smile.

Opossum ran forward and opened his mouth even wider. He hissed between showing his teeth until his throat was quite sore and his jaws ached. Groundhog chattered and stamped his feet between small, fretful noises of fear, from a small hollow in a nearby bank.

Moonbeam bounded forward, growling and tearing at the air with his paws. He lunged at the Fox. The Fox yelped and sprang up with astonishing force and speed, turned a half somersault in the air, and dived into the trees. All they saw was the tail-tip deep in the undergrowth, and then, in a flash, he was gone.

Yet Moonbeam and Opossum thought they heard a smooth, soft whisper like honey dropping from the hive. They thought they heard the Fox whisper "I shall return." But perhaps that was only the breeze rustling in the undergrowth, and Opossum thought he saw several pairs of dark eyes gleam then disappear.

Moonbeam did not relax. He stepped forward cautiously, searching the distance with careful eyes for any sign of danger. Everywhere was silent now. Behind, some rain was beginning to fall.

Groundhog, unable to restrain his grateful happiness, sprang up, rolled over and ran to Moonbeam. "Oh!" he cried with tears in his eyes. "I do think you are courageous! Wonder of wonders! How courageous you are!"

Moonbeam did not move, and Opossum remained serious. They were both watching the woods across the trail. Rainwater gathered on their backs in the moonlight, and they began to look as if they were covered with tiny gems of white-silver that Groundhog could just see in the darkness. He blinked in admiration. "How can I thank you both enough!" he exclaimed leaping up, then down, while smiling and laughing with joy.

Moonbeam still did not turn round, but backed up cautiously until he could see Groundhog beside him. "We will look for a tree hollow and den up for a while," he said seriously. "We need rest, but we had better stay together now."

"Oh! I do think so!" cried the Groundhog excitedly, but frowning in re-membrance of the possible danger he had just escaped.

"Can you climb at all?" Moonbeam asked, glancing at the Groundhog's short legs and plump paws.

"Yes, a little, but not as well as you two," Groundhog answered, feeling sud-denly very small, almost childish. "How unsuited I, a den-lover, am for these grand and dangerous adventures," he thought, pursing his lips with bitter dis-satisfaction. "But it is much too late to turn back now," he exclaimed to himself, raising his eyebrows and whimpering.

Moonbeam heard that whimper and felt very sorry for the poor Groundhog. "Well, don't worry. Pos and I can help you up and down. Let's look for a den—a nice, large dry one!" he said comfortingly, waving a paw in a wide circle. He suddenly felt very grown-up and very proud to be a Raccoon. "I have peeled off another layer of reality," he thought with triumph, and this time I have found my own nature, my own Raccoon-ness!"

Opossum did not say a word. Despite all his fear, he didn't think he had ever seen a creature more beautiful or amazing than Fox!

# Chapter SIX
## The Island of Purple Fruit

*The search for a* suitable den took quite a long while. It rained heavily most of the time, which made the search much more difficult. The first hollow was too shallow, while the second, a nice hole in a tree, proved to have a leaky roof to one side. A roomy den of several chambers located near the trail was not clean enough for Moonbeam or cozy enough for Pos. But in the end, they found one very suitable to their needs, consisting of several clean, spacious chambers at the base of a wide, hollow tree. To top all, the doorway at the front was only just big enough for Moonbeam, which meant other creatures couldn't wander in unawares, especially if they blocked the entrance with mud and twigs. And the back door, well, the back door was a real thrill! It opened up under a mossy bank of roots and weeds and overhanging Laurel, and was so secret that no one would ever be able to see it from the outside.

"Wonder of wonders!" cried the Groundhog, once he was well settled inside and had scraped the floor to hollow and soften it for sleeping. "Who could want a better den! This is luxurious! Better by far than my own den at Home!" And for a Groundhog, that was a compliment indeed!

Moonbeam had collected up some smooth pebbles from outside, an old acorn cup, and a flat, round, gold object with delicate designs on either side. He hoarded them in a corner by his sleeping area and stared at them lovingly.

"Collecting again, I see!" exclaimed Pos with some irritation.

"Oh, I know I can't take them along, but they decorate this den nicely and make it more my own. I never cared for empty dens. A home for the wind that—the wind only." Moonbeam turned the gold object again. If fitted in his hands very well. He bit the edge to test it. It was quite solid and tasted metallic like the hinges on the gate at The Great House.

"I've seen those before," said Groundhog, shrugging his shoulders with disinterest. "Once when digging new chambers above the meadow. I found a great many of them—some silver, others gold—in a square shaped log. It had a lid and was lined with strange, green, close cropped fur which had no smell of any creature I know."

"What do you suppose they are?" asked Moonbeam, mesmerized by their glow and brilliance. He thought he saw his own face reflected there as in creek water by moonlight.

"Stars perhaps," said Opossum, very proud to have thought of something original to say.

"Surely not!" cried Groundhog, quite surprised. "Do stars fall from the sky and collect like that in logs?" He shook his head as if to say that there was more in this world than he had ever dreamed of before.

"They do look like stars," muttered Moonbeam dreamily, wondering what it would be like to fly through the sky to the earth below. "Would that be something like swimming through cool water?" he wondered.

"The gold ones—like that one—might fall from the sun itself then," said Groundhog seriously, eyeing the gold piece and beginning to yawn.

"The sun!" sighed Moonbeam, blinking and curling down to rest. "It is like the sun too, and the moon, and the figure in windows of The Great House, and The Girl in The Garden.

"The Girl in The Garden?" questioned Opossum, tucking his tail under his front paws.

"Yes, sometimes she carries a lantern, a moon of her own, and it shines like this:" Moonbeam polished the gold against his fur and lay it carefully beside the pebbles and the acorn cup. He recognized on one side the face of a person such as he saw pressed to the windowpanes in The Great House when he sat there on cold, winter nights and stared in. Were there faces on the stars he thought, and on the moon and on the sun? Stamped there like an endless reflection that even cloudy, moonless nights could not take away as they did his own reflection in creek water or rain puddles. "This is quite a find!" he said aloud, very proudly.

Opossum sighed.

Soon, despite the fact Moonbeam and Opossum usually wandered about all night long, they were all fast asleep, cuddled together for warmth, dreaming their own dreams of their dens, of The Red Fox, and of glorious, silver Silversheen and of The King of The River.

Moonbeam dreamt he was in a boat, the shape of the silver, crescent moon, gliding down Silversheen to Moonlight Inlet, and that there he waved to Swift-Paws across the water. Swift-Paws called out to him and beckoned and cajoled until Moonbeam turned his boat that way and drifted in on a strong current and a strong wind.

"Chuck, chuck, chuck" the boat creaked up and down on the waves in the wind. "Chip, chip, chip" the waves said as they splashed the prow. The boat moved on "chuck, chuck, chuck" but the waves rolled high "chip, chip, chip" and splashed on Moonbeam's fur and against his nose. Higher and higher they rolled, "chip, chip, chip," flooding over his back, trickling down his nose and tickling his sensitive ears. He brushed the water away with his paws and then sneezed loudly—not once, but twice. The noise echoed in the hollow den, and he waked suddenly, feeling as if he and his little boat were being engulfed in the lapping waters of Moonlight Inlet.

He looked around the den anxiously. A "chuck, chuck, chuck" was followed by a trilling "chip, chip, chip" and something with very tiny feet of delicate weight ran across his tail.

Moonbeam jumped up. "I say!" he cried, "who is running over my tail and giving me bad dreams?"

"It's our den! Chuck, chuck, chuck," chattered a small voice resentfully and fretfully.

"Yes!" exclaimed another voice in a higher pitch, and following this exclamation with a chattering "Chip, chip, chip! We have worked for simply ages to build burrows underneath and gather foodstores of acorn, hickory nut and seeds."

"Chuck, chuck, shush!" whispered the other in a low, chastising tone. "Will you tell the whole world where our winter stores lie hidden?"

By now, Opossum, who had only slept very lightly, woke with a start and then jumped up. "Who are those?" he whispered to Moonbeam, pointing to a whole line of tiny, brown and black striped creatures who stared pertly from a shelf a little above him. They chattered, darted about, suddenly swarmed towards Moonbeam and Opossum, and just as suddenly turned and ran back to their narrow shelf, calling "Chip, chip, chip." Every now and then, they looked curiously at the Groundhog who lay asleep and was snoring quite loudly—much too loudly in fact for comfort or safety. They could see that he was more like them than either Opossum or Raccoon, but that he was a great deal bigger. He was like the Chipmunks in their legends who bravely fought, even with the snake, and crossed rivers on shiny logs to visit exotic lands, rich with purple fruits and acorns and hickory nuts as big as their heads.

"I am sorry we have taken your den," said Moonbeam softly. "It was pouring with rain outside and this seemed to be a comfy and dry spot. No one was at home when we came."

"It is quite the comfiest and driest in the Five Worlds." cried one of the little creatures with renewed pride, bounding forward and then doubling back.

"And we were at home when you came," chirped another slightly larger one, leaning over the shelf edge and staring pertly into Moonbeam's eyes. Moonbeam saw that his eyes were very dark and glossy and striped above and below with light brown fur, and that his chin and stomach were pure white, like thistledown. "We were in our burrows down below, sleeping and sorting stores," he continued, quite excited to have outwitted a Raccoon.

Moonbeam looked at Opossum and frowned. "I never heard a thing," he whispered in a puzzled voice, shaking his head.

"That you wouldn't!" chirped a Chipmunk, smiling in self-satisfaction and lifting his two front paws to show his white stomach.

"Yes, chip, chip, chip, we run as softly as new-falling powder-snow. You cannot hear us," laughed a small one twirling on the shelf and then running forward to dip in and out of the tree roots with the greatest of ease and grace. To Opossum, he looked like a rich brown leaf caught on an Autumn breeze. He had seen leaves twirling, scurrying and floating along in the woods by The Garden. There had been times when he had sat and watched them in wonder with his head tilted to one side, his eyes wide with curiosity. How could one explain their winter garments of rich red-brown or their restless dance below their old home?

"But who is that?" asked a quieter Chipmunk who up till now had sat thoughtfully at the far end of the shelf near the back door. Moonbeam followed the line of his tiny paw and saw he was pointing at Groundhog, who continued to sleep quite unconcerned by all the talking and scampering.

"A friend of ours," answered Opossum with great dignity, sidling towards Groundhog in loyalty.

"Has he been to the Island of The Purple Fruit?" inquired a timid voice, ending his question with a short "chip, chip, chip!" that somehow sounded like a question mark.

"Chuck, chuck, shush!" exclaimed an older Chipmunk, pulling the other back and looking at him with hard eyes. "Cant' you see he is not of our kind. He has no stripes, no white bib."

"But there is something the same," whined the timid Chipmunk, sliding to the back of the ledge to sulk in the shadows.

"I don't know what island you mean," said Opossum thoughtfully licking his lips and shaking his head. How much he liked fruit! Especially purple fruit! Though he liked apples and persimmons in season and had climbed trees for cherries in The Garden by The Great House. "Where is this island?" he asked, trying to sound casual as if he had no interest whatsoever in fruit.

Moonbeam looked at him sharply and turned to the row of chipmunks and nodded and said "Where?" very quietly, almost as though it was a drifting sigh or a soft meadow breeze in summer.

"There, you see what comes of chattering!" snapped the larger Chipmunk glowering at the younger one. He turned sharply to Moonbeam and Opossum and spread his arms: "No one here has ever found it," he said sadly, frowning until there were a series of wrinkles just above his twitching, pink nose.

"It is said to be east of rising Day's Light, and to drift in warm, blue waters below an eternally sunny sky," chirped a small voice excitedly.

"Oh, then we shouldn't want to go there," said Moonbeam thoughtfully in a flat, disappointed voice.

"No!" exclaimed Opossum in a ratty voice. "We shouldn't at all care for eternally sunny skies. Shouldn't be surprised if that island has melted or is full of monsters with sharp teeth and sinister jaws."

The Chipmunks looked at each other in surprise and raised their shoulders. They had no idea what Opossum was talking about. "Well, I can assure you that the Island hasn't melted and that there are no monsters there," cried the younger Chipmunk, stamping a back foot in annoyance, "or our Heroes wouldn't go there!" He said this very surely, as though there was no point in discussing the thing any further. He wished now that he had never mentioned The Island of Purple Fruit, but he never-the-less looked longingly at the Groundhog—all his young life he had been waiting to see one of the Heroes of their legends. Sometimes on windy days he thought he saw one rounding a corner, but, when he ran to catch up, he found it was a leaf in the wind. Once he thought he found the Island, but it turned out to be only a muskrat den full of flat-tailed muskrats with protruding teeth and beady eyes.

Moonbeam had been very thoughtful since his last question. He was wondering if the island was in Silversheen and if the Chipmunks had ever seen the King of The River. "Have you been to Silversheen?" he asked at last, staring into each pair of eyes, looking for that gold glint that always betrays recognition. They looked at each other puzzledly and shrugged their shoulders again.

"Where is Silversheen?" one asked, pricking up his ears in curiosity.

"Before Day's Rising Light," answered Moonbeam dreamily. "It is a wide river—so wide the distant woods look blue behind the dark line of the shore."

The Chipmunks sat silently, staring into Moonbeam's dreamy eyes. "We have never seen a river," said an older Chipmunk finally in a low voice. His chin and back were slightly grey with age, and his eyes were watery and less bright than the youngsters around him. There was in them, however, a bright glint of wisdom. "I heard stories in my youth of sparkling rivers and dark, deep seas, but I have never heard of Silversheen. Though I have heard of an eastern river called Silver-Stripe. In the mornings it was said to glow red with new Day's Light, and along it banks grew every kind of luscious fruit and nut."

"It may be the same one," said Moonbeam thoughtfully, turning his precious objects over in his gentle hands, as he always tended to do when dreaming or content or thoughtful.

Opossum passed over to him and stared down at them. Then suddenly he looked up and, eyeing all the Chipmunks, seriously asked, "Have you heard of The King of The River?"

Moonbeam gasped. He had not really wanted to share his ideas of the secrets of their adventure with so many lively chipmunks.

"Can't say we have," answered the older Chipmunk gravely, stroking his chin with nimble fingers. "Is he a Hero too, like the youngster thought that one?" He pointed at Groundhog and pursed his thin lips.

Moonbeam and Opossum looked at their plump, snoring friend and could not help but smile; their idea was so much more colourful, so much swifter, so much lighter, and so much more majestic than poor Groundhog. Strangely, their hearts went out to him now because he was just the opposite of the magnificent Fisher-King of whom they thought. It was as if they were suddenly able to see the Groundhog more clearly—to see his cheerfulness, ease of temper, friendliness and thoughtfulness as real things like wild flowers in moonlight or red berries on a holly bush.

"Ordinary but wonderful!" said Moonbeam aloud but under his breath. "'The Owl was right, Pos," he said suddenly, almost breathlessly. "Reality is made of many layers. Adventuring has more to do with discovering ourselves than a new world. I am beginning to see everything in a new light—to value what I took for granted." He found it hard to believe, but he now knew that Pos and Groundhog had become very important to him, and what is more, they had been all along, even before they met and talked about journeys at the end of the Garden. Each gave his world fresh richness and depth, difference and liveliness—one by Day's Light, the other by Moonlight.

Opossum looked at Moonbeam and smiled grimly. "You are not going to get odd again, are you?" he asked, alarmed by Moonbeam's glossy eyes and twitching paws. He remembered well all the scurrying around, collecting and hiding things, before they left. It had made him really dizzy!

Moonbeam felt a little annoyed. Here he was just beginning to make a new discovery about his world, about himself, and all Opossum could say was "You are not going to get odd again, are you?" He sighed forlornly and flattened himself to the ground.

"Well you know, "continued Opossum, looking sideways at the Groundhog, "I like him as well as you do, but I don't know about the 'wonderful' part. You did say 'wonderful' you know."

"Yes, I did," said Moonbeam quickly, with some force. "Meant it too!"

"Oh dear! Oh dear!" sighed Opossum, shaking his head. "You really can dream!" He dragged out the word 'really', stressing every letter. Each letter grated on Moonbeam's ears like claws on rock. He began to wonder if Pos wasn't a little jealous of the Groundhog, and he tried to understand why that would be. Perhaps he envied the Groundhog's usual buoyancy and cheerfulness, or his friendliness and innocent charm. Pos, after all, had none of the skills for making easy friendships, and he tended to worry and fret. But an easier answer might well be that Opossum couldn't peel down the layers of reality and peer inside like Moonbeam. Calling a Groundhog 'wonderful' might well sound odd to him when all he saw was brown plumpness, snoring in an untidy fashion. Groundhog had rolled over. His chest was bright ginger like a Fox. His tongue lolled out to one side, and it was a brighter pink than any cherry or nodding moccasin flower that Moonbeam had ever seen. The Chipmunks stared.

"No, The King is not like your heroes if indeed they look a little like our sleeping Groundhog here," said Moonbeam softly. "The King is brilliant blue and sparkling white and crowned with jet black that shines like the night. He moves more swiftly than the Swallow and his call can be heard throughout the Five Worlds from The Great House to Silversheen."

"Then we do not know him," the old Chipmunk answered solemnly.

"But he knows you," said Moonbeam, gliding his dark eyes over them. Then in a trailing voice that sounded as if he was many hills away, he said, "He knows every creature along The Creek and The River, in The Wood and in The Meadow. He has seen us all—every one."

"Well, he doesn't know me," exclaimed Pos irritably. He was getting quite exasperated with the Raccoon, and he did not at all like the idea of folks staring down at him from above when he was not aware—like a hawk, for example. He was very surprised that the Raccoon should say any such a thing with such calmness, even wonder.

"We have Heroes who know us in that way." said the old Chipmunk thoughtfully, studying the Groundhog again. Somehow, he was not surprised that the Groundhog slept on and on and on. He seemed, though so near, very distant, as if his spirit really did wander The Island of Purple Fruit.

And the Groundhog was in fact a long way away, dreaming. Dreaming of warm sun, deep grass nests at the end of long tunnels—longer than he had ever dug—and rich meadows full of delicious roots and plants. "Wonder of wonders!" he muttered contentedly in his sleep. He licked his lips and patted his paws with delight. His eyes half opened in the half-light of the moonlight that came through the back door. He looked dreamily at the tiny shelf in the tree. But oh, what did he see! What was the slinking, thin line of ginger and white behind the ledges? He growled. He tried to stamp his feet at what seemed to be the Fox, crouching with a sharp smile on his thin face. He whistled, jumped up and began to run. He knocked Opossum flying, and all the Chipmunks raced to the door in alarm, calling to each other that the hero had awakened, had returned to the land of The Woods under the Night Sky. Their chattering calls only alarmed poor Groundhog further, and he changed direction and ran straight into Moonbeam.

The Groundhog was plump, and it was quite a hefty thump. Moonbeam groaned and fell backwards on the floor.

"Good gracious!" wailed the Groundhog, lifting his paws to his face, amazed. "I am sorry!"

Moonbeam got up, dusted himself off and scowled at the Groundhog. "What on earth was that for?" he complained. "What did I do?"

"Good gracious me!" cried Groundhog again, whirling round. "Where is that Fox now?" I should never have slept!"

Opossum looked round the den anxiously and began sniffing.

"What Fox?" asked Moonbeam, frowning and hunching.

"That Fox!" exclaimed the Groundhog, pointing to the shelf. "Ginger and white with several tails!" The Groundhog began to shake. His teeth began to chatter.

"There was no Fox there," snapped Opossum, rubbing the bruise in his shoulder.

The Groundhog looked about puzzledly and tiptoed to the shelf. Several Chipmunks had by now returned to the door and were peeping in with frightened dark eyes, as wide as blackberries. Groundhog ran his paw along the empty shelf and, just as he was about to say, "It must have been a dream," he caught sight of the ginger heads and white bibs and dark eyes of all those Chipmunks. He cried out and ran to the far side of the den and tried to dig his way out through the blocked door.

"Groundhog!" exclaimed Moonbeam. "What are you doing? Please don't ruin all our work!"

"It has hundreds of eyes!" wailed Groundhog, without looking round, "and ears! Good gracious! Good gracious!"

Opossum was very annoyed, for now earth was flying back towards him from between Groundhog's legs, and he liked to keep his coat as white as new-fallen snow!

"Oh dear! Oh dear! Groundhog, it is not a Fox," Opossum cried, running over and grabbing one of Groundhog's back legs. "Do quiet down. They are Chipmunks, not Foxes."

"I didn't say Foxes," cried Groundhog, still digging. "I said a Fox with lots of eyes and ears. Dreadful! Quite dreadful!"

"It's not a Fox," snapped Opossum, pulling Groundhog back across the den floor. "They're Chipmunks—Chipmunks—quite harmless!"

Groundhog turned round and looked at them. He was entirely awake now. Nothing like digging for putting spirit in one, he thought excitedly. His paws were still swimming in the air, as if he couldn't stop. He was quite breathless.

"Never...heard...of...Chipmunks!" he blurted out, taking a deep breath between each word.

Groundhog stared at each Chipmunk in disbelief. He saw the bright brown—almost ginger—of their heads and backs, and the pure swan white of their chests and chin. Their dark eyes seemed to be laughing, but Groundhog was quite unaware why. He did not know that in a few breathless moments, he had fallen from the realm of the Heroes to quite an ordinary Groundhog with poor eyesight and poor judgment. "I can't help it if I only have Day vision," he said petulantly, even sadly.

"Well anyway, Groundhog," said Moonbeam, laughing, "I don't somehow think you will ever see the Island of Purple Fruit!"

"Purple Fruit?" questioned Groundhog, raising his eyebrows. "What are you talking about?"

# Chapter SEVEN
## The Hermit of the Forest

*The afternoon was very* cold, and they shivered and their teeth chattered as Moonbeam, Opossum and Groundhog traveled along the Laurel Ridge. The afternoon light was enveloped in heavy black clouds that left the Groundhog depressed and brooding, but made it easier for the Raccoon and Opossum to see, especially in the gloomy darkness of The Wood. Moonbeam wished that they had got an earlier start, but it had stormed all morning, filling The Wood with the sound of thunder and outlining the treetops in white lightening. Still now, rain fell all the time, and the wind blew gustily along the Laurel Ridge and around the dark corner ahead. What might be beyond that dark corner filled Moonbeam with both a pang of fear and thrill of curiosity. His encounter with the Fox may have given him courage but he was, nonetheless, nervous about the thick line of trees that the Chipmunks said marked the beginning of The Wildwood, or The Great Dark Forest, that he had heard so much about all his life, and which had been guarded for many, many Winters by the fierce Raccoons of The Great Forest Bridge. "Brigands!" Father Bright Eye had called them, Moonbeam remembered, and the name had stuck in The Garden.

Where the trail divided at the base of a huge Red Oak, they kept to the side that traveled along the Ridge, and did not follow the narrow path that dipped down to The Creek, and what the Chipmunks called maple Dell. Moonbeam could, nevertheless, see the swelling curve of Red Maple silhouettes in the distance, and he remembered well the Autumn colourfulness of their large, scarlet leaves with their three to five dramatic points, like sharp Opossum teeth. It was little wonder that the Chipmunks should live so near to the beautiful Red Maples for their seeds, stripped of their delicate wings, stored marvelously well for winter food. Beyond Maple Dell, Moonbeam saw the gentle curve of a hill, studded with the blue-grey bark of winter Beech and, nearby, the gnarled dark bark of ancient Black Oaks.

Strangely, and yet rightly, given all their fears, The Great Dark Forest started suddenly at that dark corner, just the other side of a long, narrow, silver-grey clearing. It stood there ahead of them like a magic wall dividing the world of The Creek and The Wood from Silversheen and Their Dream. The Forest looked unreal and mysterious in the gloom. Trailing wind-swept vines, including Poison Oak and Sumac, entwined the outer trees and filled the narrow spaces in between them. Winter bracken, grasses, Arbutus and Dewberry reached up from beneath to meet them and rustled eerily like the warning voices of Woodland Elves. Fine lines of silver light glistened wetly around the hollows and holes on trunks of forest trees, and sometimes the lines and their inner blackness seemed to outline a face—familiar or strange—with brooding brows, staring eyes and heavy, drooping mouths—both reproachful and solemn. The three travelers looked at them anxiously and were glad to see that they were at least not the faces of Bridge Raccoons.

"I do not at all like the look of this," whispered Groundhog, awed and afraid. "Beyond that massive wall of trees and vines, it must be damp and dark beyond anything we can imagine!"

Moonbeam nodded and frowned. He had heard too of other strange, even dangerous, forest-creatures besides the Bridge Raccoons. He looked about nervously. The faces on the tree-trunks seemed to be staring grimly at him—him especially! He thought again of Swiftpaws, and his recent dream of him calling from the banks of Silversheen seemed lost, swallowed-up, by this dense Forest dividing the worlds. Now instead, he imagined poor Swiftpaws wandering forever, lost and lonely, along narrow forest paths.

Opossum in his own way must have felt the same, for from out of the corner of his eye, Moonbeam saw Opossum's drawn, anxious face with eyes as beady and dark as two Black-currents. Opossum saw Moonbeam looking at him, but he did not speak. He was lost in the deep Opossum-silence that always came over him whenever he was in the presence of something that overwhelmed him, and the sight of that thick, high forest wall filled him with dread. He thought he saw glowering faces with hollow eyes among the branches, and the rain echoed so strangely in the distance that it sounded as though it was falling down a deep well or off the end of the Earth. "And perhaps," Opossum whispered to himself, "this is indeed the edge of the world, and this Great Dark Forest holds the edge together like the enormous rim of a cart-wheel in the stable-yard of The Great House." Yet he knew that there was a gap in the Forest shortly after one entered there, and that beyond that gap The Forest swelled upwards, rolling on and on as far as the eye could see, because he had seen that from the tree-top he climbed just before he saw Fox in The Wood.

Entering the Great Dark Forest was like suddenly ducking under deep, cold water to peer into a strange world that surged with a life and personality all of its own—brooding, dark, secret, and mysterious, and that one heart lay beating at its center like a dark-green pool.

"It is like nothing I have ever known before," Groundhog whispered, crouching down to walk as near to the ground and as softly as possible. He felt that the forest knew he was there, and that it thought of him as an intruder—a strange Groundhog from the far-distant world of The Meadow and The Garden. Somehow he expected the Forest to heave upwards like the dark-green back of a mighty dragon, or roll outwards like swift water riding smooth rocks, to throw them all backwards through the air to The Wood behind and The Creek beyond that. "It is so silent," he whispered, blinking, "and so dark".

They traveled for a long time, which seemed even longer in the gloom and rain, when suddenly the trail disappeared sharply down a dark incline where the trees, vines, and weeds were so thick that no light could enter to touch the ground below. Here, in this massy growth, no birds could be heard or the sound of scurrying footsteps of forest-creatures. No one ever comes here, not even the Red Fox, Opossum thought with dismay; this is a dead and silent world—the world before and after the days of The Five Worlds. The idea of the Bridge Raccoons of The Great Forest Bridge seemed even more frightening now, even ghostly; he imagined silent shapes with high, arched shoulders as black as night, and teeth as white as polished shells. "Do we leave The Five Worlds at that dip?" he asked nervously, pointing ahead and swallowing hard.

"No," said Moonbeam, as though he was again seeing a mysterious vision, a different reality, that the others could not yet see. "That is part of The Five Worlds as is The Garden, the Meadow, The Creek, and The River. It is not all lovely. It is not all safe." His eyes roamed over every detail of the scene ahead as they had over the body of the Red Fox in The Wood. This is the silence before the Fox leaps, before the Hawk dives, he thought, and yet this Forest has its own grandeur and charm—its own dangerous and chilling beauty. The raindrops that fell, swelled, and finally dropped from the black branches overhead, sparkled silver for a while like tiny gems, and if Moonbeam peered searchingly enough into them, he saw a whole forest world reflected there—miniature and pearly—like he imagined Fairy-Land. He called it Pearl Forest.

"Ah, you may say that!" said Opossum finally, not without a little bitterness. "Raccoons, whether of the fierce Bridge Family or not are, after all, still of your kind." Opossum said this as if Moonbeam was somehow in less danger than himself or somehow still in his own world, and for a fleeting moment it did seem that way, for Opossum had seen the wonder in Moonbeam's eyes when he thought of that name "Pearl Forest", and Opossum sensed that Moonbeam now had a secret that he would not share.

"Do Bridge raccoons eat Groundhogs?" muttered Groundhog grimly, setting his teeth.

Moonbeam did not answer.

"Well, do they?" Groundhog asked anxiously.

"I do not know," answered Moonbeam slowly. "I am of The Garden. This is not the Garden."

Opossum nodded. "I've no doubt they eat a great deal that they shouldn't!" he muttered, thinking of Opossums and pink Opossum tails. He didn't, however, think he would be very tasty, and his mind quickly returned to the berries he disliked sharing. He had no doubt they ate plenty of those!

They walked on cautiously towards the incline. There the trail seemed to wind around a stunningly tall Bitternut Hickory with grey, scaly bark tinged with yellow. Opossum recalled now how bitter their long nuts were inside the thin shells—so bitter, in fact, that even the squirrels did not like them. He remembered, too, their long, blade-like leaves and dusty catkins. How often he had climbed among their branches on Hickery Hill! It seemed strange that they should grow here too, in this other world, and yet how fitting! For the bitter nut offered no comfort and did not fill the stomach, and the tree itself always had a drawn, brooding look like a long, sad face.

Beneath, on the ground, to everyone's surprise, there were the tracks of the

Wild Turkey, and Moonbeam's eyes searched the distance for the bronze hue of their feathers and the chestnut tip of their fanning tails among the tree limbs. But, shy and wary as usual, the Turkeys were nowhere to be seen.

"I had begun to think no animal lived here besides those Bridge Raccoons," said Groundhog with a sigh, sounding a little relieved.

"Then there must be clearings here too," said Moonbeam, looking around, "though no doubt they can travel to The Wood to find their prized acorns, seeds, berries, and insects."

Opossum pursed his lips. He had little liking for this Forest, but he had no liking for open, light-filled clearings, either. He had seen Wild Turkeys of course, at dusk, but their fast running and loud gobbling unnerved him. Besides, he did not like to share his berries with Turkeys, either!

Just beyond the Bitternut Hickory, the trail swept away downhill and around a corner. Dead, rotting trees lay across their path, and the trail. Fanning grey and beige Bracket Fungi, sometimes with pure white underneath, grew on them. Moonbeam knew they were a sign of decay and change and then new growth. For did not the Bracket Fungi break down the tree-wood for food, and did not the rotted wood eventually provide rich soil for new growth? A forest might feel as if it had existed unchanged and unchangeable since the dawn of time, but forests change, spring up, grow, and disappear without a trace. Perhaps The Garden and The Meadow were once forest. Perhaps the Great House, which now seemed so far, far away, was built over a forest's thickest part—its very center. Moonbeam shook his head. It was all so hard to imagine, and yet somehow this fanning Bracket Fungi hinted as much!

Here the trail was steep, uneven, rocky, and wet, and they all tended to slide and scramble as their own body weight threw them forward on their front feet. Soon, despite the cold and the rain, Moonbeam was sweating and he could hear the other two behind him, panting.

"How steep this is!" exclaimed Opossum, more than a little exasperated. With short legs and his stomach so low to the ground, downhill travel, especially over wet rocks, was not easy.

The trail suddenly turned sharply in the opposite direction and pierced its way through a thick mass of heavy, trailing vines. "It is as well," said Groundhog, "that we did not make our journey in Summer. Who could get through here when those vines are covered with leaves and full with new growth?"

Moonbeam nodded and wondered how long it had been since any woodland creatures traveled this trail. Since the Turkey tracks, he had seen no other signs of life.

They traveled on and on, and the trail twisted back and forth, this way and that, always downhill. They were beginning to think that it never would end when suddenly they saw a wide break in the forest trees—strange, and tinged a curious blue—and the trail just as suddenly disappeared from sight. Opossum gasped!

They walked carefully to the edge where the trail had disappeared, and there their breath was quite taken away by the view before them. Below, distant and dark, swirling with white mists, was a deep ravine crossed by a curving creek that was such a bright silver it made them wonder if it possessed a strange, even dangerous, magic, and across the middle, high in the air, buffeted by the wind, was a long wooden bridge with high side rails, which shone so brightly Moonbeam and Opossum couldn't see the middle—it looked to them like a silver drawbridge, an arc of light.

"It must be The Bridge of The Great Dark Forest," whispered Moonbeam, overawed by the sight before him. Nothing in all his wildest dreams could have prepared him for this dramatic and wild beauty before him or for the magical look of the Bridge itself. Perhaps indeed this was the entrance to another world!

"Do we cross that Bridge?" asked Groundhog anxiously. He could think of nothing worse than traveling so high in the air, for so long, with all the eyes of The Forest upon him—he was sure that The Forest had eyes. How he longed now for his deepest den, down his longest underground tunnel!

No one answered poor Groundhog, for it was quite obvious that there was no other way across the ravine, and Groundhog would have liked climbing down its steep, wet cliffs, covered with slippery mosses and loose rocks, even less. Besides, there was something forbidding about that gleaming silver creek that flowed along the ravine below them: it looked somehow thick and poisonous like Nightshade juice.

"Owl said to cross any bridge we must cross before dusk," whispered Opossum in an amazed voice, without looking round at Moonbeam. The idea of crossing any bridge at all stunned him now, and this bridge was higher and stranger than any he had ever imagined.

Groundhog groaned softly. If the Wise Old Owl of The Meadow Wood had talked about crossing bridges, then he supposed there would be no escape from crossing this one! In fact, he began to think that one couldn't journey at all without crossing bridges—many bridges, some high and dangerous and buffeted by the wind, as this one was. That idea inspired an odd kind of courage and determination in Groundhog for, after all, what could not be avoided had best be faced with spirit and good-will. He set his ears upright and his eyes became glossy and wide.

"It would be unwise to go down and try to cross now," added Opossum. "We have no idea where The Bridge Raccoons are hiding. We may walk right into a trap. Besides, it is difficult to see by day. The center of the bridge is as bright as starlight!"

"But I can!" said Groundhog. "I can see the center of The Bridge. I can lead you!" The words came tumbling out, shocking Moonbeam and Opossum, even shocking Groundhog himself. He did not think of himself as brave or as any sort of leader—quite the reverse, in fact—but he suddenly felt now that this bridge crossing would be his task, his triumph or failure.

"Well!" exclaimed Opossum in disbelief, but remembering Wise Owl's words. How life does surprise one, he thought.

"If we are going, we had best go now," said Moonbeam quickly, with a sense of foreboding.

"I agree," said Groundhog, thinking that dusk by this Bridge in The Great Dark Forest, on a rainy evening, would be darker and drearier than anything he had ever experienced. He imagined evening mists swirling along the ravine and gradually rising up the cliffs, and he imagined the creek at the bottom turned to dark winter grey, then glossy black as the light faded, like a dark serpent in frothy seas.

They made their way stealthily and nervously down the rocky trail to the Bridge. They lifted their feet high and placed them firmly so as not to send rocks clattering down before them to awaken the Bridge Raccoons if they were there. They even breathed as softly as they could, rounding out their bodies to show no movement and perhaps to disguise from themselves and each other the rapid beating of their hearts.

Opossum bit his lips. His imagination painted gloomy scenes before him. He thought he heard an Owl overhead and a snake slithering through the dry leaves on The Great Dark Forest floor. In the distance, he thought he heard an animal slinking softly—perhaps a Fox, perhaps a Bobcat. Ahead he thought he saw dark shapes on the opposite bank. But what happened next happened so quickly that he never knew how he had slipped and tumbled head over heels, his pink tail flying through the air like a whip, his feet swimming helplessly before him, over the trail edge to a narrow, rocky ledge below. There he hung by his front feet and tried, without any success, to scramble back up. Rocks clattered down around him as he struggled, and then echoed in the ravine below. He bit his lips and tears gathered in his eyes. He didn't even dare cry out.

"Quick! Hold onto my feet and tail!" cried Moonbeam to Groundhog, and he leaned as far over the edge as possible to catch poor Opossum by the wrists. Groundhog held onto Moonbeam for all he was worth, leaned back and grit his teeth. Moonbeam was heavy and soon his arms ached.

"Pull!" cried Moonbeam breathlessly. "Pull hard!"

Groundhog pulled Moonbeam upwards and fell back on the trail just as Opossum popped over the edge with a surprised gurgle. Opossum was dirty, cut, and there was a large tear on the end of his nose. His eyes were red and he looked completely shocked.

"That was a narrow escape!" chastised Moonbeam, staring deep into Opossum's red eyes.

Opossum flinched. He had tried to be careful, tried so hard to watch the trail, but he wasn't used to this rough world, full of steep, winding paths and jutting rocks that seemed to jump out at him. He did not, however, try to make excuses out loud. He sensed that he was now in a world that didn't hear excuses. Here there was only triumph or failure. "Thank you both," he said meekly, gratefully. He was so glad to have not fallen among the Bridge Raccoons or to the bottom of the deep ravine.

"Well, don't day-dream!" muttered Moonbeam curtly, "keep an eye on the trail!" Opossum sighed. At least it had now stopped raining.

"No, do not dream!" echoed a soft voice that ended with a gentle trilling. The voice seemed to well out of the distance, reedy and clear, and with a swinging, down-and-up melody, rather like the sound of the Girl's old swing in The Garden by The Great House.

Moonbeam, Opossum, and Groundhog stood quite still and looked all around, but they could see no one. "It is the breeze in the branches, gently creaking," said Groundhog, looking up above at the dark branches overhead.

"No," whispered Moonbeam softly. "I have heard a voice like that before—less rich, less beautiful, but at its heart the same."

"Where?" asked Opossum, surprised.

"In the Meadow at the edge of The Wood I have heard the Wood-thrush," Moonbeam's eyes widened in wonder. Here in the forest was a richer, more magical expression of what he had heard in his own world; a voice that was both a reminder of the past and promise of a more magical future.

"Why don't you come to me? Here I am! Close by you!" sung the voice, blending high and low notes so sweetly and lullingly that the three travelers relaxed inside themselves while thoughtful expressions softened their features and glossed their eyes. Then for a fleeting moment The Forest seemed lighter and gentler and The Bridge seemed lovely rather than dangerous. It is Pearl Forest, thought Moonbeam with a gasp, here all the time under my feet, and not just in the raindrops hanging on the branches! Yet there was also a clear chillness to the voice that made each of them think of cold, running water, snow, and northern, cloud-capped mountains that they had never seen.

"But where does this voice come from?" whispered Opossum, with a start at the sound of his own voice. The silence of The Forest seemed deeper now than before.

"From above," breathed Groundhog, still looking up.

But the voice welled up again in the distance, perhaps even from the far side of the deep ravine in which it echoed:

> "Northern waters bubble by
> Through forests tall
> Far from view—far from view!
> There I line my nest so soft
> With moss and fur
> Wet with dew—wet with dew!"

"How beautiful!" exclaimed Moonbeam, in a whisper. Each reedy, warbling phrase began with a piping note that seemed in the silence like a ray of moonlight at midnight. He felt as if he now stood in a circle of silver light.

There was a rustling sound in the distance and something on earthen-brown flashing wings flew towards them and landed high above among the dark branches of an Oak. There they thought they saw a gleam of rust against soft grey, and then a speckled breast like a Thrush or Veery.

> "Beware the Weasel and Fox
> And Mink's soft hue

Close by you—close by you!
Where Lynx stalks alone
The Black Bear too,
In Forest dells—in Forest dells!"

Opossum shivered. "I do not like the sound of that!" he whispered, crouching low to the ground and looking searchingly into the Oak branches above.

"Nor I!" nodded Groundhog, who had heard many stories about Lynx, Bobcats, and Black Bears, although he had never heard of this creature called a Mink.

"It is like the warning voice of the Forest Elves of our stories," Opossum said, turning to Moonbeam. He had not understood Moonbeam's words about the Wood Thrush, and he was always suspicious of those who warned others in soft and beautiful songs that seemed only suited for singing about gentle things, bright things, like Butterfly wings.

Moonbeam wandered to the base of the Oak and peered up through its branches. There was no movement above, and the silence was again so deep that he felt as if he could have reached out with his fingers and touched it. He imagined somehow that it would feel like a delicate but elastic skin—something like the surface of a clear pool stretched across a woodland hollow, smooth and transparent.

Behind Moonbeam, Opossum sighed, and the sigh sounded loud and full in the quiet. Then the flute-like voice above sang out again in liquid notes that seemed to spill over the ravine edge and bubble in echoes over the rocks:

"Snow melts on misty mountain-tops
Above northern forests deep and green!
Hear the Porcupine walking!
Hear the Snow-Goose calling!
Quiet—quiet—they hear you!
The day and night is full
Of forest eyes—of forest eyes!"

There was a rustle and a flutter, and the songster flew up and out and down the ravine, lifted and tossed, flame-rust and earthy brown, like an autumn leaf in the wind.

"She is gone," whispered Opossum, thinking of whirling leaves in a winter wind, but thinking especially of forest eyes—yellow and green and glowing. He looked around anxiously. Who, he wondered, is watching us now? And he remembered the eyes he had seen after the Fox leaped into the undergrowth— dark eyes gleaming with surprise. "I have seen those forest eyes," he murmured unsurely, dipping his head.

"We all feel that we have," said Moonbeam, without taking his eyes off the path of that forest songster. Who was she? he wondered. Did she travel north to the land of which she sang, or did she stay in The Great Dark Forest to sing of the Weasel, the Fox, Lynx, the Bobcat, the Black Bear, and the Mink, and forest eyes that filled the night and then the day?

Moonbeam stared and stared in the path of the lonely, usually silent Hermit Thrush, who a moon from now would build her cup-shaped nest lined with Porcupine hair, and then lay four smooth, blue-green eggs. Then a northern forest that had been covered all Winter in deep snow would hear her songs, and perhaps she would sing of Moonbeam, Opossum, and Groundhog, and The Bridge in the Great Dark Forest.

# Chapter EIGHT
## Black-Tip's Band

*At the bottom of* the trail, The Bridge stretched out seemingly endlessly before them. Below, the cliffs dropped sheerly to a valley where late afternoon mists, now as white and fluffy as down on a thistle, swirled and rose. Here at the edge of The Bridge, light flooded through the trees in a bright silver pool, and Opossum and Moonbeam blinked and found that they could no longer see the opposite bank. The bridge was an arc of light.

"The world melts," Opossum said resignedly, expecting any minute the Bridge would crumble into the mist below.

"I had best lead now," murmured Groundhog, in a tone that showed he understood the plight of Night-Creatures in Day's bright light. He placed his front feet on The Great Dark Forest Bridge and lifted his brown eyes straight ahead to stare at the far end of The Bridge, which now was in darkness. A ray of sunlight racing across the treetops suddenly touched his forehead and his coat gleamed like burnished gold. He had never looked more handsome or more brave than in this crown of late afternoon sunlight.

They began to cross The Bridge slowly, carefully, one foot at a time. The ravine stretched out on either side of them, and towards the north they thought they recognized the Wood and The Creek below Maple Dell. Yet, at that distance, and from that height, both looked small and unreal, like a picture that might hang on a wall in the Great House. Somehow, they felt they would be too big to ever fit back there again.

Groundhog moved forward slowly. Somehow, as if dropping away heavy garments or as if a magic wand had been waved within him, he seemed to grow brighter and more majestic as he walked. Opossum blinked and wondered again about magic: did it work from inside out or outside in? As they neared the center of The Bridge, bright sunlight enveloped them, in an arc of light. Both were surrounded by a thousand rainbow colours that pulsed like warm sunlight on a mountain lake. Moonbeam felt as if he was a fish darting out of a tunnel into silver waters or a Swallow diving down to dip his wings in a golden pool. But nevertheless, like Opossum, he longed for darkness and the dark and pastel shades of night. He pulled into himself self-consciously.

"I am going to melt," said Opossum under his breath, sniffing out Groundhog's tracks across The Bridge. He could hear Moonbeam sniffing too, just to his side, but he could no longer see him.

"We have not far," whispered Groundhog comfortingly. "We are almost back into the shadows." He knew their need of dim light, though in that dimness he could not see as well as they.

Then suddenly, out of that silent, mysterious distance came a loud and heavy voice, crying, "What are you doing on OUR bridge?" The word "OUR" was stressed with menace, and Moonbeam could imagine a stick being waved or muscles being flexed for battle. His ears went back, his back arched, his teeth came to the edge of his lips. He peered through the light to the end of The Bridge as best he could, but could see no one. Although he recognized well enough that it was the voice of another Raccoon—rougher, harsher, more full of mockery than the voices of The Garden and The Meadow—but, nevertheless, the voice of a Raccoon. Opossum flattened his ears and did not even dare to breathe.

Groundhog thought he saw some white and black fur in the shadows ahead, and the glassy stare of glowering eyes. He lifted his head a little higher, and there, with the sun bright and warm on his back, called out, "We travel to Silversheen, to The King of The River!"

He was surprised by the firmness in his voice and so were his two friends. Has the sun brought out this bravery—the sun that reminds Groundhogs of all they cherish most? Moonbeam wondered.

There was a moment of deep silence, during which it seemed that they could have heard a feather drop to the forest floor. Then there was a stiff laugh:

## The Bridge Racoons

"Ah, you think so, Golden-One!" came the reply, full of challenge. "There are pirates on The River, brigands in The Forest! How will you pay your passage?"

Coarse laughter broke out all around them, and the three travelers realized that Bridge Raccoons, so soft and fleet of foot that they had not heard their coming, were everywhere, even swinging nonchalantly on the railings of the Bridge! Groundhog looked at them all in dismay. He saw, however, a strange, anxious look in their eyes, which they tried to hide behind various grins and laughs. He did not know what it could mean. He did not know that they had never seen a Groundhog before and that, to Night-Dwellers of The Great Dark Forest, he looked gold like noon-light itself!

"We intend to pay no passage!" Groundhog cried out strongly. "The way thought The Forest is free!"

The Bridge Raccoon laughed loudly. Like any Bridge Raccoon since the beginning of their history, he admired bravado—of which this Bridge in The Great Dark Forest was to his mind the final and best test. He remembered his own swaggering on The Bridge in his youth, when he first had come to join this motley band of Forest Raccoons. What a leader in the making I was! he thought to himself with a whistle, glancing around at his fellows and winking. He loved nothing better than the sound of strange feet on The Bridge and the chance to toss his boastful challenge, followed by the rowdy fight that he had always won.

"Ah, Iy! But you shall pay!" he called back while jumping forward. Groundhog now saw his face and was stunned. He had not imagined Raccoons could look so different, but this Bridge Raccoon was nothing like Moonbeam or the Raccoons of The Garden. This Raccoon looked cunning and boastful, and even the dark Raccoon mask on his face looked bandit-like and dare-devilish, like a famous robber or pirate that Groundhog had only met in Garden Tales.

The Bridge Raccoon was proud of the effect he had had on Groundhog and swaggered forward, swaying his hips and brandishing a paw. He muttered boastfully to himself—"Well, and am I not an astonishing sight, with my dark mask and luscious tail, my proud eye and rich forest territory!" He waved an arm and his motley band swarmed quickly and quietly in behind him. There they laughed and jeered and winked at each other, while swinging their full tails. The Great Dark Forest Bridge was entirely blocked.

It was an amazing sight, and despite the brightly coloured light around them, Moonbeam and Opossum could see a mass of dark shapes at the end of the Bridge in the shadows. They understood very quickly the danger they were all in now. Moonbeam could tell by the sound of their jeers and laughs that these Bridge Raccoons were big and muscular, although many sounded still quite young, and possibly not experienced in the ways of The Five Worlds.

Groundhog, usually so easy-going, was white around the eyes with anger and, unable to restrain himself any longer, ran forward at a charge, stamping his feet and chattering—'This Bridge was here before you and your band! It belongs to all the creatures in The Five Worlds, from Shrew to Eagle!"

All the Bridge Raccoons ran forward too. Light enveloped them and, to Moonbeam, the Raccoons were now surrounded by pastel shades trimmed with brilliant silver. With sudden panic, he realized that there were many, many more Raccoons than he had imagined, and he lunged forward to pull Groundhog back, brandishing his fists and growling loudly as he did so. Opossum sprang forward too, hissing and snapping his fifty teeth. He saw no alternative, but had begun to think the whole idea of bridge-crossing entirely foolhardy. "I shall end my days in the ravine below," he moaned to himself softly. He was, nevertheless, ready to fight, and he had been more than a little intrigued, even inspired, by the boastful voice of the brigand-leader. He liked a good boast at any time, and he would have liked to have been astonishing, head-turning, rather than silent and plain as were his kind. Besides, this was the nearest he had ever come to the pirates of his River-Dreams!

The Bridge Raccoon leader lunged forward, grabbed Groundhog round the throat and knocked him flying. He then whirled on Moonbeam, ducking his head and baring his teeth. He charged at him fiercely, growling and snarling while tearing the air with his claws. For a moment it looked as though there was going to be a dreadful fight—full of cries, gnashing teeth, and flying fur—but a young Raccoon, who was still swinging on the railings of The Bridge, gasped with amazement and called out breathlessly, "But Black-Tip, that's the one that licked the Red Fox in The Wood, and not just any Red Fox—he sent off a Ginger-Fist of The Cliff Family—the fiercest family this side of The Hollow!"

Black-Tip, their leader, suddenly pulled back and stood stock still with his hands held up in front of him, his splayed claws catching the light. He tilted his head and shook his ears. "I've told you before about those wild tales of yours!" he cried irritably.

"But it's not a tale!" came another small voice from behind him. "I saw too. It was a Ginger-Fist, I swear! And it was that Raccoon! He was with that Opossum." He pointed a sharp finger at Moonbeam, and Moonbeam shifted his weight uncomfortably. His body was still poised, ready to fight if need be. Opossum's mouth snapped shut. He had never liked the term "that Opossum!" He remembered again the dark eyes he had seen in the Wood after the Fox ran off.

Black-Tip leaned back thoughtfully and then quite as suddenly grinned widely, showing all his teeth. Two, Moonbeam noticed, were missing and he noticed now too that there was a lot of grey hair among the black in Black-Tip's tail and ears. Black-Tip was no longer young, and he did not want to try his mettle against a tested fighter, especially one who had faced a Ginger-Fist Fox. There was the possibility he would lose. "Slight, very slight," he whispered to himself boastfully, but nevertheless it was there, and there were those in his band who would have liked to lead in his place. He was careful not to show any loss of confidence to his followers and, looking carefree, laughed heartily and winked. In fact, he had never looked more sure of himself.

"A brave one, are you?" Black-Tip called to Moonbeam, hurtling forward casually and slapping him on the back. "We honor the brave here, though it is doubtful you could deal with the harsh life we lead here in The Forest. I can tell by your eyes and ears you are not a Forest-Dweller." Black-Tip turned to his followers with a strange grin that seemed to say, "you see what I mean?"

Groundhog looked at Moonbeam sharply, as he pulled himself to his feet and rubbed the bruises down his side. Moonbeam's eyes were softer, his ears neater, and his fur smother than these Raccoons of The Great Dark Forest Bridge, but Groundhog remembered well how wild and fierce Moonbeam had looked that time in The Wood with the Fox, and he suspected that Black-Tip was not quite as confident as he pretended to be. He noticed too that Black-tip's Forest Band was looking seriously at their leader as if unsure of something, but, having never been an animal who searched out leaders, Groundhog could not see the uncertainty of Black-Tip's leadership in their glossy eyes.

"Come on!" cried a shrill voice from an overhanging tree branch. "Let's see if Black-Tip, our leader, can lick the Ginger-Fist Fighter!"

Black-Tip's eyes narrowed. "Nay," he called back chidingly. "Would you have me fight a Hero, a Fox licker, one of our own kind, even if not of The Forest?" He raised a hand as if to silence any further raillery, and pulled Moonbeam towards him in a friendly squeeze, which only Moonbeam knew was cold and stiff.

Opossum flinched in horror, and thought of tricks. He was always ready for tricks, especially Raccoon tricks. He clenched his fingers, ready to spring, and bared his fifty teeth, ready to bite.

"Yes, but what about the Opossum and the Gold-One!" cried a voice. "Let them fight! What right have they to cross our Bridge?"

At this, Opossum charged forward in several short, sharp bursts, snapping his teeth at their heels and hissing threateningly, while Groundhog took a strong stand with his head down.

"They are my friends!" cried Moonbeam. "If they cannot pass freely, then we shall all fight!" He lifted his claws again, flattened his ears, and arched his back. A long, low growl came, almost unexpectedly, into his throat. His eyes rolled menacingly. He had never looked meaner or more ready to fight to the death.

"Fight the friends of a Hero!" scorned Black-tip, with one eye on Moonbeam who he did not trust. "Would that be right? Even if his friends are not of our own kind and not of The Forest, they are HIS friends."

Shouts broke out all round. Some cried, "Yes, that's right!" Others cried,

"Fight them now! They're not our kind!" But others remained silent, staring at Groundhog. He was once again surrounded by light and gleaming gold.

Given all the clamor and indecision, Moonbeam would never have guessed that by sundown he would be enjoying a large leaf bowl full of wild fruit and nuts with The Bridge Raccoons of The Great Dark Forest Bridge, at their forest camp beneath the cliffs. There, sheltered from the cold and the wind and the rain, feasting and merriment went on all evening long, and Moonbeam was carried around on Bridge Raccoon shoulders with shouts of "Here is the Fox-Licker, the Ginger-Fist Fighter!" and hearty slaps on the back. And Groundhog was not without his share of praise, for when the moonlight touched him he shone like burnished gold, and everyone remembered his brave stand on The Bridge and his golden head in the sunlight.

Opossum was somewhat left out and had to content himself with prodding Moonbeam in the ribs and whispering excitedly, "Lucky we didn't have to really fight, eh!" Not that he minded being forgotten now, despite all his fierceness with The Fox in The Wood, for he had never eaten such a luscious feast of wild fruit and nuts, and was beginning to think that journeys—even with bridges in them—were not so bad after all. Besides, being carried around on shoulders like that would have made him very seasick, he supposed.

"No one ever gets across Our Bridge!" Black-Tip exclaimed, swaggering in front of Opossum and Groundhog as he watched his Band's revelry. "Why, in our past days even the slinking Lynx of the Wild Northern Rocks was hurtled by One-Eye to the deeps below—tossed on the wind, as it were, with one flick of One-eye's wrist."

Opossum gulped and, trying to show as little wonder or fear as possible, said, "Well, but there must be some who go across The Forest to The River. Some must surely pass."

"Not on OUR Bridge," growled Black-Tip, dashing a paw through the air and clenching his jaws.

"There are other ways," a Raccoon whispered to Opossum, looking up at Black-Tip with anxious eyes—afraid he was not meant to mention this.

"You mean by Striped Cliff or South Vale or even down and over Green Island, I suppose." Black-Tip rolled his eyes knowingly. His Band had swirled in behind him and were now sitting around tensely; they knew what was coming. "And that is where you may find Shadow-Black, The Night Walker,' he added, lowering his head. Fear glinted in Bridge Raccoon eyes. None of them dared to even breathe.

"Shadow-Black?" inquired Moonbeam, staring at Black-Tip.

"He does not dare to come here. He does not cross Our Bridge—not often, anyway, and never when we are around," Black-Tip answered, boastfully. But Moonbeam noted a nervousness in Black-Tip's voice that belied his words. He sensed too the tenseness in Black-Tip's limbs, which showed in gritted teeth and hard, glassy eyes.

"Besides, he only crosses in Spring and Summer," a small voice said hesitantly from the back of the Band. "In Winter he disappears."

"Ey, he goes alright. We don't know where. Perhaps he follows the Heron south, or perhaps he follows the Snowgoose north. Only once was Shadow-Black's print found in winter forest snow—a print almost as large as our Gold-Friend here, with claws as long as Willow leaves." Black-tip stared at the ground as if that print was there for all to see.

Groundhog shivered. He had been about to say that perhaps Shadow-Black, The Night Walker, slept all Winter as he did, but his voice died in his throat, and he coughed and looked both fearful and surprised. He imagined being clutched in one paw from head to tail, like a nut squeezed in a squirrel hand.

A breeze rustled through the leaves overhanging the cliff, and everyone looked up nervously.

"But he has come early this Spring. He has already been seen, although there are few wildflowers in the wood or on the trees, and the birds have not built their nests," Black-Tip said in a puzzled voice. "It is a bad sign I dare say, I feel it in my bones."

There was a long silence during which everyone wished that everyone else would ask a question. Except Opossum, who was lost in a deep Opossum-silence that almost seemed to pulse through his body, closing his eyes, and blocking out all sound—even that of his own breathing, which had become shallower and shallower.

Then Moonbeam spoke suddenly, his voice coming out in a strange gust. "Who is he?" he asked.

"We do not really know," Black-Tip answered. "He has our rolling gait and dark night-eyes, but he is huge and dark, and those who cross his will do not survive. We have heard him above our Home in the undergrowth and in The Forest at night, under the stars. And those who see him never forget. This is why we stick together, hunt and forage together, sleep together. Our kind, as you well know, wander alone, but this deep Forest and this Shadow-Black change these things. Here we survive because we are a Band." Black-Tip glanced at each Bridge Raccoon, gathering them together with his dark eyes. Some Raccoon heads nodded, their lips turned up in shallow smiles still full of fear. Others merely stared.

"Does he have no other name?" whispered Groundhog, who could not remember ever having heard the name "Shadow-Black" in Garden Tales.

"Some call him the Spring-Waker, because he comes back in Spring," a raccoon said softly, nervously.

"Ay, but he is not the first to come," Black-Tip said gravely. All the swaggering and boastfulness seemed to have drained out of Black-Tip's voice, and Moonbeam suspected that Shadow-Black did cross that Bridge in The Great Dark Forest, perhaps quite often, and that Black-tip was powerless to stop him.

"He crosses the Bridge in Spring?" Moonbeam asked slowly.

"A black shape against the moon only!" said Black-Tip casually, as if to dismiss it. "In the Forest are other things to concern us."

"What things?" gulped Groundhog, glancing sideways at Opossum, who sat stock-still and entirely silent.

"The prowling Bobcat, the rattling snakes, and once in a while, over the ravine, The Eagle. Though he has not been seen for several Summers. Then there is the deep, winter snows and driving rains, the ice, the hail and, in midsummer, the heat," Black-Tip answered, still gathering his Band with his eyes. They in turn moved closer and, huddled together with tails entwined with tails and ears leaning against ears, stared at their leader anxiously. And Moonbeam realized that here in The Forest, different stories were told from those in The Garden, and they all worked together to give Black-Tip power over his motley crew, at least over those who did not want to lead.

"We intend to cross The Forest to Silversheen," Moonbeam said, not without some uncertainty.

"It is a dangerous undertaking," growled Black-Tip, "especially for those who know nothing of forest ways!" Black-Tip said the word 'nothing' loudly and somewhat mockingly. His boastfulness and swaggering had crept back in to his voice. A grin played on the corners of his dark lips.

"How far would you think we have to go?" Moonbeam asked calmly but strongly.

"I do not know," replied Black-Tip gruffly.

"Beyond Green Island," whispered a Raccoon at Groundhog's side, "beyond the nooning sun. By the stars and moon, it is a long way off, almost to Hollow Sky."

"Hollow Sky?" exclaimed Groundhog. Those words had a dreadful sound to him. He imagined falling down a dark tunnel that went on forever and ever—whirling in the air but unable to stop.

"The end of our world," muttered Black-Tip irritably. He never liked talking about Hollow Sky.

"I see," said Moonbeam softly.

"And you may fall off," a Raccoon voice said nervously.

"Few go that way. Some do fall off," Black-Tip muttered, turning away hurriedly. He began to flex his muscles and climb the cliff up out into the moonlight. "The moon is well up now," he called down. "Time for us to leave to forage and hunt. By dawn we will return."

The Bridge Raccoons swarmed past Moonbeam, Groundhog, and Opossum, climbed the rocks silently, with full tails held well up out of each other's way, and disappeared into the undergrowth. Moonbeam watched them go, not knowing if they would ever meet again or if next time he would indeed have to fight. "Why do they need the moonlight?" Groundhog asked, touching Moonbeam's shoulder.

"They do not," Moonbeam answered surely, "but what they hunt may."

Groundhog shuddered. "And what about this Shadow-Black?"

"Perhaps he is just a legend," Opossum said quickly, looking around anxiously and jumping at the sound of his own voice. They were the first words he had spoken in a long time.

"But there is always a core of purest truth in legends," Moonbeam said dreamily, staring at a bright star above the ravine, "covered by Time, coloured or faded like autumn leaves on a moist bank." Opossum looked at Moonbeam with wide eyes. What did he mean by that? he wondered.

The Forest was now bathed in moonlight and every tree and vine and blade of grass was outlined with silver, and where wet, glistened as if studded with precious gems of delicate pastel shades. Moonbeam stared. The Forest is different, he thought, the world this side of The Bridge is different. This is a magic world, an enchanted world, and, as in all enchanted worlds of Garden Tales, we shall meet greater dangers and greater beauty than in our own world. He cuddled down among the rocks, wound his tail around his feet, and fell asleep into troubled dreams. He searched for Silversheen and The King of The River, but only found Hollow Sky and Shadow-Black.

# Chapter NINE
## Muskrat

*The early dawn sky* was glistening silver, and it had a curious depth to it, as though it went on and on for ever and ever, getting clearer and clearer, brighter and brighter. There were no stars in the sky now, Moonbeam noticed with some sorrow, but Groundhog did not seem to mind. The sun was the only star he really cared about, and so he was heady with excitement as they traveled through The Forest, following a trail that wound away from the ravine and downhill towards a body of water where they could have a morning drink, and perhaps a wash—Opossum wasn't sure about that.

Groundhog rolled and twirled, gamboled and laughed, everything quite forgotten in his joy at the first sight of Day. Somersaults came upon him now and then, and as they got nearer to the water, somersaults came almost as soon as one had ended! He seemed really unable not to, a fact Opossum noted and disapproved. He remembered Moonbeam's shaking den and all the dirt falling around his ears, and he wondered what poor, helpless creature suffered now, as Groundhog somersaulted downhill. "They must think it is a landslide!" he nodded to Moonbeam, with an odd smile.

It was a much easier journey than it had been on the other side of the ravine, but that may have only been because the Bridge was now finally well behind them. The path itself was rocky and steep and the forest just as thick, although now quite dry.

They saw, as they climbed down the trail, that it was a wide and very deep body of water. In fact, they might have thought it was part of The River Silversheen itself, if the Bridge Raccoons had not stressed that The River was still far to the east, beyond the Forest. At the water's edge they glanced up-stream, and Groundhog was delighted to see the glorious reds and yellows of a new sunrise and, just below that, a silver that seemed fluorescent in its brilliance—a brilliance more brilliant than trout in swift water or rainbows reflected in raindrops.

"Wonder of wonders!" cried Groundhog, leaping up then down and clapping his paws. "Here comes The Sun!"

Opossum cringed. He had talked so much about melting that he was really sure that that must be what happened in Day's World. Yesterday, deep in The Great Dark Forest and on The Great Dark Forest Bridge, he had only just managed to control his fears, and here, in the open, standing right in front of The Sun itself, he was terrified. He looked down at his pink toes, fully expecting puddles to be there instead of toes, and the fact they were wet with dew and shone in the bright dawn only made this seem more than likely. "I'm melting," he whined, licking his paws to see if they were still there.

"Oh Pos, really!" said Moonbeam. "You don't believe all that stuff, do you?"

The Groundhog frowned and stepped to the water to drink. Now he would have really liked to have been alone to smell the fresh, morning air and growing warmth of the rising Sun without Opossum's whines, without the fears of Night Creatures by Day. He lifted his paws and began his digging motion again. He so much wanted to dig. He wanted to build new spring tunnels and fill them with soft, sweet grasses to lie on. He wanted to watch clover and alfalfa grow thickly by his door, to be collected and smelt and taken below for midnight snacks. He wanted to wallow there in the hot sunlight and say "Good Day" casually to the passing world, to all the busy creatures who were not content unless always on the move like the Squirrel or the Mole. How had he ever begun all this journeying? he wondered.

Groundhog stared in the water, looking at his own brown face, his dark eyes, his short ears. Opossum moved beside him and stared in too, wondering what Groundhog saw there, and wondering if he would see himself melt. He stared and stared at his own white, pinched face, pink nose, and round eyes like two Nightshade berries. But as he stared, he was horrified to see his face become fatter, darker, and more like a Groundhog. "Oh dear!" he cried. "I'm melting!" His shoulders become fuller, a strange smile appeared on his dark face, his teeth appeared—large teeth, protruding oddly. His paw raced to his mouth. "I'm melting!" he cried. "My teeth are falling out!" He shut his eyes and began to shake. The world whirled around. He thought he would faint.

"Can't you get out of my way?" exclaimed a strange voice. "This is a back door, you know—not just any place!"

Opossum opened his eyes slowly, quite expecting to have disappeared or to have turned into a Groundhog. He was now sure that that was what happened to one if you stayed out in the Sun too long. But instead, he saw a very strange creature that he had never seen before, staring at him out of the water exactly where he had been staring in. "Oh Moonbeam!" he cried in horror. "It is a Water Groundhog. The world is full of Groundhogs.'

Muskrat was not exactly flattered to be taken for a Groundhog, but he had a sense of humor and so he burst out laughing—in fact he laughed more than he had laughed in ages. Opossum was rather hurt by all the laughter, and plodded to the nearest tree to sulk behind it. Groundhog simply stared at Muskrat in silence. He had to admit that there was some strange resemblance to himself, but he was quite sure his teeth didn't stick out that much and that his tail was not so long, furless, and flat. He did, however, give a quick, nervous glance behind, just to be sure. It was not that he had ever seen such a tail on himself, but that one never knew what might happen to one on adventures. On adventures, nothing was ever at all what it seemed at first, and things had a curious habit of changing from moment to moment as though the world was very restless, even something of a revealer of mysteries. What about that Fox, for example, and those Bridge Raccoons, and now this Muskrat!

In the meantime, Muskrat was drawing himself up onto the bank with an expert's ease that betrayed his endless knowledge of banks and waterways of every kind. They all noticed, even Opossum from around the tree trunk, that he had large, webbed back feet with tremendously long claws. Groundhog's heart beat faster. This must be a fellow digger! he thought with dizzy excitement.

But Moonbeam wandered farther off. He flattened his ears a little and hunched his back. For a reason he couldn't explain, he felt some dislike for the Muskrat, and it soon became apparent that the Muskrat didn't exactly like the Raccoon either. But neither realized that their families had been enemies from ancient times, from the first time a Raccoon went down to the water to drink.

Muskrat stared at Moonbeam sourly and flipped his tail as if to say, "Who cares about you?" He couldn't, for the life of him, understand why the Groundhog kept such bad company. "I say, Groundhog," he called glibly, preening his long back toes of water weeds and gravel, "what are you doing keeping company with trouble makers? I should have thought that you had more sense!"

Groundhog was very hurt by these words about his friends. "These are very good friends of mine, I'll have you know—and brave, too! They saved me from The Fox, a Ginger-Fists of the Cliff Family!" He said these last words as if nothing after that could ever matter again to him, or anyone else.

"Oh, I'm not talking about that Opossum over there," Muskrat laughed, remembering Pos's odd expression when he popped out of the water, "it's the other one."

Opossum didn't at all like being called "that Opossum" again, and laughed at. "Well, if you must come out of the water so impolitely!" Opossum answered back rattily, pulling back again behind the tree and sitting down with his chin in his hands. He was very glad he didn't have such an ugly tail, he thought, so long and flat and dark. But he sighed forlornly and wondered what was it about himself that made other creatures call him "that Opossum"!

"Raccoons are a real nuisance!" Muskrat rattled on, making a secret grimace at Groundhog, and raising his eyebrows. "How many times they have trampled on top of my house in the middle of the water, as though it was just another pile of sticks floating by—just another island!"

Groundhog looked sideways at Moonbeam, waiting for a reply, but Moonbeam said nothing. He just stood there, completely silent, watching. He looked to Groundhog as if something was taking shape in his mind, some new feeling or idea that he wasn't yet sure of, and Groundhog felt suddenly very alone and anxious. He felt as if he was the only bridge between his friends and a distant, distant cousin, a fellow digger, and he felt now as if everything about this situation would depend on him—him alone. There were other bridges, more magical, perhaps more important, than that shining bridge in The Great Dark Forest. "You seem quite at home in water," he muttered to Muskrat, trying to lead the conversation to brighter things, to sunny banks and warm naps.

"Oh yes!" exclaimed the Muskrat excitedly. "I can swim for ages and ages without the least little bit of rest, speeded along by these large, webbed feet of mine, and this long, flat tail." He looked at both admiringly and gave a quick glance at Groundhog's. "Nothing like webbed feet and flat tails for swimming!"

he added proudly, flipping his tail and lifting a foot and splaying the toes. "You're not so good yourself, are you?" he asked Groundhog, with some vanity.

"Well—no—," answered Groundhog shyly.

Opossum popped his head around the tree again and stared. He splayed his own small hands up in front of his face—wondering—.

"Can you swim just anywhere?" asked Groundhog, waving a paw up and down the water behind.

"Oh well, I don't care for rocks or strong currents of course—much too much work, that! But I absolutely adore the feel of smooth, soft water in my hair and against my feet. There is nothing better to my mind—nothing more wonderful!"

Moonbeam looked at Muskrat more closely, with wide, dreamy eyes. He was about to say something, but changed his mind and sat down with a bump instead and began to sort the pebbles at his feet. Smooth ones toward the hill, jagged towards the water. Smooth, bright ones further up hill. Plain, jagged further to the water. He soon had four neat piles.

"Can you swim in any direction?" asked Groundhog, wondering if swimming was at all like tunneling.

"Oh yes, yes!" cried the Muskrat, jumping up. He raced to the water's edge and plunged in very quickly, head first. "I can swim forward," he called out excitedly, even boastfully; swimming upstream underwater and popping up quite unexpectedly among some distant weeds. "Or backwards!" he exclaimed, gurgling and breathless, while paddling towards the shore. "Or upside-down!" he cried, waving his two webbed back feet in the air nonchalantly. "Or in somersaults!" he called, splashing forward furiously in an energetic dive, with his tail and back legs whirling after him, soon to resurface with his head where his tail had been, to begin the whole thing over again. He did somersaults with the greatest of ease, forwards, in place, and like a small, spinning wheel, joining each one.

Opossum became quite dizzy, but Groundhog was delighted. He loved somersaults, and he particularly liked the Muskrat's. They were everything a somersault should be: gracious, carefree, joyful, dramatic, world-shaking, and uplifting! "Wonder of wonders!" Groundhog cried happily, running up and down the bank in time to Muskrat's swimming, smiling and laughing with all the joy and energy of Spring. Now he felt Spring in his bones!

Moonbeam was watching too, but his eye was more caught by the beautiful patterns in the water. The shower of water drops that followed a somersault or dive flashed silver, then gold, then red in the sunrise. It was if Muskrat was a Treasure Hunter diving for gems and tossing them in the air. Afterwards, the silver ripples on the surface of the water spread out and out in ever-greater circles, that reflected on their delicate crests the rich colours of The Forest, all the browns and all the greens. How different this was from the smooth, calm water where Muskrat was not swimming, diving, and somersaulting! Was this not yet another example of how everyday things, even everyday drabness (there was no denying Muskrat was drab to look at) could bring about beauty, colour and wonder in the most natural of ways? Moonbeam's eyes widened in wonder. He loved colour, sparkle and glossy things! He loved water!

Muskrat came to the bank again, looking rather untidy and quite breathless. He was nevertheless laughing heartily—laughing as if he would never stop—and Groundhog was jumping up and down beside him, clapping and crying out "Good gracious!" as he remembered each dive.

"Well, and I don't think I ever saw fish of so many colours!" laughed Muskrat, "and crayfish, and frogs! I must have quite amazed them! Though I suppose I am a familiar enough sight, as sights go."

Opossum tried to imagine what it would be like to see Muskrat underwater. For some reason, he thought that underwater everything would be upside-down, like the reflections at the bank's edge. He tilted his head to look at Muskrat upside-down and decided that Muskrat's appearance didn't at all improve from that angle. It made his teeth look gigantic and his tail really frightening. "Those poor fish!" he muttered to himself.

"A nice swim, a few dives, and several somersaults is just what you need for that crick in your neck!" Muskrat called out to Opossum, in the tone a doctor might use with the lazy and out-of-shape. "Slims one up too," he added, prodding Groundhog's side with a sharp finger and critical eye. Muskrat liked nothing better than being in good shape—agile, flexible, energetic, and swift. He didn't at all understand those slow, waddling folks like Porcupines and Skunks, although he had heard they could run quite fast if they put their minds to it. He looked sideways at Moonbeam. That, at least, was one thing in favor of Raccoons, he thought. They did, at least, move with ease and speed, care and purpose when they wanted to. No one could call a Raccoon clumsy or plodding.

"I'm not usually this shape," muttered Groundhog, a little embarrassed. "I've only just woken up after the Winter, and I'm a little flabby. I didn't run or leap or somersault for days on end! You wouldn't believe how many months!

Muskrat looked surprised and then a little scornful. "Won't do you any good," he said sternly, "all that sleeping. Take a tip from me and stay around more. Winter is exciting, challenging, even beautiful. You grow up fast then!"

"Well, I don't have a choice, really," sighed Groundhog sadly. "It just all sort of happens. I get more and more sluggish day by day and then—then—well—I fall asleep. It's no idea of mine, I assure you!"

Muskrat raised his eyebrows. "But you miss all the snow and ice," he exclaimed, as if mentioning a wonderful feast of every kind of fruit and nut. "This is quite a Wonderland then. Quite breathtaking!" Groundhog frowned. He felt rather left out. He had never seen ice!

"I look good against snow!" piped up Opossum proudly.

"No doubt, but my fur's waterproof and stands up to any amount of harsh weather, and mud, and knocks and scrapes. It's tough as that old tree bark over there," answered Muskrat, in a rattling tone.

Moonbeam strolled to the water's edge again and was looking in at the fish. He thought he would like to wade out a way and look about. The water felt wonderful against his feet and fingers. The bright colours of the sunrise had now painted every ripple with rich colours. It was like a meadow full of sparkling wildflowers waving in the breeze. He delved down to catch the colour in the palms of his hands. They trickled through his fingers like precious gems in a jeweler's. "How wonderful!" he whispered to himself. "How stunning! How bright! It's miracle! Pure miracle!"

"Raccoon loves water," murmured Groundhog to Muskrat, glad to direct the conversation away from his own shortcomings and to find a way to bring Raccoon and Muskrat together.

"Yes, yes, I know," nodded Muskrat seriously, looking at the Raccoon thoughtfully,

"He loves the feel of it," Groundhog continued.

"Yes, I know; I know about that," nodded Muskrat, staring at the Raccoon with wide eyes. "But no one really knows about water until they swim in it, swim in every direction, swim underneath and on top, swim in leaps and in somersaults," he added proudly.

"I say the same about earth and tunneling," agreed Groundhog, pleased with this comparison.

"I swim well enough," said Moonbeam slowly, looking at Muskrat with

*Opossum*

gleaming, dark eyes. "I had lessons once. Quite a number of lessons. All night long!"

"Oh, lessons!" scorned Muskrat. "As to lessons, I never needed any! I swam and dived before I was weaned, before I had seen anything of the world. It came quite natural—like eating and drinking!"

Opossum really couldn't imagine that. Any swimming he himself had ever done had been splashingly clumsy, awkward, and quite unnerving. He might as well have tried to fly!

"Yes," answered Moonbeam in a measured tone, "swimming comes as natural to you as climbing does to me—well almost."

"Now climbing!" cried out Muskrat with a laugh. "Climbing doesn't bear thinking of. I can't think of anything worse than scrambling about in branches high up in the air. I would never be able to hold on—what with these webbed feet of mine and heavy tail. Besides, there's nothing up there worth seeing—nothing at all!"

"Ah! Well! There you are, you see!" said Opossum triumphantly, proudly walking from behind the tree. "I can hang onto tree branches with my tail, and I assure you there is a world of adventure and richness up there—plump berries, juicy nuts, and every kind of ripe fruit you could imagine!"

Muskrat looked quite horrified and stared at Opossum's thin, pink tail in silence, but gradually his expression changed to one of disbelief and then to laughter. "What a joke!" he roared. "You certainly have a sense of humor. I quite doubted that when we first met."

"It's not a joke," snapped Opossum, drawing nearer and showing just a few front teeth. "I do it all the time. Upside-down, but not in the water."

"Well I never!" gasped Muskrat, realizing that Opossum must be serious after all. "Doesn't that give you rather a headache?"

"Not at all," answered Opossum glibly, feeling very tough.

"Would you? – well no I suppose not – But well I would rather like—Would you—?" muttered the Muskrat, circling Opossum curiously.

"Would I show you!" exclaimed Opossum gleefully "of course!"

"Oh no!" wailed Groundhog. "It's such a dangerous trick. I can't bear to see it. Do stop him, Raccoon!"

Moonbeam moved nearer. He was laughing just a little. The joy on Opossum's face gave him joy. It all made him proud to be a Night Creature. "Go on Pos!" he cried, laughing. "Show Muskrat what acrobatics you can do in the air!"

Opossum ran to the nearest tall tree, simply gurgling with excitement. He scrambled up the bark with the greatest of ease, hanging on with his toes in the most daring fashion. He ran down the tree limbs with astonishing speed, making the whole branch sway dangerously. Then he hooked his tail securely behind him and let go with a laugh.

"Good gracious!" cried Groundhog, watching his friend swinging from the tree branch by his tail, like an odd, white fruit. "It makes me ill to see it!"

Muskrat ran underneath and peered up into Opossum's face. He quite expected to see his nose turn blue or his eyes bright red, but Opossum simply smiled.

"Isn't that rather exhausting?" Muskrat asked, raising his eyebrows.

"Not at all," called Opossum, "I have remained whole days like this—asleep!"

"Asleep!" cried Groundhog, not believing one word of it. "How could you be asleep?"

"My tail sets, coils like a vine," gurgled Opossum. "I don't even know it's there."

"Well I never!" exclaimed Muskrat, again scratching his head. "I never would have believed it if I hadn't seen it with my own two eyes! But what use is all that daring and drama, except for show?" Muskrat waved a paw in front of his face, as if to dismiss Opossum's tail-hanging talent.

"I escape enemies this way," Opossum called down happily. "When enemies scramble along the branch to annoy me, I jump to the ground and am gone! See, my front feet are ready all the time." He waved one paw, then the other, as if swimming in the air.

"Oh," said Muskrat. "I see; it's a sort of frozen dive waiting to be finished—well I never!"

Groundhog whined worriedly, "Couldn't you come down now, Pos? I'm getting a sore neck, looking at you."

But Opossum was in his element now, and he refused to move.

Moonbeam ran over, stood on his back legs, and tried to reach up to Opossum, but Opossum was even higher than he had seemed from a distance, and it did look all rather dangerous.

"Won't your tail snap?" Moonbeam called up, suddenly quite alarmed.

"Not unless it freezes!" laughed Opossum, who knew well about all the dangers of frozen tails and ears. He had heard stories about that many Winters ago in The Wood.

"Oh do come down," sobbed Groundhog, quite beside himself and showing the friendliness he usually only felt for his own kind.

Opossum shook his head furiously until the whole branch began swaying again, and Groundhog was afraid to utter another word, in case it snapped.

"It is no good arguing with him," Moonbeam said to Groundhog calmly. "He is quite carried away with the whole thing."

"I should say!" agreed Muskrat, waddling back to the bank and dangling his toes in the water. He was really glad that Muskrats were not called upon to do such frightful things. In water he might try it, but not up in the air like that.

Groundhog was miserable and began chattering as he usually did when alarmed.

"It's no good, Groundhog," said Moonbeam comfortingly. "Pos enjoys tail-hanging like you do digging. After all, remember it is much more daring to burrow deep under the ground as you do, traveling to unknown places, to pop up who knows where—perhaps even under Fox's den itself!"

Groundhog shivered. He had never thought of burrowing as anything but heavenly. He blinked thoughtfully. "Surely Pos doesn't feel now like I feel when I dig," he murmured, as if his whole understanding of the world was coming to pieces like Dandelion seeds in the wind.

"I believe he does," said Moonbeam, patting Groundhog's shoulder.

Groundhog threw a quick glance at Opossum, whose eyes were closed now but who was nevertheless smiling oddly, contentedly. Groundhog sighed. "Nothing is ever the way it ought to be on adventures," he muttered under his breath.

Muskrat nodded. "You have something there!" he said. "Why just the other day I met a strange creature hanging by his toes from a branch right over the water. Said he was the Silver-haired Bat. What's more, despite that near-Opossum feat of toe-hanging, he had wings like a bird. Put together all wrong I should say, quite wrong." Muskrat shook his head forlornly, as if he couldn't imagine what the world was coming to. "Couldn't swim either!" he added to clinch the story, pursing his lips.

Moonbeam raised his eyebrows and stared at Opossum. Suddenly he couldn't help laughing. "Can't imagine you flying, Pos," he teased.

"What do you mean?" asked Opossum, tilting his head to stare at Moonbeam. "I have no desire to fly!"

"That's the thing," agreed Muskrat, nodding again. "One has to have the desire, and I have no desire for scrambling up there," he looked the tree up and down. "Only swimming out there," he pointed to the water. How happy the water made him. For him, that was shelter. For him, that was what he called Real Life.

Moonbeam nodded. It was strange how the Raccoon and the Muskrat ended up talking and agreeing, as Groundhog had wanted. There was still a coolness between them as might well exist between those creatures whose families had been enemies Winter after Winter, but there was respect too, and understanding. Moonbeam knew well enough about the inner desire Muskrat mentioned, which guided all his actions, and he knew too how important water was to what Muskrat would have called Real Life.

"Do you go on adventures?" the Groundhog asked Muskrat, almost as if he was looking for some chance to talk about their own.

"I should say not!" replied Muskrat, rather alarmed. "Who in the world wants to leave here? This water's perfect! I was born not far off and have brothers and sisters and cousins around every bend. We're all almost exactly alike!" He said these last words triumphantly, as if sameness was a great goodness in the world. Moonbeam realized that all the dramatic swimming was no more than Muskrat did every single day, season on season—it had nothing to do with what was daring and dangerous. It was a repeat performance, not a new adventure. It was nevertheless to be admired, as he had admired it. One could admire something for being itself. Moonbeam began to sense that he had a greater freedom within himself than Muskrat could ever have. He sensed that there were choices open to him that would have just alarmed poor Muskrat. His own nature was somehow more fluid or easy-going. He did not know why that was or what that would mean in the end, but it had a lot to do with adventuring, adventuring on and on.

The sun was well and truly up now, and the whole water and bank was flooded with light. Light dappled The Forest, touched the tree bark and fallen leaves, splashing each one with gold. Moonbeam was dazzled by the brightness. The shape of things appeared as light, drifting shadows against a bright background. Light filled every detail. Moonbeam was amazed but no longer anxious about the bright vision before him, fuzzy around the edges which were shadowy and strange.

"Wake up, Opossum!" he called anxiously. "We will have to travel on before the sun gets straight over head as happens in Day's World. Then light may be too bright for us."

Opossum woke with a start and, fighting against instinct to sleep when it was light, paddled in the air. He had quite lost his sense of direction and had quite forgotten he was hanging by his tail from a tree. He looked around and gasped. The brightness was stunning. He could see nothing clearly. Raccoon looked like a whirling blob of stripes and dots moving toward him. Groundhog looked like a fallen tree limb or a hollow in the earth, and he couldn't see Muskrat at all, not at all! He let out an anxious squeal and showed his fifty teeth to Day's World.

"Oh dear! You're not going to ask me to come down in this!" he cried, as if being asked to go out in a thunderstorm.

Groundhog bounded up and down and ran toward Opossum excitedly. "It is wonderful down here!" he called up with complete honesty. After all, what could be better than sun-filled grasses, warm earth, and all the lively colours of Day, especially after the gloom and rain yesterday in the Great Dark Forest?

"Wonderful!" scorned Opossum. "With monsters hidden behind every tree! No, I'll not come down there!"

Moonbeam sighed. "If they're hidden behind every tree, they can find you up there just as well as down here! Come on, we're moving along!"

Opossum shook his head furiously. "You melt, if you wish," he said solemnly, as if saying Goodbye. He waved one pink foot at Moonbeam and closed his eyes.

"Do you think you can't melt if you're asleep?" asked Groundhog, quite puzzled.

"That's right!" snapped Opossum, getting not a little tangled in his own ideas.

"That makes no sense!" argued Moonbeam, more than a little annoyed. "Besides, you were up and about yesterday in The Forest!"

"I can't help that!" sighed Opossum. "It's not my idea. Day is all back-to-front from the beginning, and yesterday was different; the Forest was not full of sunlight!" He remembered, however, how frightened he had been and how his fear had nearly made him fall in the ravine. He didn't plan to try that again!

Muskrat, who preferred Night's World but moved from Night to Day and back again without the slightest loss of ease, thought Opossum very funny and couldn't help laughing. "Back-to-front," he cried, holding his stomach because he was shaking so much with mirth. "Well I never! But then, I suppose it is an opposite of Night's World. Why not think backwards, then it will all come out right in the end." He laughed and laughed, quite delighted with his own wit. He prided himself on having a sense of humor. "Comes from having so many brothers and sisters," he whispered to himself—which perhaps was true.

Moonbeam winked at Groundhog. "Well, goodbye Muskrat!" he called. "Glad to have met you. We have a good deal of journeying to do, you know, and have to be off. Isn't that so, Groundhog?"

Groundhog stared. "Well—yes—yes—I suppose so," he muttered unsurely, watching Opossum anxiously. He knew how independent Raccoon could be, and he wasn't sure whether he would leave Opossum or not. He felt suddenly very torn inside and began planning every kind of excuse for not leaving yet. He had doubts anyway that Opossum could keep holding on like that, by his thin, pink tail. He really did think it would snap.

Opossum eyed his friends sideways from under half-closed eyelids. He didn't want to be left behind with Muskrat. He couldn't stand all that swimming and so much water; he had grown used to good company and was in no mood for lonely walks and lonely naps. He even liked Groundhog now.

"Ah well!" muttered Muskrat. "Hate even the word journeying, but I wish you luck and all that. Are you heading anywhere special?"

"To Silversheen!" chimed Groundhog, looking at Opossum again.

"Ah well, that's a long way off. I've never been there, but I had relatives there once, all along the waterside." Muskrat sighed almost wistfully and began to slip slowly into the water. He wanted to go back to his lodge now and his family. The mere mention of journeys made him long for Home.

"I don't suppose you've heard of The King of The River?" asked Moonbeam, with glossy eyes and lifted paws.

"Once!" called Muskrat, gurgling through the water and beginning to swim away from shore. "He knows all my kind—every one. "I've heard he has wings and can swim and burrow too. There must be nothing like him in all the Five Worlds!"

"And what about Shadow-Black, the Night Walker?" called Moonbeam.

"He comes in Spring, by Green Island, but I've never seen him. They say he is huge and fierce and does not take kindly to questions. Beware! Beware!" Muskrat cried, as he waved goodbye and ducked under the water, leaving a gold ring that circled ever wider and wider until it touched the shore. To Moonbeam's day-vision it looked somehow like cornfields swaying in the moonlight, or Buttercups opening in the morning sun, or, perhaps, even a gold crown circling, on and on. Groundhog gasped. He couldn't imagine anything more wonderful than a creature with wings, which swam like a Muskrat and tunneled like himself. He indeed would be King of The Five Worlds! But he shuddered again at the name of Shadow-Black. Would they meet him unawares in The Forest, and if they did, how would they survive?

# Chapter TEN
## Friendship Lost

**M**oonbeam and Groundhog had reached the top of the hill just inside the edge of The Forest when Opossum ran up behind laughing. "Tail-hanging gives one a huge appetite!" he exclaimed, looking very pleased with himself. "I am famished and couldn't dangle another minute without a hearty meal."

Moonbeam smiled knowingly. Opossum hated to admit that he didn't want to be left behind, and Moonbeam suspected he wasn't really hungry. Opossum usually never ate by day, and besides he had eaten a great deal of nuts and berries before they left Black-Tip's camp—and that on top of all the feasting of the evening before. Opossum, nevertheless, made energetic attempts to search for food, scurrying this way and that and exclaiming "Ah, ah!" every now and then. All of which Groundhog accepted well enough, because he himself never ate till after sun-up. Besides, Groundhog had little talent for acting. He was what Moonbeam would call simple or straightforward, as Day-Creatures often tended to be. There was something about Night, Moonbeam felt, that demanded more, developed the character more, for good or ill: Night-Creatures seemed more complicated, more dramatic, more independent and more cunning.

After that, they followed the trail on and on, downhill, uphill, over logs and under low branches, high on top of rocky banks with the wind in their fur and down by the water along muddy ledges. They slept in bank-dens and tree hollows, under overhanging rocks and, buffeted by the wind, in the niches of high branches. They ate whatever they could find and sheltered from the rain whenever they could.

Then one morning they followed the trail downhill, past a small shallow clearing and on over bumpy ground covered with roots, hollows, and pebbles. The water swung in at the bottom of the hill and lapped gently against a tree-lined, sunlit bank, and as they drew nearer they realized they were at the head of a very small and very pretty cove rounded by a wide and strange trail. The trees along the cove's edge reflected in the water and joined their tops in the center. There fish jumped, and Groundhog thought he saw large Carp basking just under the surface in the sunlight. A Rabbit bounded down the hill, nibbling grasses along the edge.

They stood silently on the trail watching the view, while they caught their breath after their bumpy downhill walk. "What kind of a trail do you think this is?" asked Opossum, but before anyone could answer, the ground beneath their feet began to shake and rumble as if it had come alive beneath them and was shaking off dreamy slumbers. The Rabbit cartwheeled through the air and was gone.

"Quick! We shall be thrown back to The Meadow and The Garden, where we belong!" cried Groundhog, remembering his thoughts about the dark-green back of a mighty dragon. But before Moonbeam or Opossum could ask what he meant, they heard the loud voices of running men, followed by the barking of dogs and bellowing of what sounded like huge Bulls.

Opossum let out a shrill squeal, and yelling, "The ground is breaking! The world is melting!" ran into The Forest, stumbling over roots, tripping in hollows that seemed to his vision like deep wells, and ducked under the trees and was gone.

"Good gracious!" cried Groundhog, bewildered and alarmed, running to the side of the trail and searching the undergrowth for any sign of the familiar, now well-loved, pink and white of Opossum.

"Come!" cried Moonbeam to Groundhog, his ears pricked up to catch each sound. "I hear men traveling and dogs running! We are in danger!"

But before either of them had time to run and duck into the undergrowth, men ran round the corner shouting and waving sticks. Dogs barked at their heels and behind them cattle clattered down the steep incline pulling large, rolling barrels, perhaps of wheat, perhaps of corn. The ground shook and the rumbling sounded like thunder, and reminded Moonbeam of those dark stories, common to all the creatures of The Five Worlds, of earthquakes and disappearing woods, of deep ravines that opened up overnight. How many times had Old Grandfather TaleHoard told them those strange tales!

A dog rushed towards them, snapping and prancing wildly, showing all his sharp teeth. Groundhog ran into the trees. He ran and ran as fast as his short legs would carry him and dived headfirst down a narrow hole at the base of a large Oak Tree. There he shivered and whined and listened and was glad he could not smell Fox.

Moonbeam tried to follow but the cattle, pushed forward by rolling barrels, rushed between them, leaving Moonbeam facing that large, snarling and snapping dog. He arched his back, flattened his ears, showed his teeth and growled, but the fear of being treed by men and dogs overwhelmed him; he lunged sideways and jumped into the water. The dog leaped in behind him, barking and growling and creating a huge wave that surged forward over Moonbeam's head. Moonbeam struggled to surface, gulping for air, fighting against a downward push as strong as winter wind. At the same time, a strong current pulled him downstream; knocking him into hidden logs and rocks, between which he only just managed to catch his breath. The water was cold and deep, and he had never more wished that he was an excellent swimmer like Muskrat, or even that he was now a Muskrat himself with a flat, swinging tail and webbed feet. Events had changed all his desires.

He did not dare to try to look behind, but he could hear the dog barking and splashing noisily, and now and then swells of water overlapped him, thrusting him forward then drawing him back. Luckily, despite all his fear and tension, he was able to remember how to run and cross a current as his Mother had once taught him—in imagination only, for they had never seen high, swift water. He swam out strongly, as far as he could to let the current carry him forward, away from the dog, far away—he hoped to safety!

He swam on and on, further and further until he began to feel he would not be able to swim much longer. Behind, the men on the bank were yelling and waving sticks while their cattle bellowed, and the dog in excitement and confusion lost control in the current and ran into the bank where he got tangled in weeds and branches and was soon covered with black mud. Moonbeam still did not dare glance round, but he understood what had happened from the sounds picked up by his sharp ears.

Suddenly, he saw what looked like a rather large rock in the middle of the water in the distance, except that Moonbeam couldn't remember ever having seen a rock of such strange colours—it was whirled with red and gold stripes on a black as velvety black as the center of a Black-Eyed Daisy. Day's bright light caused him to squint. Water trickled into his eyes. Now quite exhausted, he often stopped swimming and merely floated towards the rock, which shone beckoningly bright in the sunlight, like a freshly painted farm gate. Moonbeam closed his eyes. His limbs ached. His head whirled. In dream-like flashes he saw the edge of The Garden. He saw the green, flowing robes of The Girl.

The train of men and dogs, cattle and barrels was long, and it was a long time after that before Groundhog found poor Opossum, halfway down a hole. They wandered back to the water's edge, and there Opossum sobbed and sobbed. Tears ran along his white fur, gathered on his pink nose and dripped onto his pink feet. Nothing, absolutely nothing Groundhog could say comforted him in the least.

"If only I hadn't run!" he wailed miserably through his tears.

"It was nothing to do with your running. It was that dog, that dreadful dog, and those barrels!" comforted Groundhog with a squeeze.

"If only he hadn't jumped into the water! Did he really jump?" sobbed Opossum, more loudly than before.

"Yes, I heard the splash," answered Groundhog in a half whisper, staring at his feet.

Opossum lifted his front feet to wipe the tears off his nose, which gathered there just as fast as he could wipe them away. "Then he is drowned," he said in a low voice.

"Not necessarily drowned," said Groundhog softly. "He was a good swimmer you know—not a Muskrat or anything—but a good swimmer in any case."

Opossum gulped and coughed. "But he is nowhere out there, you see," he said, pointing up and down the water.

"No, I know, but he might be further downstream by now. Given the current, he couldn't swim back here," Groundhog said, looking up and down the trail where such a short time before they had all walked together happily, even merrily.

"Muskrat might have actually been useful if he hadn't run off like that. He might have saved Raccoon!" said Opossum fretfully, winding his tail around his feet as if for comfort.

"There was no foreseeing this event," said Groundhog firmly. "Besides, Muskrat didn't run off anyway, he merely left."

"Ran off! Left! It's all the same!" sobbed Opossum. "And I was no better. Indeed, a good deal worse, for I was his friend!" Opossum's misery somehow made him look smaller and thinner and more sharp-faced than usual. Perhaps because he sat crunched up tightly, nose down, with his thin, pink tail trailing over skinny feet. It seemed strange, even to Opossum himself, that he, who had always liked to be alone by himself, should have grown so fond of Raccoon and feel so upset by his loss. "One grows used to friends much quicker even than red berries found by chance," he muttered, flicking the tip of his tail and looking up at Groundhog.

Groundhog didn't know what to say, but he knew that for many that was all too true. Although he had not thought that that would be the case with Opossum.

"I have never known such loneliness before," said Opossum tearfully. "In fact I have never really known loneliness at all." He almost wished that he had never met Raccoon if it meant he must now be so unhappy, but he knew deep down that that was a cowardly wish as well as quite pointless. "It's not just," he muttered finally, with big tears rolling off the end of his nose. "It's just not just!"

That life was not always just, Groundhog knew only too well, but he didn't know whether to urge Opossum on or suggest they turn back. He was miserable too, of course, but apart from the fact he believed they would find Raccoon again on up the trail, having lost many friends Summer after Summer in The Meadow and The Garden, he had never imagined they would all be together forever as Opossum had. His long Winter-Sleeps divided his life in an odd way and made each fresh Awakening seem like an entrance into a new world of new friends and new adventures; the world of the year before always seemed shadowy and strange like a half-remembered, soon-to-be-forgotten dream. And so Groundhog knew that if they hadn't parted before, they would part when Winter came and, after that, who could tell what would happen!

Wild Mallards with metallic green heads and yellow beaks had drifted to the cove's edge and were quacking noisily, quite unconcerned by Opossum's crying or Groundhog's movements. Opossum had seen Mallards before. He had seen their strong flight on summer evenings across The Garden by The Great House. Seeing them again now brought him a strange longing, almost a restlessness, that welled up through his sorrow like a small, bubbling spring of clear, fresh water.

He wiped away his tears and looked out over the water. "Let's walk on and see if we can find Raccoon," he said softly, rising and shaking his fur free of earth and grasses.

"I think that would be best," nodded Groundhog, paddling forward, now uphill and towards a sun-filled glade full of birds darting and singing joyfully. The singing seemed out of place now. Groundhog felt that the world should be completely silent while Raccoon was missing and Opossum sorrowing. But life would go on, he thought with a sigh, as it always did, swelling forward before them, hidden around corners, like a full and glistening stream, golden in places with the joys of new-found friends, red berries, and warm dens; and pitted here and there with shadowy darkness—other sorrows like this sorrow

They were walking and thinking, barely talking, except to point out a hollow here or a root there that might trip them up, when something large and dark suddenly tobogganed, whistling and chuckling, down the bank and ran across their way to the other side where it did a sort of sudden winding dive like chimney smoke twisting in the wind, and began to slide towards the water.

"I say! I say!" it called out to them excitedly, twisting its head to look back over its shoulder and smiling gleefully as if life could be no better and no morning more beautiful. "Why not toboggan a while with me? Believe me, this is no morning for plodding uphill unless you mean to slide down."

Opossum looked askance at the broad, whiskered face with its dark, wide nose and squat ears. The smile on the face irritated his inner sorrow like a heavy hand ruffling his fur backwards. He looked at Groundhog. "What is it?" he whispered, afraid if he spoke out the creature would get into a long merry explanation. He looked, to Opossum, very pleased with himself and only too willing to talk.

"How can you be sliding about like that when the world is quite falling apart, quite gone to pieces?" cried Opossum, unable to hide his irritation or his sorrow, although he did not want to talk at all.

"Falling apart!" laughed the creature, staring at Opossum in disbelief and amusement. "I assure you it is not! It is quite like always, only better, for tobogganing that is."

Groundhog stared and stared. The animal before him now was strangely familiar, and its face made him happy and warm inside. Summer memories flashed through his mind until he found himself staring at the same shape, the same face and the same smile. "An Otter!" he cried, clapping his two paws together. It was like finding family.

"Um, yes," nodded Otter, pleased to hear the note of friendship and recognition in the Groundhog's voice.

Groundhog continued to stare, remembering his young Otter-friend who once, many summers ago, had shown him glimpses of another world and had talked to him about nothing but fish, fish of every variety—speedy fish, colourful fish, slim fish, slow fish, fish one caught easily and fish that always got away!

"Though perhaps it is not quite like always," the Otter suddenly exclaimed with a shake of his head, "for I did see a very odd sight this morning in the water, not far from here in fact."

Groundhog braced his body and gulped, quite afraid to ask what that odd sight might be. Opossum looked at Groundhog with wide, tearful eyes that were now glinting with a kind of cold terror. His heart was beating loudly within, and his feet had begun to tremble again. "What kind of sight?" he asked anxiously, not even daring to look at Otter's face. He just stared at the ground, quite ready to hear that Raccoon was drowned or had been eaten by a Dog or, worse still, had been grabbed by one of the Day-Monsters who lurked behind all this tinsley brightness with their sharp teeth and cold eyes. At least he could take some cold comfort from the fact that Shadow-Black was not out and about by Day.

"Well," laughed Otter in an amazed tone, raising his eyebrows until his already round and ringed eyes looked rounder than ever. "Well, I saw a Land Raccoon building a log house like a beaver, or perhaps it was a dam; I really have no idea." The creature shook his head again and muttered, "Well, well," once more. The thought so amazed him that he forgot all about sliding and just sat there staring as he had that morning by the waterside.

Opossum let out an excited squeal so loud that both Groundhog and Otter jumped in fright. He then sprang up and ran one way and then turned suddenly and ran the other. He was laughing wildly and gurgling. "He is alive, Groundhog!" Opossum shouted at the top of his voice. "Raccoon is alive!" He spun round and round on his pink toes, crying "Oh! Oh!" in a shrill voice every time he saw Groundhog's two brown eyes.

"Quite crazy," muttered Otter, staring at Groundhog and tapping his head with a webbed finger.

"Where did this Raccoon go then?" asked Groundhog anxiously, grabbing

Opossum by the shoulder and trying to calm him down. Opossum squealed irritably and pulled himself free.

"I have no idea," intoned Otter, shaking his head. "Downstream, I suppose. Perhaps to one of the Beaver islands. A friend of theirs, I suspect."

Groundhog smiled and laughed a small knowing laugh that sounded rather strange to Otter, who began to think that the Opossum was not the only crazy creature in The Forest that morning. He had often been warned about The Forest. How many times had Uncle Swift-Water told him to stay by the water's edge and not wander in The Forest.

"Could you show us where you saw him and point out the way he was traveling?" asked Groundhog quickly, nodding his head at Opossum who was feeling rather dizzy after all the wild dancing around.

"Oh yes!" said Otter cheerfully. "But you really will have to slide, you know. It doesn't pay to go downhill any other way, especially on such a warm, sunny morning."

"Well we don't slide!" chimed Opossum, trying to smile at Otter now but finding this whole business of sliding or not sliding very upsetting. He might have been tempted to try, but he couldn't imagine what he would do with his feet or how he would keep his tail from becoming tangled around his body like a summer vine. Besides, he had no idea what to do with his head—if he curled it in, he would be entirely the wrong shape for rolling, and if he stretched it out, he would end up with very sore ears and quite dizzy. "My coat would get all covered with leaves and earth," he added, not wanting to say he didn't know how to roll.

Otter ran his eyes up and down Opossum's snow-white coat. "Very handsome, but in water one needs to glisten and not be seen against the dark depth of deep green and blackberry black. You are like Winter Ermine with dark eyes like summer berries in sunlight. You would be seen from one bank to the other!"

Opossum fidgeted and bit his lips. He did not know if he had been complimented or told he lacked something.

"Opossum hates to slide, but I love somersaults—somersaults of every kind—especially early morning ones when dew is fresh upon the grass and sprays against my nose," Groundhog exclaimed, springing up and laughing with delight at the very thought of it all.

Otter's eyes sparkled. "Well follow me, fellow somersaulter, into the wonders of the water, the way of Land-Raccoon, the Beaver friend!" He said this as if a grand poet of old, with an heroic flourish. Then suddenly he turned and ran uphill. His long, heavy tail swished through the undergrowth and sounded like a breeze rushing through gold cornfields beside The Garden. At the top of the hill he turned and let out a shrill whistle that could be heard a long way off. "Come Ot—tt—ters all!" he called chatteringly, looking round with eyes so full of joyful enthusiasm that Opossum wondered what the Otter was going to do next. Could sliding downhill really give such joy—a joy that now seemed, from Otter's expression, to be both solemn and deep, and returning like the cycle of the seasons or the search for spring dens?

"It is like somersaulting," whispered Groundhog, understanding the rituals that surround all new beginnings of old, time-tested joys.

Otter let out another whistle and ran forward past them at a speed so great that he created a strong breeze full of the familiar smells of woods and meadows as well as the more unfamiliar ones of waterweeds, river mud, and fish. Once across the trail, Otter folded his forelegs close to his body and leaped high and long, like a streamlined toboggan, onto the grass. There he pushed his shoulder to the ground and, swinging his large tail sideways, rolled downhill. His eyes were wide and his whiskers twitched with enthusiasm. He looked as if he had never been so happy in all his life.

"Wonder of wonders!" Groundhog cried and, unable to resist the inspiration of Otter's rolling, leaped up too and somersaulted with more energy and daring than ever before, unless it was on that day when he met Raccoon and Opossum in front of the Raccoon's front door. But, before he had even got half way to the water, a commotion broke out all around him. Shrill whistles were followed by loud chattering; the sound of swishing tails was followed by flashes of sleek silver and dark-brown fur among the trees. Otters of every size and age were running, rolling and tobogganing towards the water from every direction. Groundhog stopped with his mouth wide open.

Opossum, who had been walking stiffly behind, bemoaning his fate, could not believe what was happening. Otters whizzed by on either side with strange Otter-smiles and bright eyes. Soon he heard loud splashes as they plunged into the water. There they rolled about, splashing and gurgling, sliding and diving with high-pitched laughs and low chattering.

Groundhog was enchanted! He had never seen such grace and power. Muskrat may have swum marvelously well, but the Otters seemed to mold the water around themselves like a second skin. They brought the water alive and gave it the beauty and brilliance that Groundhog had always thought belonged to the water itself! Now he realized that all the gurgling, bubbling, surging, and spilling of water were the result of some other energy, like this acrobatic swimming of the Otters.

They swam too quickly for Groundhog's eyes and could stay underwater for ages and ages, or so it seemed. Whenever they finally surfaced, they would call out to Groundhog and Opossum, with their heads held up high above the swells they had made and tread water quite effortlessly, quite gleefully, as if they were the happiest creatures alive—which at that moment they probably were. It all made Groundhog feel a little strange inside, a little lost. He didn't think he had a niche in life that fitted him or suited him as well as water did the Otters. He loved to dig, and he loved the smell of fresh earth, but tunnels and dens were somehow too closed up. And then he loved to gambol and somersault in long meadow grasses or amble through The Garden looking for fallen fruit and juicy roots, but out in the open he never felt really safe or quick enough on his feet. How different for an Otter! In the water an Otter was both free and safe—both at Home and on a grand adventure. Who else in all The Five Worlds could say the same?

Opossum ran down the last part of the slope and landed beside Groundhog with his front feet awkwardly pinned under him. He struggled to get up again while he watched the Otters playing in the water. Almost against his will, he became fascinated by the flowing and graceful swimming. Against his will, he was forced to admire and sit back oddly, with some toes still pinned under him.

The Otter who had first crossed their path uphill surfaced nearby and lay on his back in the water, resting. He peered at them sideways with his two front feet across his chest. His eyes were bright, even questioning—he obviously was wondering what effect his own swimming had had on them. Not that he was vain or boastful about it, but he had learned over time that what was quite natural to him, and Otters in general, stunned the other creatures. And there was something about the expressions on their faces that always made him see himself from the inside out, so to speak.

When he first began to swim, he had known only the inner joy and excitement and the wonderful feeling of the water rushing against his body, but in the faces of others he learned something else; he learned that he had created a little beauty, a little brilliance. So now he saw himself as something of a showman, even as artist—generous by nature, he loved to give pleasure.

"Wonder of wonders! You all have quite taken my breath away!" Groundhog called out to Otter, with all his usual good nature.

Otter's face flushed with real, deep pleasure. "If you both move along the bank with me, I'll show you where I saw that Raccoon. It's not far—just round this corner."

Otter swam out ahead, rounding the corner like the wind, leaving the other Otters behind playing. Groundhog wondered what it must feel like to leave things behind so quickly. It must give one a different sense of Home, he thought. Though he knew will enough that Otters did have dens; dens of which they were quite fond. Dens they dug in banks with secret, underwater entrances; dens where they could cuddle down on a nest of grasses, reeds, and leaves, and sleep and dream—just as he did. Though the dreams, he thought, must be different, more rapid, more varied, more breathtaking.

Groundhog and Opossum scrambled along the edge of the water and around the corner. The bank jutted out sharply and was thickly wooded with trees and shrubs. A breeze wafted by and it was full of the smell of fish and Turtles and mud. In the distance the sky had grown dark, and they thought they saw rain at the far edge of the water.

"He was traveling out that way!" Otter called, pointing at what looked like a large island with muddy banks and stick-like undergrowth.

Opossum gasped. The island looked very far away to him, and it was so thickly covered with weeds and shrubs that no light came across it; it looked very dark. Then, when he ran his eyes along its banks, he saw that it was very long, and that beyond its eastern end there was yet another island, even bigger and more woody than the first.

"Gracious!" moaned Groundhog, sitting down with a bump. "Are you sure?"

Otter nodded, not at all sure why they should be so bothered by it. "It's a nice island," he chuckled cheerfully, flipping his tail. "Wonderful banks for digging! Great slides for snow-rolling! I spend days and days there each Winter! We all do!"

Opossum, who didn't like islands of any kind, looked at Otter forlornly. If Raccoon had landed there, where was he now? Was he hurt or asleep, or had he traveled on, on to the next island, or even back to the mainland? "Is there any other way to the island?" he asked Otter, almost in a whisper.

"No, no, there is no other way. Just across the water—swimming," he replied softly, even comfortingly. Now he had calmed down a little, he sensed their sadness and their fear.

"Then we will have to swim," said Opossum, surprised by his own words and trying to hide the fear that gradually crept over his face. He would hate to get wet, hate to swim, but what else could they do? Dear Raccoon might by lying over there in need of help, lying in all that mud and stick-like shrubbery, hurt and miserable. Opossum's eyes filled with tears again. He had run away when he was needed, so now he would swim to the island and find his friend.

But he was not really sure that he could swim so far. He stretched out his front legs and stared all the way down them, right down to his ten pink toes. He wriggled his toes thoughtfully as if trying to understand what it meant to be an Opossum, or rather to be inside an Opossum skin, for his spirit and ideas seemed to be changing. One thing all the adventuring had taught him was that being an Opossum was nothing like being anything else. He had different weaknesses and quite different strengths and possibilities than other creatures, and he wondered secretly, hardly daring to even admit it to himself, whether he wouldn't have rather been something like Muskrat or even Otter. He winced. Well, it's no good being dissatisfied, he thought to himself, the world would be a ridiculous place of it was full of nothing but Muskrats and Otters! The trees would be empty, the meadows lonely, the rivers crowded. Besides, there would never be enough clams and crayfish and frogs and fish to go around!

Otter had been watching the movement in Opossum's eyes and knew he was puzzling over something. "That Raccoon was a friend of yours, I gather," he said, pulling himself out onto the bank and shaking the water out of his sleek fur. It shone in the light.

"Yes," said Opossum softly, staring at Otter. "Yes, he was."

"Then why not let me go around the island and search for you. It would be easier for me; I know the island well," said Otter, seeing all the anxiety in Opossum's eyes and wishing only to see a look of pleasure.

Opossum shook his head. "No," he said firmly. "We will swim out there to look, though your coming along would help a great deal. Is the water deep?"

"A little," answered Otter, looking out across the water. "Especially in the middle there. The bank is rough and jagged too; you have to know where to land."

Groundhog moved to the water's edge and dipped his toes down in the water. It was cold as ice and the mud was slippery. Both sent chills of anxiety through him that were deepened by the fact that the sun had gone behind clouds, and it had begun to drizzle with rain on this side of the water too. He didn't want to say, but he was not sure whether he could swim at all! He was nothing the shape of animals that swam. He felt he knew that only too well. He had no webbed feet, no long, wide tail, and no trim, streamlined figure. Perhaps I shall sink, he sighed to himself glumly, but without the least idea of giving up.

Meanwhile, Opossum walked into the water and stared at the far bank as if willing himself there. The cold water stung his naked feet and tail and felt like winter snow against his stomach. He remembered foraging for food in snowdrifts and shivering in his den afterwards until he finally fell asleep. It seemed strange that the coldness of midwinter should still be here in this water lapping at his feet. Coldness always made him sleepy, in the same way daylight did. He struggled to hide a yawn. He would have to fight against himself to get across the water to his friend. But if I get across, he thought, I shall have leaped out of this Opossum skin of mine in some way; I won't be an ordinary Opossum any more!

# Chapter ELEVEN
## Strange Tracks

*T*he first few moments of swimming were terrifying for Opossum and Groundhog. Their legs were so short that they moved very slowly and clumsily, and it made their hearts beat fast and caused them to pant quite loudly. How often their mouths and eyes filled with water and then, in their efforts to cough the water out, gulp for air and clear their eyes, they would flap about and slip back beneath the water again! It was all very frightening, especially as the bottom was already a long way away and the water so murky from the rain that they could not see logs and rocks until their feet hit them.

Towards the center, the water was even colder and their legs and feet became numb. Opossum began shivering, and Groundhog, who loved warmth and sunny skies, groaned aloud. Even the shrill whistle and quick chattering he usually gave when alarmed would not come to him. His throat seemed as numb as his feet and he was out of breath. Nevertheless, beneath all the numbness and groans, Groundhog was rather pleased with himself. He had had no idea he could swim and no idea, once out in the water swimming, he could just keep on swimming. He didn't like it! It was certainly unnerving. Yet he was rather proud, and, underneath it all, he expected Opossum was too.

But all Groundhog's pride and pleasure disappeared suddenly when he heard Opossum scream "HELP!" shrilly, and saw him slip under the water, gasping for breath. Groundhog turned and tried to swim towards Opossum but the current pushed against him, and he was overcome by a deep fear that made his heart pound. If Opossum were hurt or too tired to go further, he would not be able to carry him to shore! Opossum resurfaced, cried out again and slipped back under.

"He's tangled in old vines!" Otter cried to Groundhog, unexpectedly surfacing beside him. "Try to hold him up while I untangle his feet and tail!" Otter ducked beneath the surface, and Groundhog tried with all his might to tread water and hold Opossum's head above the surface. Opossum gasped and cried and tried to kick his back legs free from the vines, which only seemed to tighten the more he struggled.

"Keep still!" cried Groundhog fearfully. "Leave it to Otter!"

Otter chewed the vines away quickly, and then without even thinking about it came up under Opossum and let him lie across his chest like any spring Otter pup one might see on a river.

Opossum closed his eyes and filled his lungs full of fresh air. He felt dizzy, his heels and ankles ached. He thought he might have cut his toes, but he felt too odd to look down at them. Otter's sleek body swayed in the water, and Opossum thought of swinging branches and soft breezes, and in a flash, vivid and full of colour, he imagined he was back in the meadows and fields by The Garden. He heard Night-birds calling; he heard Owl calling; calling out across the Meadow Wood, "Who, who are you?"

"I'm Opossum!" he cried out to the sky, snapping open his eyes and finding with surprise he was still out in the water floating on Otter's warm chest. "I feel fine now," he said unsurely, slipping back into the water and beginning to swim again. He felt somehow now as if Owl was watching him, and he did not want Owl to see his mistakes or his fears. The rain began to fall more heavily around him, but he swam on, on and on.

It was a very, very long time before they reached the island, but they did finally land there—and in one piece! They scrambled up the bank exactly where Otter told them to, but even then, in their eagerness, got caught on some rocks and weeds. One would have thought that, totally exhausted, they would have fallen fast asleep, but they were so amazed to be there—Otter had certainly had his doubts once or twice—that they couldn't stop talking and laughing, recounting every detail of their swimming adventure.

"Well I thought I was quite done for!" exclaimed Opossum for about the twentieth time, with great gusto and not a little pride. After all, he had swum to the island, and he doubted any Opossum had ever done that before. His thought or dream of Owl was soon forgotten in his excitement although he did have a feeling Owl had seen him. He couldn't explain that. He had seen no outline of Owl wings against the sky, and it was not Night. He put it down to nerves and swallowing too much water.

"Yes, I was worried," said Groundhog cheerfully. "Especially when you began to scream out. Thank The Five Worlds we were not all drowned!" He laughed a short laugh that was tinged with all the nervousness of a narrow escape.

"Oh, Otter here wouldn't have drowned! Would you!" Opossum cried out proudly.

"No, that I wouldn't!" cried Otter. "On land I might well come to grief but not in the water—especially water as familiar as this."

"Ah well, you can't drown on land," sighed Opossum. "That's the great advantage of it. If you're the drowning kind, that is." Groundhog nodded rapidly in agreement.

Otter burst out laughing. "Drown on land! My word, wait until I tell the others that!" He had not heard such a good joke in a long time.

Opossum blushed under all his wet, white fur at the idea of Otter telling all his friends and relations about his foolish words and clumsy swimming. What a sight I must have looked, he thought, with quite a new vision of himself bobbing about, screaming, blowing, and panting! So that's what Owl saw if he really was there!

Groundhog saw the look of shame that had crept into Opossum's eyes. "Don't worry, Pos. You looked quite splendid, like a great adventurer chased by pirates while diving for gold!" he comforted, patting him on the back.

Opossum's eyes lit up. He had always thought that there were pirates on The River. He had even played games about that, and he hoped more than anything he had looked a little like an adventurer, even if not a great one.

"Do you think that Land-Raccoon is here?" Groundhog asked almost in a whisper, a little surprised to hear himself use Otter's words. That must come from being in the water too long, he thought with a smile.

"Somewhere around here," Otter answered, sounding much vaguer than Groundhog would have wished. "We should search for tracks and smells. That's quite the quickest way to find him, especially if you think he may need help.

Though I for one think he looked rather well on that log. Are you sure he's not used to floating about?"

"Oh no!" exclaimed Groundhog. "He's never been out of The Garden this far before. He knows nothing about deep water. Nothing at all!"

Otter shook his head forlornly and wondered whether the Raccoon had not indeed drowned. He wondered too about this place called The Garden where no one knew about deep water. Otter decided rather quickly, with a deep sigh and sharp shake of his two short ears, that he wouldn't want to go there.

"Please don't sigh like that and shake your head so!" pleaded Groundhog. "Raccoon has to be alright. He just has to!"

The tone and paws pressed together touched Otter's kind heart, and he wished more than anything in the world to be able to find the Land-Raccoon and bring him back to his friends. "I was only sighing over places without deep water, not about your friend the Raccoon," he answered, sounding very mysterious to Groundhog who had never thought of The Garden as a place without water because he had never had any desire to swim. "Perhaps you two should circle and search the island in the path of sundown," Otter pointed upstream, "while I search the other way. We'll meet on the other side. When we've done that, we can travel inland skunk-fashion to cover as much ground as possible. I've no doubt we shall come up with something before dark, even if only tracks."

Opossum stared at Otter questioningly. "It all sounds like a good idea, but what on earth is skunk-fashion?" Opossum could not imagine any good coming of that!

"In wavy lines!" exclaimed Otter proudly. It was not, after all, every Otter who knew about Skunks! Some had never even heard of one, much less seen one!

It did not take long for them to finish making their plans, and Groundhog and Opossum were soon scurrying towards the western end of the island, running back and forth sniffing for smells and looking for tracks. It was difficult in the heavy rain, but they knew it was best to search now before the rain washed all the smells and tracks away. Besides, wet and cold already, what could more wet and cold do? Groundhog suffered more than Opossum because he never went out of doors in bad weather and slept all Winter. He was not, however, surprised that such a lovely sunrise should be followed by rain. Red morning skies were often followed by storms.

Opossum had had to search for food in all kinds of storms, including snowstorms, and he had learned a swift run with his head down and his tail swinging behind so that he shook off the rain as fast as it fell and never let it drip into his eyes or ears.

They both felt rather lost without Otter, who knew the island well, but they had to admit that splitting up was a good idea. This way they could cover more ground more quickly, which appealed especially to poor Opossum whose imagination painted ever-gloomier pictures of Raccoon's plight. Every rumble of thunder overhead made Opossum wince because it reminded him of the barrels rolling downhill. Every hint of a track in the mud made him start. Every new smell caused his heart to pound.

"Really, I'm not at all sure now that Otter did see Raccoon, that is, OUR Raccoon," Opossum said miserably, stressing the word "OUR" with deep affection, as though he was mentioning a great treasure like winter hoards of juicy roots and berries. "I can't imagine him floating about on logs, drifting downstream. Can you?"

"Well, I think it really must have been our Raccoon," said Groundhog confidently. "Raccoons don't float about on logs as a rule, and our Raccoon is the Raccoon that fell into the water. I am sure it was ours unless of course others fell in too, which is always possible. Creatures do fall in from time to time, or so I have been told. Though one never knows the truth of these things."

Opossum nodded his head at each word but, because of the noise of the rain against his ears and, because he was busy looking at the ground in front—he thought he smelt something familiar, sweet and gentle—he soon got all tangled in them and in the end, he wasn't sure how many Raccoons Groundhog said had fallen into the water or how often that sort of thing happened. He pursed his lips anxiously and stared about, wide eyed.

Then that same sweet, gentle smell welled up again around his front feet. It filled his nose and lungs. A thrill of excitement ran through him. "Willow!" he said in a loving and surprised way. "I smell Willow—the fresh insides of Willow tips!"

"How do you know it is Willow, especially the insides of Willow tips?" asked Groundhog, sniffing.

"There is a tall and wonderful Willow in Deer Meadow—just below The Garden and nor far from my den. Have you never seen it?" Opossum answered with a longing sigh. How long it was since he had thought of Home! "The tips are often chewed and eaten. Perhaps the Deer or the Rabbits browse on them.

Anyway, I have found them on the ground, sweet smelling in the evening air, like young grass." He remembered now its dusty, yellow catkins—those furry flowers—and its slender leaves and long, sweeping branches that touched the ground.

Groundhog blinked and wondered. "What chews them here then?" he asked anxiously.

Opossum did not answer but scurried on, running back and forth, sniffing loudly. "As I thought, there's something else here too!" he exclaimed, whirling round in a circle staring at the ground. "Something even more familiar! I think I smell a Raccoon! It is very faint, but it's certainly Raccoon fur, wet Raccoon fur. There is no smell like it in all The Five Worlds!" He gave a strange gurgle of nervous excitement and ran on ahead. Then suddenly he let out a high-pitched squeal, jumped forward and dashed round the corner as fast as his legs would carry him. Groundhog's heart jumped into his throat.

There, just as Opossum expected, he found Raccoon tracks plodding up the bank with a surprising large drag mark to one side, as if the Raccoon was carrying something long and heavy. Opossum ran inland, following the tracks uphill to a downy place among the weeds, but there he saw what filled his heart with dread. He saw a heavy flattening in the undergrowth where the Raccoon had laid down, and all around were large prints of strange feet—webbed feet with long, split claws. Opossum placed one of his own feet in the strange track and saw that it barely filled the back half. Opossum groaned. "Oh no!" he cried. He sat down with a bump and his dark eyes filled with tears.

"What's wrong now?" cried Groundhog, running up behind quite out of breath.

"Raccoon has been eaten by Day Monsters!" Opossum whined, beginning to shake. "I told you they had long, sharp claws. No one ever believes me!"

Groundhog circled the flattened weeds and studied everything carefully. He had never seen such footprints before, and he remembered Black-Tip's description of Shadow-Black's track, almost as large as himself with claws as long as Willow leaves. "They are not big enough for Shadow-Black, The Night Walker," he said softly, almost in a whisper. He hoped more than anything that Opossum had not heard the fear in his voice.

Opossum started and looked at Groundhog with sharp eyes full of worry. "Shadow-Black?" he said, as if he had not thought of that before.

Groundhog bent down nearer the ground. The prints were nothing like an

Otter's. They were something like a Muskrat's although much bigger in every way—longer, wider, more deeply set. He froze inside. "Giant Muskrats!" he whispered to himself with horror.

"What did you say?" Opossum asked in a startled tone. "Giant what?"

"I didn't say anything," said Groundhog, quickly shaking his head. "Look Pos, are you sure that this was our Raccoon? I admit it smells something like, but one can't be sure."

"It smells very, very like," sobbed Opossum, staring at the tracks around him.

"Well, these tracks don't end here. They travel inland between those hillocks. They cross that muddy patch beyond. They disappear again among the weeds in the distance," said Groundhog, trying to prod Opossum out of his dark imaginings.

"Oh I know. I know," moaned Opossum, dipping his head and flattening his ears. "I saw that too. But don't you see the other tracks, thousands of them, going that way too, surrounding him, pushing him inland?" Opossum's imagination had quite run away with him although he was right about the tracks.

Groundhog sighed. Against his will he was drawn to Opossum's gloomy outlook. The tracks did make everything look rather hopeless. But that adventures undertaken happily should end unhappily was, he suspected, quite common. He had never thought that the world that existed beyond his cozy den and tunnels was safe, he wouldn't even go outside when his own body might throw a long, dark shadow on the earth for all to see. After all, he had his enemies—The Red Fox, The Hawk, The Bobcat—and this strange-footed creature might well be another. However, although his gloom and fear brought a lump into his throat, he said, "Look Pos, we ought to follow these tracks. We are but two—but you know—you never can tell—."

Opossum looked at Groundhog and frowned deeply. "We could never fight so many," he said weakly, scraping the ground with his feet.

"But they may have left Raccoon somewhere and gone off," said Groundhog coaxingly. "He may be imprisoned somewhere, waiting and hoping. We can't just leave him there."

Opossum blinked and thought again of rough river-pirates. "Like pirates," whispered Opossum breathlessly, feeling a glimmer of Opossum-courage grow deep inside himself—colourful stories, full of dash and daring, always thrilled him.

"Yes Pos, like pirates," Groundhog answered. His voice was a little flat, but Opossum only noticed the word "pirates".

"Come on then!" Opossum called, running down the hillock on the other side and following the tracks across the mud. "Raccoon may be alive and in danger. He may have been captured by pirates!"

"Yes, that's it," Groundhog nodded, following behind and trying to look hopeful but feeling cold fear in his heart. He had never seen so many large, clawed prints, not even in nightmares. His only comfort was that it had now finally stopped raining.

The tracks were not easy to follow because the rain had already washed many away. In fact, if there hadn't been so many to start with, they might never have been able to follow them at all. "These creatures, whoever they are, are all different sizes. Some tracks are large, some small, and some in between," Groundhog exclaimed as they crossed the mud.

"What do you suppose that means?" asked Opossum, circling them cautiously and staring at the tracks in the mud.

"Well," said Groundhog, scratching his head, "they're all the same shape so I suppose the same creature comes in different sizes."

"Well," murmured Opossum slowly, "Opossums do that too. I have seen much larger Opossums than myself and much smaller ones too, and the newborn are no bigger than a bean! That's why they stay well hidden in the mother's pouch for two whole moons."

Groundhog raised his eyebrows. "By then any self-respecting Groundhog would be off on his own!" he chided with a crinkled brow.

Opossum flinched and swayed his head. "Well these weren't, you know," he said, pointing down.

"What—do—you—mean?" Groundhog asked slowly, anxiously.

"Well here the young of more than one Spring seem to travel together with adults. What creatures do you know who do that?" Opossum sounded afraid again as though that idea made these creatures more frightening than ever.

"I know of none," whispered Groundhog, looking about. Every rustle in the undergrowth made them jump.

"Well it must be for a reason," whispered Opossum, crouching down to peer closely at the tracks. "Everything in The Five Worlds has a reason, or so I have been told. After all, no one wants to move about in such a crowd with no time alone and no independence."

Groundhog held his breath. How well he knew now what was coming and how little he wanted to hear it!

"Unless they stick together to hunt and take prisoners," Opossum whispered quickly, looking up with fearful, dark eyes like two beetle backs. He now thought he knew the secret of the muddy tracks and beneath all his anxiety flickered a gold glint of Opossum-pride.

It was perhaps this pride that kept him going on their wet and rough trek across the island. Pride and the darkness of Night, which sent energy down his legs and into his tiny toes and even along his thin, pink tail to the very tip. Night pulled the island closer around Opossum like a magician's dark cape; inside he felt secure and hidden. But Night made Groundhog feel that the island was much bigger than it really was, and the moonlight, glinting here on a stone and there along a gnarled root, made each dip or hollow look large and dangerous. Groundhog's heart was forever jumping into his throat with fear.

"Look!" cried Opossum, pointing ahead with a pink finger. "Look, there's a pond!" Below them was the glassy stillness of a large pond rimmed by dark banks and crossed by a narrow, black strip of what looked like a bridge.

"How beautiful," sighed Groundhog, thinking that the pond looked like a large bowl of magic, silver liquid. But he did not think that for long. For as they ran across the last hill and down to the narrow flat of mud at the pond's edge, they saw what filled them with sorrow—the Raccoon tracks disappeared into the water, surrounded by the prints of the creatures with the long, sharp claws.

"They must have dragged him to their den!" cried Opossum, peering into the water and trying to see the bottom. "There is no hope of finding him now. We can't dive through the water to their caves on the bottom." Opossum imagined now a whole world deep, deep down on the pond bottom, stretching to the very center of the earth and reaching far out to a sea of high, cresting waves like the one Moonbeam had described so often.

Groundhog stroked his chin thoughtfully and pursed his lips. "Otter could go down there," he said slowly. "Anyway, how do we know they didn't just all swim across and come out on the other side?"

Opossum clicked his tongue. "Is it likely?" he asked in a heavy tone. "Why swim across when there is a bridge?

Groundhog had not paid much attention to the bridge—he had been too worried by the water and the footprints—but he looked up at it now and tilted his head on one side. "Is it a bridge?" he asked in a puzzled voice, pondering the strangeness of everything around him. A pond here was strange, especially one that mixed beauty and sorrow in the way this one did. But a bridge was even stranger, especially one so thick and full that it looked more like a wall. It was nothing like that high-flung Bridge in The Great Dark Forest where he had faced Black-Tip and his band.

"What else?" answered Opossum, with a flick of his tail and shake of his ears.

"Well it looks like a wall to me. There's no way under unless you duck down like a fish," answered Groundhog, furrowing his brow again.

Opossum stared and tried hard to remember everything he had ever heard or known about walls—Orchard walls, Garden walls, Meadow walls, House walls. He had never heard of water walls. He ran his eyes across the top. Now with moonlight shining along its edges, it did look more like a wall, a very thick wall that went all the way to the water-bottom. "My!" he exclaimed at last. "It must be the wall of an underwater town. THEIR town, I suspect," he said, pointing at the tracks.

Groundhog sighed. "Well, whatever it is, if we cross that way, we can at least see if Raccoon came out of the water on the other side."

Opossum looked suddenly terrified. The thought of crossing the pond on top of the wall filled him with dread. "But we might fall in," he cried out. "It might be a trap. They might capture us too, and I know very well I can't breathe under water. I found that out not so long ago!"

"They can capture us just as well here!" exclaimed Groundhog with a sharp nod that made poor Opossum shiver all over. "And how do we know they didn't come out on the other side of the pond and go uphill into the woods over there!"

Opossum began to sniff and moan as he always did when he was upset, but as he had no answer and certainly no other suggestions, it was not long before he found himself leading Groundhog across the wall. It was wide and sturdy but was not smooth on top, and they had to pick their way gingerly over and between branches, twigs, and stones that stuck out at odd angles and hit their faces. "You were right, it seems," whispered Opossum, tripping in a hole and then knocking the side of his head against a branch. "It must be a wall. No bridge would be so uneven on top or so dangerous."

"Yes, true," Groundhog murmured, quite exhausted by the effort it took to stay on top of the slippery branches covered with waterweeds and moss. "Quite perilous for walking, this!" he sighed irritably, as if blaming whoever had built the wall for their thoughtlessness. It would, after all, have made a very fine bridge if it had only been finished off properly.

It took a long while to reach the far bank, and more than once Groundhog wondered if they would ever get there. The far end of the wall was in deep, black shadows because the moonlight was hidden behind the spreading branches of woodland trees. Groundhog couldn't see where he was going. Luckily, Opossum's white back showed a little still in the darkness, and Groundhog followed as closely as possible. This had its problems as once or twice poor Opossum squealed out because Groundhog had trod on his tail.

When they finally reached the other side, they searched up and down the bank for Raccoon tracks but found none, none at all, not even the tracks of the creatures. "Then we may as well find Otter," said Groundhog sadly, "because Raccoon must certainly be under the water." Tears filled his eyes in the darkness, and he fought hard to hold back a sob that welled up in his throat. Until now, Groundhog had really had hope that Raccoon was safe somewhere—alive at least—but now that hope seemed lost. How well he knew that Raccoons couldn't live underwater for long, and they had been on the banks of this pond a long time. The tracks in the mud were not fresh when they came. Not even an Otter or a Muskrat could stay underwater so long! The moon moved deeper down into the woods, and it became even darker than before. Groundhog looked around anxiously. He could not see Opossum's white back anymore, though he could hear Opossum's uneven breathing. He guessed Opossum was crying.

# Chapter TWELVE
## Out in the Water-world

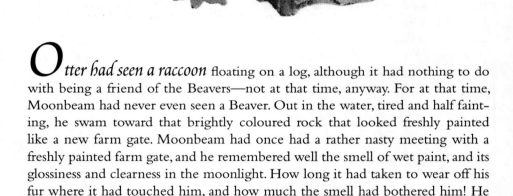

O*tter had seen a raccoon* floating on a log, although it had nothing to do with being a friend of the Beavers—not at that time, anyway. For at that time, Moonbeam had never even seen a Beaver. Out in the water, tired and half fainting, he swam toward that brightly coloured rock that looked freshly painted like a new farm gate. Moonbeam had once had a rather nasty meeting with a freshly painted farm gate, and he remembered well the smell of wet paint, and its glossiness and clearness in the moonlight. How long it had taken to wear off his fur where it had touched him, and how much the smell had bothered him! He squinted and stared at the strange rock and wondered if he really should try to not touch it, and if there was something wrong with it.

He had, anyway, very little choice about the matter or so it seemed. For the water swept him into the path of this odd rock, while the rock also seemed to be moving toward him. Moonbeam was quite sure that this must all be in his imagination, overheated after such a fright and so much swimming in Day's bright light. He tried however, in one last burst of strong swimming, to move aside and at least get a better view of the rock before grabbing on, but the rushing water as well as the rock's strange way of moving wherever he did, left him quite unable to ever avoid it. Anyway, he was tired and sore enough now to welcome grabbing onto anything, even a rock so mysterious and so colourful. He lunged forward and grabbed. The rock somehow ducked beneath the surface, dragging him down with it. Moonbeam thrust himself back up, coughing and gulping for air, and pulled himself up over it. The rock was almost too slippery to hold onto, and the tighter he held, the more difficult holding on became. The rock tossed one way and then the other, plunged and surfaced, rolled and broke free. All his fears surrounding the stories of Swift-Paws flashed through Moonbeam's mind; had he ended his days here at the bottom of the water?

"Do you have to cling on so?" exclaimed a squeaky, whispering voice. "Can't you fend for yourself like others do?"

Moonbeam stared and stared. His eyes were full of water and light, but he thought he saw a small head, two beady eyes, and slim yellow lips in the middle of a yellow striped face staring at him from under the rock.

"Don't look so surprised!" added the voice angrily. "Haven't you seen a Turtle before, or are you quite unfamiliar with us independent types who know better than to hold on where we're not wanted!"

"Well I'm sorry!" gasped Moonbeam, "but I'm so tired from swimming."

"Shouldn't be out at all if I was you!" snapped Turtle. "You're not built for it, you know!" He looked Moonbeam up and down and said, "Well, well, well!" in an odd way, as if he had never seen anything so wrong for swimming in all his life. "There's a rock over here just a little underwater. Perhaps it would suit you. I often rest there myself although it is not warm enough," he said earnestly, not wanting the creature to grab him again, and very much doubting that Moonbeam could swim any further. "Not at all the shape for swimming," he muttered to himself, dipping out of Moonbeam's way.

The rock was there sure enough, and Moonbeam pulled himself up onto it and sat half out of the water looking very forlorn and tired. His hair hung flat down around him in a most unbecoming fashion. He wasn't exactly vain, but he did hate to meet a new creature, especially one so critical, while looking nothing at all like a Raccoon. He stared at his reflection in the water unhappily. What on earth do I look like, he thought, tossing the water out of his ears and eyes! I might as well be a Weasel, with a pointed face like that!

"You really should give it up, you know," the Turtle squeaked, paddling around the rock and grasping on with his front feet which, Moonbeam noticed, were striped bright red.

"Give what up?" shivered Moonbeam, looking sadly at each distant bank.

Now he would have to swim back, and who knows where Opossum and Groundhog were by now! He might well never see them again, he thought.

"Swimming," the Turtle answered glibly. "I would say you're a bit too wide for it, and your tail is too long and full of fur. But then, you meet all types out here—all types! What are you?"

Moonbeam looked at him sourly. He thought the Turtle rather odd looking too. And so he pursed his lips and stuck out his chin and refused to answer.

"Oh I know now!" chuckled the Turtle, waving one of his black and red front feet in a circle splashing Moonbeam's nose. "I have it! You're one of those—one of those—Skunks I've heard so much about. All black and white and striped! That's it, isn't it?"

"No," said Moonbeam slowly. "No it isn't! I mean I'm not!"

The Turtle looked puzzled. He scratched his head and leaned it to one side. "Well, let's see. Oh yes! That's it! I know now! I'm right now! You'll see. You're a Ringtail! Black and white and rings all over!"

"No," said Moonbeam irritably, "I'm not!"

"Well I give up," said the Turtle with a deep sigh.

"I'm not playing a guessing game with you," said Moonbeam peevishly, looking about and trying to decide where he should swim to next.

"Oh!" said the Turtle in quite a disappointed voice. "I thought you were. Isn't it a bit late to be formal? I mean you were hanging onto my shell you know."

"I thought you were a rock," said Moonbeam sharply, staring into the Turtle's dark eyes.

"A rock!" whined Turtle. "How could you?" I'm nothing like! I mean have you seen colours like me on rocks? Glorious yellows and brilliant reds! A rock indeed! No indeed!" The Turtle's dark eyes flashed, and he shook his head from side to side. That's what comes from living in shells, Moonbeam thought, gives one a narrow outlook on the world and a short temper.

The Turtle began to sway to and fro in the water, waving one foot at a time in the air and nodding his head. Moonbeam wondered what the Turtle was doing until he realized he might be showing off his bright red and yellow stripes, as if to prevent, once and for all, all talk about rocks. Perhaps he feared too many creatures thought of him as a kind of rock. This was not the first time he had been grabbed! He doubted it would be the last!

"Do you live in that shell all the time?" asked Moonbeam, pursing his lips

and then beginning to shiver again. How much he hated being so wet and shape-
less!

"I should say! Well I wouldn't at all care to go about unshelled as you are.
You're so unsafe, so soft and squelchy. I should wear your shell if I was you. It
doesn't pay not to," the Turtle answered proudly, looking Moonbeam up and
down with a sharp eye that took in every detail of Moonbeam's soft shape. Turtle
shook his head and wondered what the world could be coming to when creatures went out so rashly leaving their shells forgotten at home. He believed every
creature had a shell somewhere. Although he had to admit, many had lost them
and never found them!

"I don't have a shell," said Moonbeam, feeling suddenly rather foolish. He
was after all a long way from shore, and the top of the rock was too small. His
tail trailed in the water whenever he relaxed his body, and the chill water lapped
against his toes.

"No shell!" whispered Turtle in surprise. "You do alarm me! How did you
lose it, and how on earth can you face the day without it? The water world is
sometimes dangerous, you know!"

"Oh!" said Moonbeam sharply, "I can fight!" He raised his paws and splayed
his claws. He lashed in the air, showed his teeth, and flattened his ears fiercely.
The whole show was made doubly frightening because he was getting at each
moment into a worse and worse humor!

"Yes, I see," said Turtle boredly, yawning. "You do look different. Very frightening, in fact. I'm more of one piece, personality-wise. I'm always the same. I
don't change. I can't remember ever looking that way or that other way, to be
precise."

"What other way?" asked Moonbeam, not understanding what Turtle
meant.

"Why! Frightened! When we met, you looked quite frightened. I have never
looked frightened or fierce. The world does not much alarm me, and I alarm no
one else in return. I bask and doze and search the soft water bottom for juicy
weeds, loll on floating logs with friends, and trundle back to my same Home
each Spring. When enemies attack, I pull into my shell and wait. It's best to wait,
always wait." The Turtle closed his eyes sleepily. Sunlight glinted on his wet head.
A smile of pleasure touched his lips. He loved the sun more than anything!

Moonbeam became very silent and very thoughtful. It seemed strange to
him that anyone as colourful as Turtle should be so dull. Moonbeam was sure that

Turtle would have little patience with talk of adventures, especially adventures to see The King of The River. He saw quite clearly now that colourfulness was very useful defence or camoflauge to creatures like Turtle who, underneath it all, wanted a quiet life, basking on logs in warm sunlight. He couldn't imagine a worse fate than basking about on logs in the water.

"Surely it is not always best to wait?" said Moonbeam, stressing the word "Wait" until the word itself sounded dull like a huge dull shape blotting out the light of the sun, the moon, and all the wide show of sparkling colours on the distant horizon. He stared at Turtle.

"Oh yes!" Turtle breathed quickly. "One can always wait, even for meals."

"But it isn't pleasant!" exclaimed Moonbeam, standing almost pigeon-toed on the rock and turning in a circle. He was growing cramped and bored and both made him nervous. He reached out with his front paws to explore the feel of the water. It was cold, but lovely and smooth.

"Waiting is quite wonderful," drawled the Turtle, remembering warm lollings with friends along the islands and coves, "especially if you have a few friends to chat with about this or that, about green vegetation up-stream and down-stream, about trusty logs and wading pools." Turtle sighed deeply. "But you know," he said fretfully, eyeing Moonbeam deeply, "you never told me about yourself. I mean except for that shell business, or lack of it I should say. I'm not usually the curious type, but one likes to know what to expect. I might meet another of your sort one day, and next time I would know to look out for this shell of mine."

Somehow it seemed like a stranger question than it would have if he had been asked it in The Garden before all the journeying had begun. Now Moonbeam felt as if his character was changing, filling itself out in directions he had never thought of, moving towards an end he still couldn't even imagine. He felt like a small boat crossing a large sea. To say he was a Raccoon sounded flat and dry and final, and said nothing about any of this or his adventure. Nevertheless, he said, "I am a Raccoon" with a frown and sounding rather puzzled. In fact, the words went up at the end as if asking a question. So much so, the Turtle jumped and was surprised to hear an answer!

Turtle waved his head from side to side sorrowfully, as if he couldn't imagine a worse fate than being a Raccoon. "Are you sure?" he asked seriously, staring at Moonbeam with pursed lips, sucking in his cheeks and blowing air out. "You don't exactly sound sure."

"That's because I'm changing," said Moonbeam quickly. "But then, when

I've stopped changing, I suspect I shall still be a Raccoon." He looked down-stream into the bright sunlight. Trees moved in the breeze, and the world seemed to sparkle with gold and silver.

"Change is something I can't stand," whispered Turtle anxiously. "I will be as I am one hundred years from now—one hundred years at least! I couldn't bear the idea of waking up one morning and finding I was quite different—a stranger in my own shell."

"Yes, well," said Moonbeam softly, "that's what comes of having a shell. When you don't have one, you feel different about life in some way. I suppose because Home is never exactly the same place from one year to the next."

Turtle shook his head. He didn't really know what the Raccoon was talking about, but he did understand that life without shells must be very different. Being grabbed must be doubly unnerving! "I suppose that's why you were out swim-ming!" cried Turtle, with sudden inspiration and a wide smile. "Doubt you'll change into a Turtle though."

"The swimming wasn't my idea," said Moonbeam, turning round again and shaking water out of the tip of his tail. "I was being chased by a dog."

The Turtle's eyes widened, and he tapped a striped foot on the rock several times. "You see what I mean about that shell of yours; if only you had one. You could have avoided all this swimming for which you are not in the least suited."

Moonbeam merely sighed. "The question is now how I get back. You know the waterways well, should I just swim straight out for shore or is there an easier way to get over there?" Moonbeam pointed to the distant bank and moved his finger up and down the shoreline.

"What you need is a nice cozy log," said Turtle dreamily. "Large, but not too large, smooth, but with hand grips down the sides, silver like the water, and preferably with a little moss for nibbling."

"I don't nibble moss!" said Moonbeam, annoyed.

Turtle looked surprised and then a little relieved. He hoped that meant more moss for him. He couldn't stand those striped logs he found all too often, espe-cially in Winter, which had not one patch of green anywhere! In fact, in Winter he imagined that the land, all the way to The River, was covered with giant Turtles who ate the trees and banks bare. Raccoon was after all a land-creature and might well know about the Mystery of The Trees.

"Have you ever seen the Giant Winter Turtles?" he asked slowly, bowing his head in embarrassment. He did not like to admit that there were things about Turtles he didn't know, couldn't even guess.

Moonbeam looked surprised. He didn't at all know what Giant Turtles had to do with his plight, but as he certainly didn't want to meet one unawares in the water, the thought it best to find out what he could. "No, I haven't. Have you?" he asked, sounding both alarmed and interested.

"Can't say I have, but I thought you, being a land-creature and all that—," muttered Turtle, eyeing Raccoon carefully. "Anyway, I've heard they eat all the green, every spot of it, when the weather gets cold. It makes life very difficult for others," he added with a deep sigh.

"Well there aren't any giant Turtles on land that I've seen, not in The Garden or in The Wood, probably not anywhere throughout The Five Worlds from The Garden to The River," Moonbeam said, turning round and pointing at the land in every direction as he circled.

"Ah well! We differ there, you see," said Turtle, sticking his chin out stubbornly. "There have to be Giant Turtles because of the way that green disappears, almost overnight. It stands to reason."

"It doesn't stand to reason at all!" said Moonbeam, raising his eyebrows. "There's nothing reasonable about it. It all has to do with the changing seasons."

Turtle sighed solemnly. "Oh yes, I've heard all about that, more than I can say. But no one ever explains these seasons, so much gossiped about and so little understood. My belief is that that word is just another way of saying Giant Turtles. How else can anyone explain where all the green goes, even my precious moss?" He began swimming around the rock as if he really didn't want to be contradicted again and didn't want to hear Raccoon's answer.

Moonbeam raised his eyebrows, made a wry face, and sighed loudly. "The green falls to the ground," he said firmly, "and there it turns red and gold and yellow and finally brown."

"Oh my! Oh my!" exclaimed Turtle in a mocking tone. "Whatever will you tell me next? I suppose the sun falls out of the sky at night and all the stars by day!"

At that Moonbeam was dumbfounded. What could he say? He had ideas of course about the sun and the stars as Opossum and Groundhog had, but he didn't feel in the mood to argue with Turtle about mysteries he was so uncertain of. Besides, he was afraid in the end he might get all tangled up again in Opossum's melting theory. Nevertheless, perhaps out of exasperation, he couldn't help blurting out "Some folks think they melt!" he laughed.

"Oh my!" squeaked Turtle. "Do they?"

"Yes," answered Moonbeam hastily, trying to look very sure. "Yes, they do!"

Moonbeam slipped on the rock and his tail went under water again. Rebalancing himself, he looked around. The two distant banks seemed a very, very long way off. He looked up. Clouds had gathered. Upstream the sky was almost black. It's going to rain, he thought.

"Look! Look what's here! A nice log that's just right for you!" cried Turtle suddenly.

Moonbeam looked behind and saw a fairly large log drifting slowly downstream toward them. Turtle flapped about excitedly and swam out to haul it over. "It's just the kind," he squealed. "Perfect, absolutely perfect!"

"For you, you mean," said Moonbeam drily, sniffing.

"Oh no, not for me! It's just right for you! Here, hang on! It's yours!" Turtle answered, thrusting the log toward Moonbeam.

Feeling that it must be now or never, and not enthusiastic about the long, cold swim back to shore, Moonbeam lunged forward and grabbed the log.

"Gracious!" cried Turtle. "Careful now! Careful!"

Moonbeam rebalanced himself and, hanging on with his front feet, tried to push off from the rock. The water felt freezing cold around his middle and he shivered. He couldn't imagine a worse life than drifting about, hanging onto logs, and he said so rather loudly.

"You don't look quite right," exclaimed Turtle, scurrying about from one end to the other and looking at Moonbeam's legs with a critical frown. "Couldn't you move more forcefully? You won't go anywhere like that!"

Moonbeam thought of the girl in The Garden, his queen. He thought of Silversheen and The King of The River. He filled his lungs with air, tightened his leg muscles and kicked. The log streaked forward rapidly and then drifted on downstream so swiftly that Turtle had a great deal of trouble keeping up. "Well I never!" Turtle laughed, gurgling through the water. "I had no idea you had it in you. You'll make good speed to shore. I shouldn't doubt you'll land before it rains."

Moonbeam was laughing too, now, and had to admit that this log-hanging had its uses. He rested and drifted and then kicked again. He swirled forward. The water lapped against his chin and whirled around the log at either end.

"Oh my!" cried Turtle in the distance. "Oh my, yes!"

Moonbeam's heart was beating fast with excitement. Soon he would be back on the bank. Soon he would be able to get thoroughly dry and look once again like the Raccoon he was. Soon he would be free to search for the dear friends he had lost. Suddenly he felt rather grateful to the Turtle. He turned a little on the log, clumsily, with water hitting his face, and called back loudly, "Thank you! I hope we meet again some day under better circumstances!" He thought he heard a high-pitched laugh come back to him across the water, but he wasn't sure. He could no longer see Turtle. The bright, shiny shell had gone. The water seemed somehow empty, flat and grey under the clouds. It began to rain. A Swan appeared and disappeared in the distance ahead, like a bright, twinkling star.

# Chapter THIRTEEN

# On Green Island

*T*he trees along the banks swayed in the wind that always seems to come before a storm. Their branches seemed to beckon Moonbeam and, on the wind, he thought he smelt short, fresh whiffs of Chestnut Grove, Oak Way, and even The Garden. Again he remembered the girl with her dark auburn hair and her floating green robes billowing out behind her like Willow branches in the breeze. Her eyes were as dark as the sky behind him now, and yet the gentleness in them had been so different than the harshness of this storm-burdened sky. Realizing this, his memory of her grace and queenliness gave him courage. He swam more strongly, and the log sped forward more surely.

Raindrops pattered around him on the water, now making round, dark hollows rimmed with silver where they fell. Rays of sunlight darted through the clouds now and then and tinged each raindrop in its way with gold, giving the rain and the water an astonishing beauty all its own. But Moonbeam knew that there was going to be a bad storm, and that as the rain fell more heavily, everything would change. The water would become murky, the sky black, and the rain a cold sheet that would come through his fur as cold as snow. He imagined too that the water would become rough and, perhaps, rise up in high-cresting waves like the blue-green sea Great Grandfather The Fisher believed went on forever beyond Silversheen. "Such a fine line," he muttered to himself, "between beauty and danger," and he thought of the rich red fur of the Fox, the glistening white-ness of deep winter snow, and the velvet black stripes of the Bee.

That moment of silvery beauty on the water passed just as he had expected. Thunder crashed overhead, and lightening, silver tipped with gold, flashed across the sky like the jagged crack on a hatching egg. "And if Opossum were here now, he would say that the sky fits over us like a shell, and that now it is cracked it will fall!" Moonbeam exclaimed with a sharp laugh. Rain poured down in heavy sheets; wind swept the water into waves that splashed Moonbeam in the face; the air became as cold as ice. Soon he could not see where he was going and, without the log for support, he would have found it difficult to swim, perhaps impossible. He tried as hard as he could to keep going in the direction he had started in, but the wind kept blowing him back and turning the log in circles. Several times he lost his grip and went under. Several times he got caught on logs and rocks under the water and had to get himself and his log untangled again. Soon he was tired, breathing hard and had sore legs and stiff fingers. But the tree–lined banks, whenever he caught glimpses of them through the rain, got no nearer.

He had been drifting and swirling for a very long time when he quite unex-pectedly ran up onto a muddy bank straight in front of him. He scrambled out of the water and up over roots, dragging his log with him—he had no doubt he would need it again once the storm passed. He had no idea where he was. He curled up under a bush, his log in his arms and fell asleep. To a Raccoon, cold and tired, that was the most natural thing to do, especially in daylight, and especially in such a storm.

Asleep, he dreamed of Swift–Paws and rich red berries. He dreamed they met by Silversheen and built a den there. His precious log propped up their doorway. He clutched his treasured log and snored. Perhaps now he understood Turtle. What a den it was—all decorated with Laurel flowers and gilded with Butter-cups, soft inside with deep green mosses and Thistle-down! In the center there was a Banqueting Hall where they entertained their friends and other weary travelers. There they told marvelous tales full of colour and adventure while they drank Blackberry wine from fruit-skin cups. He stood clutching their door-post, looking out at the star-studded sky reflected in Silversheen, and then he looked in at the merry, dark eyes of Garden Raccoons who would return Home with tales about their glorious Hall, about Opossum and Groundhog and The King of The River and, of course, about Moonbeam.

"But watch out!" Opossum cried. "Watch out, the world is melting! The doorpost is slipping!" and Moonbeam clutched it more firmly. The doorpost swayed and pulled, and he was dragged across the floor behind it. Everyone in the Hall jumped up and ran to the door, and as they passed him their faces changed, becoming more round, more brown, something like a Groundhog, and yet not a Groundhog. But before Moonbeam had time to understand what was happening, the doorpost swayed the other way and pulled loose from the roof. Moonbeam was flung across the room and pinned down under it.

"Hang on!" Opossum called. "Hang on!"

Moonbeam hung on, but the doorpost was being pulled or dragged away from him. He clutched and clung and dug his nails deep into the wood until his fingers ached.

"But what good is the log to you?" came a deep, rasping voice, "and it is just right for us!"

"It is my doorpost," answered Moonbeam dreamily. "It holds up the roof of my Banqueting Hall."

"You're wrong there, you see!" the voice answered with a slight laugh. "It holds up nothing! Besides, that's not the way to build a house, any house, much less a Hall."

Moonbeam half opened his eyes. He thought he saw a large, brown face with a wide nose and tiny, annoyed eyes staring down at him. Beyond he saw the blood-red sky of Day's End. How long I must have slept, he thought, it is evening!

"What good is it to you?" cried yet another voice and Moonbeam, looking around, saw another brown face, and a little to the side of that at least four more—smaller ones, more anxious, with eyes that darted about unsurely.

"It is my log!" answered Moonbeam, still seeing his glorious Banqueting Hall in his imagination and still tasting the Blackberry wine on his lips. "It has done me a great deal of good. It saved my life!"

"But how?" asked the creature in return, pulling again at the log. "You cannot eat it or build with it as we can, despite all this talk about roofs and Banqueting Halls, which we well know Raccoons don't go in for. And then neither could you hollow it out and curl up inside like a Vole or Chipmunk—you are too big!"

Moonbeam sat up and curled his body up over the log to protect it, as he knew well how to do. He flattened his ears and swatted the air with one hand, and as he spoke he showed his teeth, which looked both sharp and white in the evening light. "I intend to keep this log until I'm sure I'll be doing no more swimming. It's just right for floating about on."

"Great Timbers!" exclaimed the creature, backing up and looking both surprised and worried. "There's no need to get all upset! If you want to float about on it, float about! It's all the same to us. Although it is a waste of a good log." He looked at the log lovingly, longingly, and reached out to it with his front paws. He had not seen such a beautiful log in a long time. It was already trimmed, and he could see that it came from a high, high branch near the top of a tree. That was always where the bark was tastiest and softest. Once peeled, it would be perfect for building—strong and close grained. He sighed deeply.

Moonbeam saw the look of desire in the animal's eyes and wondered what it was about the log—this log in particular—that appealed to him so. If it had not been for his dream of the Banqueting Hall and for fear of more swimming, he would have left it there. He was not, as a rule, especially fond of logs, but he could see that that was not at all the case for the creature staring across at him now. That creature was obviously very fond of them, in fact somehow totally taken by a desire to collect them. Moonbeam sensed that the animal thought of little else day after day. "And what would you do with this log?" asked Moonbeam curiously, eyeing all the creatures around him.

"My sweet branches," exclaimed the second largest, while pawing the air, "there's a world of doing about a log!" All the animals flexed their fingers in a busy way as though they couldn't wait to get their hands on a log—any log—but especially Moonbeam's log.

"Yes, I see," said Moonbeam, backing up and pulling his log further under him. The more they desired it, the more he wanted to keep it. "But what kind of 'doing' do you mean?"

The creatures looked at each other in absolute amazement. They couldn't believe that there was any creature in all the Five Worlds who didn't know what marvelous things could be done with logs, although they knew full well that there were many, including Raccoons, who never put that knowledge to any use whatsoever.

"Well?" asked Moonbeam, rounding his eyes and pursing his lips.

"Oh!" cried a young one running forward. "It is all too wonderful to even describe. You have to 'do' for yourself to really know, or be a Beaver like us. We know by heart!"

Moonbeam had heard of Beavers and all their clever building, but he had never seen one, and now he was looking at them he knew that he had imagined something quite different—something bigger, grander, with long arms and legs. "How do you build so well and carry so much?" he asked, not wishing to offend them but really puzzled.

"With our teeth!" the young one replied.

Moonbeam was surprised. He ran his tongue along the edge of his own teeth very slowly, feeling all their sharpness and smoothness. He knew that although they did wonderfully well at tearing, pulling, and biting, they were not exactly suited to carrying logs. Indeed, he doubted he could do that at all.

The young one saw Moonbeam's tongue moving across his teeth and knew what must be passing through the Raccoon's mind. "Oh, our teeth are perfectly suited for carrying! They stick out, you see, and we have flaps of skin behind to keep out water when we swim. Nothing could do better!"

"But why always build anyway?" asked Moonbeam in a puzzled voice. His dream had made him a little sympathetic to house and hall building, but he still understood nothing about the delights and seriousness of building Beaver dams. He could think of so many much more pleasant and necessary things to occupy his time.

The large Beaver, who had moved nearer again and who was still looking at Moonbeam's log with longing, chuckled at the word 'build'. His small eyes filled with a wistful yet happy expression. The last shreds of evening light flickered in their centers like two tiny flames. "What wonderful dams I have seen in my time," he intoned dreamily, "sweeping across the water in gentle curves as smooth and even as a rainbow or tree rings. Such beauty! But then I am a poet! Dams are built for safety and winter food, and there are those who never notice their beauty—those who think only of their stomachs like hoarding Squirrel or Chipmunks." He looked anxiously at one of the young Beavers who was pursing his lips and raising his brows mockingly, while leaning casually against a clump of roots.

"But times have changed," said the Beaver with a sigh, as though trying to accept a new world and a new lore about which he knew nothing. "In my day we gathered to chant the famous poems of the Great Dam Builders, and we began our dam-building with prayers and ended with joyful songs. Now we chant nothing. We do not even gather on the set days."

Moonbeam was spellbound by the Beaver's words. The mystery in them intrigued him, and then he saw the same dreamy look in the Old One's eyes that he had seen in his own reflection on the water. He felt he was somehow looking into a mirror, and yet he knew that while this Beaver dreamed of times past, he (Moonbeam) dreamed of times to come and of The King of The River whom he had not yet found. "I dream of the future," Moonbeam said softly, not so much making conversation as trying to understand himself.

"Ah yes!" said the old Beaver knowingly. "The young dream of the future and the old, like me, dream of the past. Between us we somehow hold the present together like woven reeds along a river's edge or threads in a Spider's web, glinting in morning dew. Between us we create History. But still we should chant. We should sing of things past and of things yet to come and not to come."

Moonbeam stared. It was dark now, and he could see much more clearly than before. It was a great relief to no longer have to squint and frown to keep out the light. He felt too the usual surge of energy inside him that came with night. He began to prowl restlessly around his log.

"Ah yes!" said the Beaver, eyeing Moonbeam's prowling with a knowing nod. "Night is the time for building and for all good things."

Moonbeam nodded.

"Perhaps you would like to see our dam?" asked the other adult Beaver with excitement, jumping forward and smiling, showing front teeth the colour of chestnuts, much larger and thicker than Moonbeam's own.

"Oh Mother," cried a young Beaver, with a short laugh. "Raccoons have no interest in dams—no interest whatsoever!"

"Well there you are not quite right," said Moonbeam thoughtfully. "I have heard they are very sturdy and make marvelous bridges across the water. Uncle Long-Ears traveled across one once in the early morning, in Winter. I have heard that Great-Grandfather Fisher fished from one in his youth, so long ago."

"My branches!" said the largest, sitting back to remember old times. "Why there are many who are grateful to us; many who fish from our dams. Our ponds too are favored. Otters, Minks, and Deer all come to them to feed and drink. I see them often."

"Then you would like to see our dam?" squealed another Young One, running up to Moonbeam, clenching and unclenching his hands excitedly in the air as if feeling for logs.

Moonbeam had noticed this Young One before, who had until now been sitting, half asleep, on his mother's tail as little Beavers often did. He could not resist this coaxing question; he had a soft heart for all Little Ones. However, he decided then and there that he had better hang onto his log in case he needed it again. The vegetation around him was scrubby and low and any trees looked a long way off—he might not find another log easily. He thought again about Opossum and Groundhog and a look of pain crept into his dark eyes. Nevertheless he said, "Yes, yes I would," as cheerfully as he could, and tried to smile.

The Little One already knew that such smiles hid worry, even sorrow, and he wondered what could be bothering the Raccoon.

"Well, it's not far," said the large Beaver, "if you would care to follow along."

And Moonbeam did follow them. At first they ran energetically along the bank's edge, diving out into the water now and then, and then they ran less comfortably across the land toward the trees. They stopped every now and then to sniff the air for danger. "We don't like to go by land," said Mother Beaver—the Little One was riding on her tail again and yawning widely—"but sometimes when you are looking for new timber, it is the only thing to do."

"But surely this way travels inland," murmured Moonbeam anxiously. Now he saw the direction of their dam, he was really worried.

"Oh no!" said the Mother breathlessly, running on, "the middle of the Island is quite in the other direction.

Moonbeam's heart jumped. His blood ran cold. "Island?" he repeated in a bemused voice. "Did you say island?"

"Sweet timbers! Yes, this is an island. Green Island, to be exact, " answered the Mother, puzzled that Raccoon did not know. What was the world coming to when Night-Creatures no longer knew where they were and were not!

"I had no idea!" said Moonbeam in a flat, chill voice. Though perhaps that was not quite true. He had suspected something was wrong, but he had not known what. One thing was for sure, he knew nothing about islands. He wracked his brain to try to remember anything he had ever heard about them. Then in a flash that filled him with dread he remembered what he had heard about Green Island—Shadow-Black, The Night Walker, came that way in the Spring. Black-Tip had said that, Muskrat had said that. He turned quickly to the Beaver Mother, but she had run on ahead, and he did not want to shout. Moonbeam looked around anxiously and tried to calm his fears at the same time—it was not yet quite Spring, he reassured himself, so why worry the Beavers with his own fears? Wasn't life hard enough?

The journey across Green Island was a rough one. Roots, hillocks, and dells were everywhere—all mostly hidden by a stick-like shrubbery and weeds that caught on Moonbeam's fur and flicked in his face as he ran by. As they neared the other side of the Island, Moonbeam sensed the Beavers' excitement. For perhaps no one liked to arrive Home as much as a Beaver did!

"See! See our beautiful dam!" the Old One called back to him, with an enthusiasm quite as great as when they had built it, many, many Summers earlier.

Moonbeam found that he was almost at the water's edge again but on the other side of the Island. The Beaver dam stretched out in an even arch toward the opposite bank, and all around stood gnawed tree limbs, woodchips, twigs, and saplings stripped of bark. "It must take a long time to build such a dam," Moonbeam said slowly, fascinated by its gentle curve—its fine shape.

"Yes, my branches, yes!" exclaimed the Mother with mock irritation. Nevertheless, Moonbeam could tell that she was very proud.

"We start with shrubs, cut and placed trunk-end upstream, in a line across the water-way," the Old One said, staring at his workmanship and pointing out the features to Moonbeam, "and then we pile rocks, mud, and branches on top until the dam is high enough and quite water-tight. It all takes ages and ages, but what a marvel our pond is afterwards! Have you seen a better?"

Moonbeam, of course, did not know much about ponds. He thought he had seen one once with his Mother when he was very small. But that memory was shadowy and distant like a dream. Perhaps, indeed, it was a dream. But, if he was to dream of a pond, the perfect pond, then he thought he might as well dream of this one. The water was smooth and clear and looked like silver in the moonlight, and the sweep of the banks, melding into the curve of the dam itself, made a half-circle as even and graceful as the half moon. "It must be the best in the world," sighed Moonbeam dreamily, "the very best."

The Beavers puffed out their chests and looked very pleased. "And you haven't even seen our lodge yet," the big Beaver exclaimed joyfully. "It is still better."

Moonbeam could tell from his words that the Beaver thought of their lodge as part of the dam even though it wasn't built on it this time—only fairly near by. But the dam was built to protect the lodge and provide food for those who lived there, and so the two were one in the Beaver's mind, like a nut and its shell, or a seed and its fruit. It was quite pointless to admire the dam without seeing the lodge or vice-versa.

"Is that the lodge?" asked Moonbeam, pointing to a heap of sticks in the water. It was shiny in the moonlight and repaired with new mud.

"Why, my timbers, yes!" cried a Young One, with breathless excitement to see again the Home he loved so well. His eyes widened with happiness, and thought suddenly of all the comforts of Home—soft beds, warm rooms, old smells. All Winter, with the mud frozen like a castle wall, he had stayed cozily hidden there, going outside only at night and mainly underwater to find the saplings they had stored for food. When the weather had warmed a little, and it came time to go further afield to find new wood to repair the lodge and dam, he had been sad to leave, even for a short while. He was feeling much more adventurous, though no beauty in the outside world could bring this joy of going Home.

"Our lodge," said the old Beaver, sitting back on his haunches thoughtfully, while chewing a willow tip, "is the center of our lives. We're homely types—family folks. Come Spring, a lodge is full of the noise and affection of three generations. Sparkle-Eyes here has been with me since I built my first dam and lodge many, many Springs ago. We hope to live in this one for the rest of our lives." He looked at his mate with deep affection, and she smiled coyly, dipping her head in pleasure. "We care little for the wide world or for those outside family," she said softly.

And how else could they build such dams and lodges that changed the face of Nature, or lead such complicated lives, unless they all worked together in contentment and deep pleasure? Moonbeam thought. How Opossum would have hated that crowded lodge, noisy with Little Ones in the Spring. Yet because of his loneliness, how little Opossum ever changed the face of nature or even provided for his own safety and comfort.

Moonbeam wanted to ask the Beavers about Silversheen and The King of The River, and yet he was not sure now whether his questions would be welcome. Adventures, and the world beyond this little pond, were quite obviously disliked, perhaps even feared, and so he bit his lips and decided to say nothing for the time being. Besides, he was delighted with the pond and the dam and the lodge and felt somehow calmer and more content than ever before.

"Life is strange," he thought aloud, shaking his head. "One moment I am thrilled by adventures and the next I am thrilled by a quiet Home in the middle of a quiet pond." Then which, he wondered, do I really want, or do I want both? He thought again of the Hall in his dream, on the banks of Silversheen, and saw that his dream had put both together in a way life never had. Will that be possible? he asked himself, frowning—will I wander all the way to The River to find a real Home at last? It was the first time he had thought about not ever returning to The Garden, and pain filled his eyes—he longed again to see the Cherry Tree by The Great House and the Girl in green.

"I hope we have not made you unhappy," said the Mother Beaver with concern. She had seen the frown and the flicker of pain in Moonbeam's eyes.

"Oh no!" cried Moonbeam quickly. "It is just that I suddenly thought of my own Home—the one in the future and the one in the past—and I felt homesick.

"But Homes are for the present," said the Old Beaver sincerely. "Homes of the past and of the future are of no use to us. It is the lodge that weaves the past and future together. Without a lodge, we are nothing, we would not be Beavers."

Moonbeam stared at him and thought suddenly of Turtles' shell. He stood silently thinking when a loud, slapping noise that he had never heard before anywhere made him jump nervously.

"Quick!" cried the Old Beaver. "To our lodge!"

"What's wrong?" cried Moonbeam, grasping the Beaver's arm and arching his back. Visions of Shadow-Black raced through his mind, quickly followed by others of the Bobcat and the Eagle.

"That's a danger signal! Quick, follow us!" rasped the Beaver, running to the water and diving in headfirst.

Moonbeam had no idea what to do. There were no trees on this side of the water—the Beavers did all their cutting on the far bank—and he couldn't remember having seen any really deep holes nearby as they approached the pond. Well, he thought, there's nowhere to hide so I see no way out of it! He ran to the water, dived in and swam toward the lodge. There, unable to find a door, he panicked and flapped about in the water. He slipped under, coughing and spluttering, and found himself being grabbed by a Beaver and pulled briskly up and underwater passage.

There was a lot of hustle and bustle inside the lodge. Everyone was bumping into everyone else. But eventually they sorted themselves out and Moonbeam, still gasping for breath, found himself in the most comfortable Home he had ever seen. There were, he saw, two doors at one end; at the other was a platform covered with woodchips. The wood walls were tightly packed with mud, and Moonbeam could find no chink through which he might see the night sky, except at the center of the roof. He glanced up and then cuddled down in the warmth.

"Those holes above are for fresh air," Mother Beaver nodded, brushing the woodchips and settling the Little Ones down.

"You have to have that you know," said the old Father Beaver. "When the water ices over outside, the only air we have comes down through those holes." He sat back and began to comb out his wet fur with the split nails on his webbed hind feet.

"I must say, you have done a good job here!" exclaimed Moonbeam enthusiastically, glancing all around the cozy lodge.

"We're busy with repairs at present," the Old Beaver answered tiredly. "It's a long job after the Winter, but it has to be done before more Little Ones arrive in early Summer. Then there's never time! One can't move for all the playing and racing and splashing and goings-on!" He looked at his mate and frowned.

"Well, children need to play!" she exclaimed. "That's how they learn about our life! Don't you agree?" She turned to Moonbeam with bright eyes warm with affection.

"Yes, I think so, he answered uncertainly. "I remember playing. Sometimes I still do."

The old Beaver sighed. "Life's a serious business," he intoned. "If it wasn't for me, none of this would be built. These Young Ones can't ever settle to it until they are off on their own." He leaned back against the wall and closed his eyes.

"What's under this lodge?" Moonbeam asked. "I mean, what keeps it afloat?" He looked down at the wooden floor and tried to peer between the cracks.

"Ah, you won't see anything that way!" exclaimed the Father Beaver proudly. "We built a sturdy island of rocks, mud, and branches. There's not a crack anywhere—not one. I assure you. Why, I was down there yesterday repairing, but it didn't need much. A work of Art it is, though I say so myself."

It seemed strange somehow that once in the lodge no one ever again mentioned their alarm outside a short time before. It was as if they felt nothing could touch them here in their comfortable Home. It was as if the outside world was a planet away, and they were whirling around alone somewhere far from danger and difficulty. The warmth made them all sleepy, and soon the Young Ones fell fast asleep, while the old Beaver dozed and chewed his Willow twig. The Mother combed the children's fur as they slept and hummed gently to herself. She sang about the Maple and the Willow and pungent marshes full of reeds.

Moonbeam stared at the little pieces of night sky he could see through the holes above. Home, he thought, a Home! And then he thought of gleaming Silversheen, red–gold in sunset. It began to rain heavily again and he lay cozily listening to the patter of rain on the Beaver's roof.

# Chapter FOURTEEN
## Old Magic

*It was a long night* for Opossum and Groundhog, sitting hunched up at the wood's edge waiting and waiting for Otter. Opossum tilted his ears nervously as he listened to a pair of Minks, sleek-bodied with chocolate-brown fur, hunting in the dark at the far edge of the pond. How he wished the splash of their dives and sound of their glides were Otter's as he had at first thought. But Otter did not come, and Opossum began to think that he had forgotten them and returned to The Forest to chatter "Come Otters all!" to his friends and roll again down the banks.

Just before dawn they saw a Great Blue Heron glide down to fish in the pond. In the misty dusk, his feathers glistened silver from the dew, and he looked magical, like a figure in a winter dream. Opossum blinked in the light and pulled into himself. He closed his dark eyes and fell asleep, with his nose tucked onto his chest and his pink, front feet touching each other.

Groundhog sat and stared over the undergrowth at the pond. Dawn flickered on the water and banks. Silver light touched the rims of the dark tracks on the other side. I do wish Otter would come! he thought anxiously. And it was just as he thought that that he saw something large slink and then crouch low to the ground in the shadows of the undergrowth just across the water. The Minks must have seen it too, for there was a splash as they turned suddenly downstream, and

Groundhog saw their long, streamlined shapes, shining in the light, dart away from him like falling stars on a clear night. The Heron gave a noisy squawk and flew upstream over the Island—his great wings silently lifting and falling.

Opossum woke with a start and sensed Groundhog's tenseness—stretched tight like a ripe fruit skin. His own fur bristled. "What have you seen?" he whispered sharply, without looking around.

"A large, dark shape across the pond—a hunting shape," Groundhog whispered.

Opossum squinted and blinked and tried to see across the pond. He found he could still see fairly well. The dawn light was faint and full of shadows. He stretched his nose into the air and sniffed. Heady smells left him wide-eyed and stunned. The morning dew seemed to have unlocked the spicy and sweet smells of the woods behind and water below. And sifting through these, noting what he knew and what he didn't, Opossum did smell the wild and strong scent of the hunter, strangely mixed with the fresh, green smell of waterweeds and grass. He saw too, or thought he saw, dark ear-tips much, much larger than his own, curving into the sunlight.

"Hey you two!" cried Otter, who appeared quite suddenly out of nowhere at the far end of the water-wall. Opossum and Groundhog's hearts jumped into their throats and they signaled to Otter to be quiet and hide. But Otter only laughed at their odd movements and called out, "What are you two doing up there asleep? I've been looking for you for ages! Did you see those tracks?" He was laughing and smiling and his whiskers twitched with silver in the light.

Then, with the speed of a ray of sunlight racing across a valley, and without time for Opossum and Groundhog to think, the hunter sprang from the undergrowth. He bounded across the mud flat toward Otter. His long, lean body stretched out between each bound. His back feet came down just where his front feet landed before them. His dark, narrow eyes caught the light and flamed out like fire. A breeze wafted across the water from the woods. The undergrowth rustled. Branches rattled. Opossum bit his lips and held his breath. The hunter stopped suddenly and turned. He peered into the woods with narrow eyes. He smelt Opossum and Groundhog on the breeze.

Otter took a deep breath, raced to the water and dived in. He swam out and out, further and further, to what looked to Opossum and Groundhog like a pile of sticks and mud in the middle of the pond. There he disappeared.

The hunter, without even looking at Otter, sprang to the water-wall and fixed his narrow eyes on just the place where Opossum and Groundhog sat hidden. He gave a strange hissing sound and bounded toward them.

"Quick, to the woods!" Groundhog whispered into Opossum's ear, pulling Opossum by the shoulder. Groundhog felt a strange hardness and coldness in Opossum's shoulder that did not feel like the Opossum he knew. He was filled with fear.

They turned quickly and scrambled up the bank into the woods. It was a very nasty climb as the bank was full of holes and hollows, roots and broken branches. Opossum could see that the ground was much smoother at the top and covered with deep moss. But Opossum never reached there. For just as they climbed over a large log caught on a jutting shelf, the hunter sprang out at him with glowing eyes like the fire itself. Opossum cried out, dived away, and rolled down the bank to land in a dirty heap at the bottom. Groundhog ran as fast as his legs would carry him into the woods.

In the darkness of the trees, Groundhog could see nothing. He heard the soft pad of footsteps, but they grew fainter and fainter, moving away downstream. "IT went back to the water," chattered Groundhog to himself. He listened but heard nothing. Everywhere was silent. "Pos!" he called in a whisper. But there was no answer. "Pos!" he called again softly. But there was no reply. He crept out from the trees and picked his way back downhill. He saw the edge of Opossum's back in the dawn light. He thought Opossum had never looked so white before.

"Well Pos," he said a little tearfully, brushing the earth off his fur and shaking the leaves from his feet, "let's get out of here! I don't want to meet another of whatever that was!" He gave a nervous chirp, but Opossum didn't say a word. "Oh come on" Groundhog pleaded, afraid Opossum was going to play an odd part like he had when he did all that tree-hanging nonsense. He could see Opossum was not hurt in any way—his fur was not even torn. He leaned forward, crouched on the ground, and shook Opossum gently, but Opossum didn't move.

"Oh no!" cried Groundhog. "What has happened? Pos! Pos!" But Opossum just lay there. His eyes were shut, his body was ice-cold, and his pink tongue lolled to one side. Groundhog put his ear to Opossum's chest. He couldn't even hear him breathing. His eyes widened with horror. "Then it's all over! They are both gone!" he cried, "and all I can do is to go back to The Garden!" But the thought of The Garden and The Meadow made him miserable. He tried to imagine all their greenness and flowers but saw only a dull, empty shape, empty of life, of friendship, of joy. "Oh Pos! Pos!" he sobbed, running a paw across Opossum's ears.

In the lodge, in the middle of the pond, Moonbeam heard the sound of sobbing. At first, half asleep and dreamy, he thought it was a Mistle Thrush or perhaps a Nightingale. But slowly, between dozes, he became aware that the noise was more familiar than either of those and that the chattering at the end of each fresh sob reminded him of old friends, especially of Groundhog. The lodge was very warm now, and full of the sound of deep breathing and contented snoring. Mother Beaver was even asleep now, leaning over her little ones just where she had been before Moonbeam dozed off.

Moonbeam stood on all four feet, forcefully shook himself awake and listened. The sobbing was softer now and the break between each one longer. It sounded in fact more like a tired hiccup. Then, almost without thinking, he ducked down the dark Beaver tunnel, pushed out, and splashed his way to the top of the cold water. There, hanging onto the side of the lodge, he searched the banks and woods with sharp eyes until he at last saw Groundhog sitting in a heap, his head low, on the far bank below the woods. "Groundhog!" he called, waving wildly, "GROUNDHOG!"

Groundhog heard the call and looked up. He had never been so shocked in all his life. He stared out across the water but couldn't see a Raccoon anywhere, much less their Raccoon. "Now," he said to himself, "I hear voices of friends long gone." He had no doubt that Home, in The Meadow by The Garden, he would forever hear the voices of Raccoon and Opossum. He would never find peace again.

"GROUNDHOG!" Moonbeam called again, diving into the water and swimming toward him. "GROUNDHOG! Dear Groundhog!"

Groundhog heard the splash and the sound of the swimming and the voice he loved so well, but he was too frightened to move. He had heard of ghosts. He had heard of the tricks of the Wood Elves.

"It's me! Raccoon!" Moonbeam called out as he neared the shore.

Groundhog didn't answer, but he lifted his head a little and looked out from under two fat paws. In the dawn light, running to him, he saw a very wet and very thin Raccoon, but he wasn't sure it was Their Raccoon until the light hit Moonbeam full on the face, showing his wide smile and bright eyes full of friendship. "Raccoon!" he moaned. "Where did you come from? Is that really you?" His head was still tucked under his paws.

"From the pond," Moonbeam answered quickly, "but it's a long story."

Groundhog jumped up and hugged Raccoon round the shoulders. "You've no idea what we've been through," he moaned. "A Night Monster with eyes of fire sprang out at us while you were in that city beneath the water. Poor Opossum is lying over there in that hollow. I think he must be dead." He waved his finger nervously at Opossum's still, white body.

Moonbeam didn't understand a word Groundhog said. He thought he heard something about Night Monsters and underwater cities, but he didn't think he had time to ask any questions. He ran over to Opossum and peered down into his face. Opossum had never looked so odd before, but Moonbeam was sure he was not dead. There was a faint pulse in his wrist and some warm breath came now and then from his pink lips.

"He's still alive, Groundhog," Moonbeam said gently, "although I must say he is in a bad way. Did he hit his head?"

"Not that I know of," sniffed Groundhog sadly, "but I couldn't see. I did hear him roll down the bank. And it is covered with rocks and roots." Groundhog glanced unhappily at the bank. "I don't like it out here," he added, frowning.

"Well, it would be better to take cover," Moonbeam agreed. "I don't think we could ever get him to the Beavers so we might as well carry him into the woods.

Groundhog listened to the word 'Beavers' with some anxiety. He hoped Raccoon didn't mean that city under the water. Just in case, he said, "Not there!" in a frightened voice. "Good gracious, not there!"

Moonbeam looked up at Groundhog but thought any words about the comforts of Beaver life would have to wait. "You lift his back legs and I'll carry his head and shoulders," exclaimed Moonbeam, placing his hands under Opossum's shoulders. Between them they lifted Opossum off the ground. He was less heavy than the time he had fallen over the cliff by The Great Dark Forest Bridge. Worry and walking had thinned him down.

They had almost climbed the bank and gone into the darkness of the woods when Otter appeared out of nowhere—as usual. He was panting and his red tongue was at the edge of his lips. "What's happened to Opossum?" he sputtered, flapping his thick tail and tensing his back. Moonbeam looked round with startled eyes, which ran quickly up and down Otter's body. He had never seen an Otter before but was glad to meet Otter's gentle eyes and to smell the delightful smell of water and fish.

"This is Otter!" said Groundhog quickly, seeing Raccoon's surprise. "He was helping us search for you."

"Otter!" said Moonbeam, sifting through his memories. No, he had never seen an Otter before, but he had heard something about them, and remembered too what Groundhog had said about one all that time ago near Whiteoaks.

"Yes!" said Otter very politely and with a shallow bow. "But what has happened to poor old Opossum?" Opossum looked awful to him, with his sunken cheeks and lolling, pink tongue—now rather dry from being out in the air so long.

"We have no idea," whined Groundhog. "That hunting animal—that Night Monster—came. I ran. Poor Opossum fell. When I came back to find him, he was just lying there. I thought he was dead." He gasped between words as if about to cry again.

"And is he dead?" asked Otter, staring at Opossum. "There are no cuts or scratches! The Lynx didn't touch Opossum as far as I can see." And that seemed strange to him. For he had seen the flame of hunger in the Lynx's eyes—a flame he remembered well and always looked for, a flame he saw in uneasy dreams in deep Winter when snow covered the banks and turned The Forest white like winter-mink.

Moonbeam and Groundhog jumped at the word 'Lynx'. Had they not been warned long ago about that hunter? "The song in The Forest!" said Groundhog, looking at Moonbeam.

"How did it go? 'Beware where the Lynx who stalks alone!' Was that it?" Moonbeam cried, trying to remember those words that had echoed down to them from the treetops.

"In Forest dells! It was in Forest dells!" exclaimed Groundhog. "Is this a dell? Is it?"

"I would not call this a dell," said Otter, glancing around, "but the Lynx does indeed stalk alone, though he does not like to swim unless he has to, and so I usually escape rather easily. But what about Opossum? What has happened to him?"

"He's still breathing, though faintly," said Moonbeam softly. "I feel his pulse too, now and then, like rain dripping from a high branch."

Otter followed them up into the woods while the sunrise flooded the banks and pond behind. Everything it touched turned a glimmering red, like flame Lily or the dusting of ripeness on an apple. Then a little later, at the edge of full daylight, the grass and branches along the banks seemed to leap out in gold light, and birds began to sing all around them.

They lay Opossum down in a mossy place and covered his cold body with a blanket of leaves and grass. And while Moonbeam and Groundhog sat at either side of Opossum, with narrow faces full of fear, Otter went to fetch the Beaver who, he said, knew everything there was to know about the water-world.

Later, all together—Moonbeam, Groundhog, Otter, and the Beaver family— sat round Opossum, staring at him and whispering. But although Opossum lay there before them, they felt he was a long way away—far from the woods and the pond, far from their sorrows, even far from his own danger. The young Beavers grew restless and were soon scampering around in the undergrowth, gnawing on twigs and feeling logs with excited fingers. They stared lovingly up high into the tree branches, following the tree trunks until their eyes hit the sky, and they blinked in the light.

Moonbeam looked up and down the far bank, searching through the sunlight for his log. It was still there, just where he left it. It shone out in the sun, waiting, it seemed, waiting for his return. "My log," he whispered softly.

Suddenly Opossum sprang awake with such force and strength that it seemed as if he had leaped through an opening about to close. All of which added to the feeling he had really been somewhere else—a long way off. The other all jumped back, and it was a few moments before they showed their happiness that Opossum was alive and well. And it was true that Opossum felt as if he had burst through some layer of reality like a flowering bulb. Indeed, he had found out something new about himself and about all Opossums, though he didn't know that yet. He was surprised to find himself surrounded by Moonbeam, Groundhog, Otter, and a family of strange animals he had never seen before, and surprised too to find that as he sprang awake, he shook off a mass of leaves and grasses under which he had been buried. He remembered the hunter well enough. He remembered the gaping jaws and jagged teeth. He even remembered the wild and strong smell. He gave a startled look around and an odd gurgle then exclaimed, "Did I faint?" in a surprised voice.

If Opossum had fainted, he couldn't imagine how he was alive now. He had seen the flame of hunger in those dark yellow eyes. He had seen it. He had stared deep down into the center—deep down like looking down a well—then everything had gone black. It seemed as if he had fallen into that well, and it had no bottom and went on forever and ever, but somehow ended here in this pile of leaves surrounded by friends and strangers. "I feel as though I have been cuddled down somewhere, in some core of myself, some secret center, warm and cozy and far from this world," Opossum said with a shiver.

"It is an old trick," muttered the Father Beaver, still munching on his Willow twig, "and it is not changed by the time of year or the light, I am told, though I have only seen it once before and then by moonlight. They say the moon changes all things. I had not really thought it happened by day."

"Well, it was day, dawn anyway," said Groundhog, looking at Opossum as if Opossum was no longer the Opossum he knew. It made Groundhog sad in a way although he didn't know why.

Opossum shivered again. He sensed everything had changed. He looked at Raccoon with anxious eyes. "How thrilled I am to see you again!" he said lovingly, "but I knew you were here. I have smelt you for a long time. Was I asleep?"

"We were wondering that," said Moonbeam, eyeing Opossum up and down and then giving him a big hug.

"And?" said Opossum quickly, tensing his legs.

"We think you were not," said Moonbeam with a broad smile that showed more than a little pride in his friend Opossum.

"Oh!" said Opossum, surprised but somewhat glum. He didn't like change, and he sensed change all around him, in their eyes, in their faces, in their smells, and in himself. The Five Worlds seemed large and cold, strange and comfortless.

"Well, but I have not seen it for so long," murmured the Beaver seriously, still staring at Opossum and still chewing his twig. "Is this your first time?" he asked Opossum.

Opossum felt a wave of cold panic run through him. "So long! First time!" he said to himself fearfully, biting his lips. What had happened?

"Well is it?" asked Groundhog breathlessly.

"Yes! No! I mean I don't know what you're talking about. I've never met an animal like that before." Opossum crouched down and leaned forward. He looked as if he was going to run for it.

"We aren't talking about the Lynx," said Beaver, shaking his head. "Is this the first time you've ever played dead?"

"Played dead!" cried Opossum. "I did no such thing! I was full of fear—from head to tail. I fainted. I'm surprised that that animal didn't eat me!"

Beaver laughed loudly. "Lynx likes to catch his food himself; he won't touch what's already dead; that is, unless snow is thick on the ground and food really hard to find, which here by the waterside that only ever happens in midwinter."

"And you did look dead!" exclaimed Groundhog to Opossum, with a nervous grin. "Raccoon here says your heart slowed down and you were hardly breathing. It reminds me of my own sluggishness before those winter-sleeps of mine."

"It is not unlike that," said Beaver slowly. "Perhaps it is very much like that."

Opossum pursed his lips and frowned. "But I didn't do it on purpose," he exclaimed. Light flooded through the trees and hurt his eyes. The woods seemed to be opening up all around him.

"Perhaps not on purpose Pos, but Opossum-like. Opossums do it, Beaver says," said Moonbeam with a wink.

"I don't believe I've ever seen anything so clever!" cried Otter, jumping around Opossum with eyes full of pleasure. He saw Opossum now in a whole new light. He had even forgotten that Opossum didn't like to slide.

"I have heard something about 'playing dead'," said Opossum with a nod, "but I have never seen it. I thought I would know when it happened. I thought it would be different."

"But it would not look real if you knew, if you only acted it," said Beaver, "It is Nature not Art."

"I would say it is magic!" cried Groundhog, grasping Opossum round the shoulders, "Inner magic!" Opossum remembered his own thoughts about magic, and whether it worked from the outside in or the inside out.

"Well, and Nature is magical," said Beaver thoughtfully. "It works with all of magic's marvel, and all of its colour and drama, all of its mystery and surprise—the birth of the Butterfly, the opening of the egg, the green of Spring, the beauty of the ice crystal. I have seen them all—every one, every miracle."

# Chapter FIFTEEN
## Night Shadows

*They stayed a day and a* night and yet another day with the Beaver family, listening to all the Beaver stories of the pond and The Forest beyond. And it was hard to remember when they had heard such wonderful stories. For the Beavers had stored up many stories over the Winters and knew how to tell them with colour and dramatic pauses that chilled the night. They were nothing like the stories of the Otter-Folk, which were always filled with play and laughter and much diving and rolling. These were instead stories of building and growth, danger and loss, and the deep joys of Home. In the end, no one could say where Nature ended and Art began in Beaver life.

The final goodbyes on the other side of the pond were simple and quick. At dusk, the Beavers could think of little else but logs. Their bodies became twitchy with excitement, their eyes became glazed and their noses sniffy. Soon the sweet smell of Willow on the breeze beckoned from the west end of Green Island. It wafted across the water from what they called Lone Island and what Otter called The Island of Dawn. For it was there, he said, he first saw the dawn; the light sifted its way through the Willow branches like silver Thistledown. The Beavers said their goodbyes and cried out pleasant things always a few paces further west and soon they disappeared round the corner.

The swim back to the mainland and The Great Dark Forest was easier for all of them this time. There was no rain and the sky was clear and full of stars. It looked like a gem-covered canopy, fringed with the red of sunset. Otter led the way, streaming out across the water, his head shining in the twilight. Soon his chirps and chatter and echoing calls were rewarded by a circle of Otter-Folk. They swam toward him from each direction, rolling and diving and cresting the water as they came. Moonbeam, who had never seen Otters swimming before, was stunned as he sped forward with his log, which he now shared with Opossum and Groundhog.

On the far side, the Great Dark Forest brooded high above at the top of a cliff, and the land running from the bottom of the cliff to the water was covered with small, grassy hills and dells. It smelt sweet and spicy too, and would soon be covered with wildflowers. Water Lilies might even spring up along the banks. This was a favorite place of the Otters, and they called it Green Water Glade. For it was here in early Spring that they came from all around to bask and slide, and play and feast. And it was here, under these banks, that they liked to build their dens and cuddle down to sleep with their arms around each other as do their kind.

Otter went with them across Green Water Glade to the bottom of the high cliffs. "I never climb those cliffs," he said, amazed again by their height. "If you follow Water Glade to the east along the bottom of the cliff, you will find a sort of stairway in the rock. It was made long ago by Forest Creatures traveling up and down to bathe and drink. It is a long stair. I am told it ends in a part of The Forest called Dreamer's Elbow. From there, I suspect, you will want to go east and keep close to the water." He frowned deeply. All the laughter had gone from his voice. He found this part of the Forest upsetting and he was sad to leave his friends. Like all Otter-Folk, he loved his friends. They and the water were his greatest joys.

Groundhog looked up anxiously. The last light of day lingered on the cliffs and the trees along the top. Water Glade and the water behind were in deep shadow. But gradually the moon appeared above The Forest and, luckily, it was a full one that flooded the land all around them with pure, white light.

"But is that the same Forest where we met you?" asked Opossum, pointing up. This Forest looked very different to him.

"Yes, the very same!" said Otter, "though this part is less well known by my kind. We have no reason to go there. Green Water Glade fulfills all our needs; it is the most lovely place there is!"

Opossum stared upward. Somehow the Forest seemed now both more dangerous and less frightening. After all, he knew about danger now, and he knew that The Forest was full of danger, but he also thought he could deal with most of it. Hadn't his talents turned out to be much, much greater than he had ever expected?! He had found out he could swim for quite a long time, find long-lost friends—friends he never thought he would see again—and escape a Lynx by playing dead! And Beaver said there was no other creature he knew in all The Five Worlds who could do that! In fact, he had discovered he was rather special, and now he thought he wouldn't want to be anyone but Opossum—not for anything!

It was some time later when the moon was high above the trees and glistening on the water behind that they said their goodbyes and gave their hearty thanks to Otter. They did so with many hugs and handshakes and gulping back of tears. Friends, after all, are not so easy to find, and The Great Dark Forest did not seem to promise any! And Moonbeam had to leave his precious log. Now smooth and bleached pure white, it shone in the grass.

In the moonlight, the stair at the east end of the cliffs was easy to find. It swept steeply upward, overhung on both sides by tree branches and weeds. The steps were a little high for them and pulling themselves up was hard work.

"This stairway must have been made by larger animals than us!" muttered Opossum, but without his usual tone of irritation.

"Who could they be?" asked Groundhog, glancing around with dark eyes full of shadows.

"Deer for one," said Moonbeam calmly, "and that Lynx for another." He thought too of the Fox, of Men and Dogs, and of Shadow-Black, and as he thought about these things he heard a rustling sound a little ahead of them and then the sound of hooves on the stairs. The three travelers stopped still and glanced at each other. The hooves clattered on the rock.

"Deer!" Moonbeam nodded. "Coming down! Step aside quickly! It sounds like a large herd!"

They pulled themselves into the cliff on the dark side. Groundhog even found a comfortable hollow for his back. How beautiful the Deer looked in the moonlight as they streamed down the stairway, their antlers silver, their eyes gleaming! And who could say of what they hoped as they whispered to each other about the rich green of Green Glade and the clear water beyond? Moonbeam thought he caught the word 'Silversheen' on dark lips. It sounded like a breeze rustling through Lilies. "Have you been there?" Moonbeam blurted out suddenly, jumping in the path of the dark-lipped Deer.

"Where?" the Deer asked looking down at Moonbeam, but still walking on.

"To Silversheen!" Moonbeam said excitedly.

"Our kind may go there. Yes, I have been there."

It was the first 'yes' Moonbeam, Opossum, and Groundhog had heard, and their hearts jumped into their throats. But the word 'may' bothered them. "Do you need permission? Is there some kind of rule?" Moonbeam asked slowly.

"An ancient rule though I don't know what it is. I only know my kind may go there," the Deer answered unsurely.

"And is it beautiful?" Moonbeam cried out, clasping his hands.

"Very, very beautiful," the Deer answered with dreamy eyes, "but the banks beyond are even more beautiful. They are greener than here; the trees are taller; the dew is sweeter. Day's first light floods that undergrowth while this is still in darkness. But we shall never go there! It is too far to swim; the water is deep and wide; in the South it goes on forever."

"Will you go to Silversheen again soon?" asked Moonbeam.

"Soon. In the Spring. In Winter it is too cold, the wind howls across the water, the water beats the shore. In Winter we go to Green Water Glade," the Deer answered. Then the Deer clattered on downward. And once they had all passed, Moonbeam, Opossum, and Groundhog began to climb upward again.

"But which way is it to Silversheen?" Moonbeam called down after them.

"East from Dreamer's Elbow. Downhill, uphill, over the top!" a voice called back. "But do not take the ancient trail of Shadow-Black, trod by his Grandfather and Great-Grandfather before him!"

It was a tiring climb for them, and even though the night was cool, they sweated and panted and had to stop often to catch their breath and cool off. Dreamer's Elbow jutted out over the white cliffs, giving a clear view of Green Water Glade. Dreamer's Elbow was a wide, sweet-smelling glade of short grasses. Moonlight flooded brightly in there and caught on the dew and on The Forest edge, which stood darkly around the glade in an even curve. In fact, the glade looked almost like a silver lake, except that it was crossed by trails that came uphill from the west and went downhill in the east.

Moonbeam stared at these trails. They were not at all alike. One was wide and grassy. Another was heavily traveled and covered with roots that were shiny and smooth and well weathered. And yet another was narrow and winding like a Skunk trail. And then not far from this was yet another, which was wide and well worn and marked by sleeping areas along its sides, or so it seemed.

"Which way do we choose?" asked Opossum, quite bewildered. He sniffed strongly, and he thought he smelt Spring on the night air. He thought he smelt trees full of swollen, red tips that would one day burst into leaves and blossoms. Why one more day or two of warm weather and all this will break out in beauty, he thought, and a tide of energy ran through him. "If we hurry, we might meet Spring on the banks of Silversheen," he exclaimed with wide eyes.

Moonbeam nodded.

They chose the Skunk-type trail because it seemed the safest and crossed the glade toward The Forest in the West. The glade was full of sounds in the night silence, and the air was full of the smells of creatures, for creatures of every kind traveled back and forth to the water below all night long. Sometimes as they walked they heard snatches of conversation rustling through the grasses or murmuring overhead like leaves shivering in the wind.

"Forest Creatures," Moonbeam whispered. "Voles and Ferrets, Nightjars and Nightingales!"

The Forest on this side of Dreamer's Elbow was dense and dark—so much so that the ground lay in deep shadow even at noontime. To follow the trail, they scrambled over logs and across deep dells, pushed their way through thickets and waded over streams, climbed up rough rocks and ran across open, light-filled glades. They slept in caves and tree-hollows, in tight bank-tunnels by steam-beds and under thick roots. They ate and drank on the run and didn't bother to shelter from the rain unless it was so heavy that they couldn't see ahead of them. Night after night came and The Forest just went on and on and on before them, downhill, always downhill.

By day they found their way by the sun and by night by the moon and stars. Opossum would stare at the stars with blinking eyes. How much he loved them! And how much he still wondered about them as he had long ago near Whiteoaks. He knew something more about the Five Worlds since then, but nothing more about the stars except, perhaps, their patterns. Those he had learned to know and find. By those he now could tell his way.

Eventually they had to leave the Skunk-like trail because it curved into the north. They found another, well worn and narrow but much less winding. It was old too like the Skunk trail and disappeared in places altogether, to pop up unexpectedly on the other side of a hill or steam. "This is not easy to follow, but it helps us avoid all that tall undergrowth and briars. It would be awful to have to find our way through all that!" exclaimed Moonbeam.

"I should say!" cried Opossum, who could think of nothing worse than having his nose and stomach scratched by sharp sticks and thorns.

"Shush—," whispered Groundhog. "What's that strange noise?"

"Isn't that hooves? Don't you hear hooves thundering in the distance?" said Opossum, twitching his ears.

They all stopped and listened. Moonbeam put his ear to the ground, and a long way off he could hear the muffled thud of hooves. "Deer in flight!" he exclaimed, flashing his eyes from side to side, searching The Forest beyond for any sign of danger. "Come!" He ran to a hollow Oak tree and scrambled up inside. Opossum followed, sniffing loudly, his mouth dry with fear. They grabbed Groundhog by the wrists and swung him up after them.

Inside it was musty and damp. They slipped on the wood, which had been polished smooth by years on years of sleeping Forest Creatures. "Shadow-Black! It's Shadow-Black, the Night Walker!" a voice cried out in the darkness, and outside the whole Forest sounded as if it had come alive. Every creature that lived there seemed to be running, running northward, scrambling up into the trees and through The Forest to Water Glade. The Deer came around the corner like the wind and thundered across the grass. On their heels ran the Mink, the Weasel, and even the Fox. Then silence suddenly fell, stretched like a skin over everything, even over the trees, the breeze and the falling night dew.

And Shadow-Black's footsteps came as they were sure to come, after his name was cried. For no animal cries his name by day or night who has not seen him, has not heard him, has not smelt him. In all The Five Worlds, the name of Shadow-Black is used with care. He appeared on the edge of The Forest, frosted by the moon, with eyes that somehow did not catch the light. The three travelers held their breath as he shuffled toward them across the silver grass. They had never heard the sound of such footsteps before—low and closely placed, yet strong and firm. They remembered Black-Tip's words—a black shape against the moon only, with dark night-eyes and prints almost as large as Groundhog and claws as long as Willow leaves. Taller than the men they saw at The Great House, Moonbeam thought with a shiver. They heard the slap of a paw against the bark of a tree, and the low, tearing sound of claws drawn deep across the wood.

Moonbeam drew closer to his two friends until all three were pressed together, and each could hear the beating of the other two's hearts.

Then, suddenly, the smell of a large and powerful animal filled the hollow where they were, and claws dug deep into the bark just a little below them. The whole tree shook. Every branch rattled. Moonbeam, Opossum, and Groundhog pulled back from the opening and pressed themselves against the back wall. But there the floor was old and flaky and could not bear their weight. They found themselves falling through it, and the more they tried to scramble back up, the more the wood broke loose in their fingers. Outside they heard a long, low growl that echoed through the trees.

Moonbeam, Opossum, and Groundhog hung there, gripping the wood above until their fingers were sore and nails torn. They dared not even breathe. Then, finally and suddenly, the floor above gave way all across with an echoing crack! And they fell down and down, head over heels, wood chips flying, to land in a heap on top of each other at the bottom of the Oak tree. "Whatever you do, don't move!" whispered Moonbeam, trying to blink dust out of his eyes and hoping that he wouldn't sneeze.

Everything fell silent again, though Moonbeam knew Shadow-Black was still there listening, probably startled by all the noise in the tree. He rolled his eyes upward and saw a touch of moonlight on the edge of the hole they had come in. It was a long, long way above them. In fact, now that he saw how far above, he was very surprised that he had fallen so far without breaking any bones. He looked at the other two anxiously. Opossum looked shocked but not in pain and Groundhog, who blinked and peered as he tried to see his surroundings in the dark, looked oddly calm, just as he had looked before they crossed The Great Dark Forest Bridge.

There was a long, thin slit in the tree trunk on one side through which came rich forest smells and just a reed of silver light. Moonbeam, silently and slowly, crawled toward it and placed one eye against it. He saw nothing but grass and undergrowth and another gnarled Oak nearby. Everything shone with dew, so fresh and full it made Moonbeam thirsty. He ran his tongue along his lips. "I cannot see him!" he whispered so softly that the other two could hardly hear.

Opossum leaned across him and sniffed. His eyes rolled in fear. On the night air, cool and damp, he smelt the same smell—strange and powerful. It filled his nose and made him cough. He remembered something faintly like it, a whiff somewhere on the evening breeze, but he couldn't remember where or how long ago.

Moonbeam could tell from Opossum's eyes and nose that he had smelt Shadow-Black and indeed, Moonbeam could smell him now quite strongly. He must be just around the other side of this trunk, he thought with a frown. He knew that Shadow-Black, like all Night-Creatures, would be able to hear the slightest sound, and so he pushed himself down into the earth and roots underneath him. He felt sure the ground would muffle his breathing, and Opossum and Groundhog must have thought so too for they did the same.

Their first glance of Shadow-Black through the chink in the tree trunk was startling. The moonlight hit his face suddenly as he came round the corner. It flooded over a broad nose with dark pitted nostrils, and then on over a huge head with ears that jutted sideways from a wide forehead. Behind followed a wide and powerful body, arching deeply at the back into thick, furry legs. Moonbeam shuddered as light caught those long, front claws. They were indeed as long as Willow leaves!

"Who travels my ancient trail, trod down by my Grandfather and Great-Grandfather before me?" growled Shadow-Black, placing his forefeet firmly beneath him and stretching his great head upward.

Moonbeam, Opossum, and Groundhog looked at each other, startled, and did not try to answer. What could they say? They did not think that they were on his trail, but the trail had wound about in such a way that they may well have crossed it without knowing it, but they felt Shadow-Black would not listen to their excuses and so they pressed down further and tried to muffle even the sound of their own breathing.

"None of The Forest comes this way! Neither the Bobcat nor the Mink dare follow my trail. The Fox slinks along its borders. The Wild Boar has moved further south. The silent, stalking Lynx has long gone north to chase the hare in the snow. Do you alone return after all these years?" Shadow-Black growled.

"Yes, I return to Eagle Bridge, the Home of my ancestors," a proud voice answered firmly from overhead.

Moonbeam stared at Opossum and Groundhog in surprise. Then it was not them that Shadow-Black had spoken to. Perhaps he did not even know that they were in the hollow tree at his side. Moonbeam hoped so, peering out again. He looked overhead for a shape to go with that firm voice, but he could see nothing but deep sky and the full moon.

"I have heard stories about Eagle Bridge," Shadow-Black said gruffly, swatting the air with a large paw, "but this is not the way! It rests in the Spring bed of the moon." He pointed out south across The Forest.

"But we never fly that way!" the answer came, with a rustle of unfolding and folding wings, and Moonbeam suddenly saw a shape open and close against the light. "Besides, I do not travel on the forest floor. I do not travel on the trail of your ancestors. You may be lord of The Forest, but I am lord of The Skies. This is my realm. Here all feel my power!"

Shadow-Black laughed mockingly and slapped his upheld paw against the earth. "My domain stretches as far as your eyes can see! I own The Sky also! My trail rises upward between The Forest trees, higher and higher, until it touches the moon herself!"

"I have seen you in The River powerfully swimming; I have seen you high in the trees searching for honey and fruit and the rich, inner layer under the bark; but I have never seen you in The Sky. Here you have no power, you have no rule!" answered the other.

"There are stars formed in my shape," answered Shadow-Black, rising up and standing on his back legs with his front feet held high in the air. "No Eagle's form rests in the stars."

At the word 'eagle' Moonbeam was filled with excitement. He remembered Ringtail's marvelous Eagle stories, and he remembered now how he had been told that the Eagle's massive nest of sticks was just beyond Moonlight Inlet on that spit of land called Eagle Bridge—a spit of land that no-one he knew had ever seen. Yet there were some who said they had seen The Bald Eagle, as he was called, high above, a speck of darkness in the sky. And now Moonbeam himself was one of those lucky few. For above, a black shape against the moonlight with broad shoulders and dipping tail, The Eagle sat, majestic and calm.

"Oh yes, we are there too and have been since the beginning The Five Worlds! Our wings stretch out to embrace the sky!" Eagle answered quickly. "But we should not quarrel now. We do not ever travel the ground and it is long since we crossed this way, and then but once before Spring and once before Winter. Your kind, anyway, have never liked Eagle Bridge.

Shadow-Black growled irritably and, lowering his body back to the ground, prowled to Eagle. He stared above, blinking in the moonlight. "In Winter it is cold and thick with snow; in Summer it is hot and has not enough deep shade," he said slowly.

Now Opossum and Moonbeam saw Shadow-Black's dark eyes glinting. They were small and round, and there was in them a puzzled look as well as a look of respect. The same look of respect that all the other creatures gave Shadow-Black. "Besides," Shadow-Black went on after a long pause, "Hollow Sky is not far beyond." He said this with almost the same tone of anxiety as the Bridge Raccoons, although he tried to look calm and dipped his head and swung one huge paw forward.

"There is no Hollow Sky!" exclaimed The Eagle proudly, stretching out his snowy head, opening his curved beak, and lifting a gnarled foot. His long claws caught the light like sparks. "The world goes on forever and ever. Whichever way you fly, it is there below you—rich browns and greens; sparkling blue waters and the white of snow; swaying fields full of Mice and Voles; trees full to overflowing with leaves and fruit; Birds and Butterflies and Honey Bees; hilly pastures bright with wildflowers and insects; cloud-capped mountains climbed round by Mountain Goats and deep, mossy grasses; Pines that touch the sky; and skies that lie, flat and blue, on the back of the sea!"

Shadow-Black panted at the Eagle's rapid flow of words. How much he had seen and yet how much there was to see! The flame of adventure caught fire in his eyes—a gold glow beside the silver from the moon.

Islands that drift in mighty rivers; Rivers that spill into swirling seas, full of glistening fish that jump in the sunlight; the Sunlight that turns the waves gold at dawn.

Moonbeam's heart raced. Speak of Silversheen! he cried inwardly. Longing overwhelmed him. Restlessness raced through his fingers, it tingled in his fingertips, it spilled out into the night. Silence fell suddenly in The Forest. The Eagle turned, leaned forward, and peered. His pale-yellow eyes narrowed. And eyes, which could see the small Mole on the hillside as he soared through the skies, saw Moonbeam's dark eyes through that slit in the tree trunk. Shadow-Black's eyes darted that way too and fastened on his. They were full of fire.

Shadow-Black sniffed. The Eagle tilted his yellow beak. Opossum grabbed Moonbeam's arm and pulled him back from the crack. Moonbeam didn't understand how they suddenly knew he was there. He had not spoken out loud, and he had not moved. Though it was true he had changed quite suddenly inside and that change seemed to have welled out of him onto the night air. In fact, everything looked different to him now. The hollow he lay in seemed hotter and smaller and the moonlight outside looked more beautiful, more inviting than ever before.

"They have seen you!" Opossum whispered, alarmed as usual by Moonbeam's dreamy stare. It always made Opossum wonder if Moonbeam really knew what was going on.

"Then we had best run for it!" said Groundhog, searching in the dark for tunnels and doorways.

"But we are safe in here. They cannot get in here. They are too big," Moonbeam answered slowly, still staring at the sliver of moonlight that came through the crack. How he longed to get out of the tree, cross The Forest and find Silversheen!

Then unexpectedly a large paw slapped the trunk and the slap echoed all the way down to where they lay. It seemed to ring and ring in their ears, closing in on them in ever-tighter circles. When the sound died away, they heard claws drawn deep against the tree layer under the bark, tearing the bark away. Then they heard the bark whiz through the air and land in the undergrowth a long way off. "Who is it who listens to our moonlight talk? Who has given you permission to make a Home on my trail?" growled Shadow-Black.

There is no one there!" said the Eagle, opening his wings and plunging down to a lower and nearer branch. "It is the Spirit of the trees—The Spirit of the night."

Shadow-Black gave a gruff laugh and stretched his nose out in front of him. He sniffed again more loudly. "No, Eagle, you are wrong—how wrong! That is the smell of Raccoon. They live in the West by my Bridge, which they like to call their own when I'm not around. But who has the most power, I should like to know? Who stops who on that Bridge?" Shadow-Black asked, leaning forward and slapping the tree once again.

Opossum placed his hands over his ears and shook his head. The whole tree seemed to be ringing and moving.

"I do think we should try and get out," whispered Groundhog, reaching around, still searching for a way out.

Moonbeam frowned deeply. Pain flashed across his eyes. The warmth, the closeness, the dampness, and the ringing all made his poor head ache. He felt trapped and longed to be free—longed to see moonlight on his nose, longed to feel the breeze in his fur!

"I tell you, there is no one there!" said the Eagle with a sigh. "The smell is old, worn and faint—left from the past. Nights and nights ago a Raccoon may have slept there. He is not there now!"

Shadow-Black frowned. He didn't like Eagle's tone. Who, after all, knew more about tree-hollows? Who in all The Five Worlds knew more about them than he did? "Well I can prove it to you easily enough!" he exclaimed with a low growl. "I'll reach in and pull him out!!" He turned again, smiled oddly at the tree and began to climb up. The whole tree shook and rang, branches lurched and bark fell around on the ground below.

Moonbeam, Opossum, and Groundhog all ran around in a circle looking for a tunnel out. They scrambled and fell and ran into each other.

"Do you hear that?!" cried Shadow-Black, glancing at Eagle, but Eagle didn't answer.

"This way!" cried Opossum, pulling Moonbeam and Groundhog after him. "I've found something!" And the three travelers ducked down a dark opening just as Shadow-Black poked his face through the hole up above.

# Chapter SIXTEEN

## The Green Queen

*They were gone before* Shadow-Black had time to push a paw long and deep into the tree hollow, but they did hear his growl of disappointment and Eagle's pleased cackle.

It was a long, wide tunnel full of the smells of many animals, including those of the Fox and Snake. They moved carefully, glancing nervously round corners and peering deeply into sleeping rooms piled with dry grasses and slender twigs. They knew that the tunnel would end and open out back into The Forest because some of the sleeping rooms were for animals too large to have come in through the tree before floor fell from under them,

"Be quick! Be quick!" a reedy, twittering voice called and a long, slender, brown-backed Weasel flowed past them down a side tunnel. They were glad she was too busy to notice them, for the Weasel can be quarrelsome and a fierce fighter whether of The Meadow, The Woodlands, or The Forest.

Then, suddenly, they heard a rattling, and in a wide side room, deep with grass and fur, a Rattlesnake uncoiled and looked at them with angry, yellow eyes.

"RUN!" cried Opossum and, pushing Groundhog before them who could only just see but could smell each turn in the tunnel on the damp air, they passed the Rattlesnake at breakneck speed and disappeared around several corners before he had time to strike. In fact, anyway, these were lazy days for him. The weather was not warm enough for much adventure and he was content, between naps, to stare proudly at his beautiful new skin, richly patterned with dark diamonds outlined in gold.

Moonbeam, Opossum, and Groundhog smelt fresh air now, wafting past them full of forest smells and full of the smell of something quite wonderful, something they had all forgotten. "Berries!" cried Opossum gleefully. "I smell berries!"

They tumbled out into the open, one on top of the other, unable to stop running and surprised to find the tunnel end so suddenly. Before them was a moon-flooded glade, smaller and neater than Dreamer's Elbow and, across the middle, was a gurgling stream. Beside the stream sprawled trailing Bearberry with its mealy, red fruit. It was not Opossum's favorite, but it was nourishing, and he was hungry. Wintergreen grew not far away. The bright-red and fragrant winter-berries had all gone now, but Groundhog loved the taste of its leaves, especially in early Spring. Beneath, in the grass, were lovely Fairy-Ring Mushrooms with their hill-shaped caps and slender stems.

"This is quite a treat!" exclaimed Moonbeam, running forward and wading into the cool water to fish.

The glade was quiet and seemed quite magical to them. No breeze rustled the grass and no birdcalls filled The Forest behind. Even the gurgle of the stream was faint and distant like the memory of a stream in a dream. They fished and ate and sipped the water in silence—water that was lighter and more delicious than they had ever tasted before. It was in fact more like the dew mixed with nectar that they sipped from flower-cups in The Meadow by The Garden. It reminded them of Home, and yet, it reminded them that at Home they had dreamed of streams like this—streams of dew and nectar flooding down past berries and mushrooms and fragrant leaves.

"This place is very beautiful!" nodded Opossum, who seldom used that word and thought it suited Moonbeam's ideas better than his own. It was, he felt, a word that belonged to adventurers.

"Yes," said Moonbeam, looking around anxiously, and he suddenly realized how little they had been on guard and how dangerous their excitement over the stream and berries and juicy leaves had actually been. For sitting high above on a bowed tree limb was a tall, dark shape with raised shoulders and glistening white head. It seemed pointless to run, pointless to hide. The Eagle's amber eyes glared down at them, piercing through them and somehow, Moonbeam felt, reading his mind, seeing his ideas of The King of The River. He flattened himself to the ground with his front feet still in the water.

"You are still here then!" the Eagle said seriously, without even blinking.

Opossum jumped; his head snapped round; he leaned protectively over his precious berries. He was stunned by how huge Eagle was.

"Shadow-Black says this glade is his. He calls it Bear-Patch, and he does not like to share his Bearberries!" Eagle said with a stiff laugh. "You are not yet far from his ancient trail, you know!"

They had suspected that, and too the glade had a mystery about it as if it belonged to someone else—someone powerful, even magical.

Moonbeam cleared his throat. He feared the Eagle, especially out here in the open with moonlight around his feet—his own shadow like a dark twin beneath him. He wondered too why Eagle had pretended not to know they were in the hollow tree when he must have known all along. Moonbeam tried to hide his fear as best he could and strut his own shadow proudly. "We know we are not far from Shadow-Black's ancient trail, and we do not plan to stop here much longer. But what of you, brave Eagle? Is this your glade also? Is the trail your trail?"

The Eagle spread his wings full. Moonlight caught on the feather-tips like raindrops. "Eagle Bridge is my Home, and my trail crosses The Forest to the south, sweeping over trees and hills and streams in a way no ancient earth-trail ever could. And no one can follow my trail but my own kind; it is not marked; it is secret; it is invisible to all but The Bald Eagle."

The three travelers stared at Eagle. How wonderful such a trail must be! How full of magic! "Do you fly to The River, to Silversheen?" asked Moonbeam, knowing the answer but wishing to know more about the way, not only there but to Moonlight Inlet where he had dreamed of building his Banqueting Hall and giving great feasts.

"To the River! To my Home!" cried the Eagle, and his voice lifted up, high over the treetops, and his eyes again blazed out like fire. Then Moonbeam saw what he most feared.

"RUN!" cried Moonbeam. "RUN!"

The Eagle swung off the branch, his large feet circling forward, his claws splayed to catch the light like sparks. He parted his beak and gave a cackling cry that split the silence and echoed all around them. Moonbeam, Opossum, and Groundhog ran each in a different direction, but Groundhog slipped on his short legs in the dark at The Forest's edge and The Eagle dived down; his claws caught hold of the fur of Groundhog's brown back. But Groundhog leaped forward and, in a gigantic somersault that sent leaves and earth flying backwards in The Eagle's face, landed deep within the trees, rolled down a steep bank and ducked down a deep hole. There he calmed his breathing and pressed himself to the ground. Silence and darkness closed around him. He fell into a strange, unnatural sleep.

When Groundhog woke up, he didn't know how long he had been there— how many suns had risen. It seemed an age, and yet also, only the night before. He felt stiff and sluggish and feverish, and it was only after he had crawled from his hiding place into the dappled forest sunlight that he realized he was in pain. His whole back felt as if it was on fire. His legs ached. His head throbbed. His eyes were sore.

But then, suddenly, gentle warm hands closed round him and he was lifted and placed on a mossy bank. Cool spring water was held out to him in a cupped hand and he had no alternative but to drink. He was too ill to run or move and his fever made him unbearably hot and thirsty. He drank slowly, unsurely. Then he looked up.

"My Sun-Lover, what has happened to you?" Who tore your fur?" a soft voice asked, and he saw a lovely face with gentle blue eyes, framed by cascading auburn hair that touched his sides and trailed across his forehead—shielding him from the sunlight and, he felt, from any harm. He fell back into a deep and healing sleep.

Every day she came to him, bringing him water and grasses and roots, and every evening she carried him back to the hole where he had first hidden. She bathed his burning forehead in cool spring water and washed his wounds and wrapped them in he knew not what. But each day he felt a little stronger and in the morning he would greet her as she came over the dip in flowing green robes that billowed out behind her like Willow branches in the breeze.

"My Green Queen!" he called her, and he did not fear her. She smelt of wildflowers, of summer blossom, of delicate foods, and her eyes were always calm and had none of the flame of the hunter—none of the narrow cunning of Lynx and Eagle.

Then one morning she carried him to the stream, the same stream where he had been with Opossum and Raccoon, and she shielded him while he bathed and then ate the Wintergreen. It was sweeter now. The tips were longer and greener. And so he knew a long time had passed since he was there before. He looked around as he sat at her side, searching for signs of his friends. But he couldn't find any, not even a smell. In fact, the glade seemed different now. It smelled different. It was coloured differently. The moonlight and sunlight touched it differently. Spring was just round the corner—it might even come that night.

"You are stronger now," the Green Queen whispered, stroking his fur. "Your wounds are healed, and though I would like to take you with me, I must set you free to go to your own den, wherever that may be." Tears filled her eyes. The sun shone her auburn hair red. Groundhog felt strong now. Energy raced through his limbs when he was touched by the sun. His fever had gone. His head was clear. And so he knew, without a word, in a day or two she would not come again.

The first day he did not see her, he wandered around hopelessly. He munched the grass unhappily and drank from the stream while looking over each shoulder in fear.

But as he returned down the dip to his hole, a voice called out, "Groundhog, are you well now? We waited and waited!" He turned and saw Moonbeam and Opossum running toward him. They both looked thinner and their faces were drawn. The glow had gone from their eyes.

"We have been so worried!" Opossum exclaimed with a sob.

"The Green Queen came and took care of me!" Groundhog said, surprised by the world, surprised by all its mystery.

"Yes, we saw, and we waited," answered Moonbeam. "She was The Girl from The Garden—The Golden One—she comes from her world always bearing gifts to our world—this time the gift of healing. It is only her kind in all The Five Worlds who can heal others; we can only heal ourselves."

"And you are well now, aren't you?" asked Opossum anxiously.

"Yes," whispered Groundhog. "Yes, I am."

"We could not come before now," said Opossum tenderly, touching Groundhog's shoulder. "Shadow-Black comes here by night to eat and drink at the stream. We didn't want him to know where you were. We were afraid."

"But not of Her!" said Moonbeam breathlessly. "We watched Her, but we did not want to disturb Her. She knew how to look after you and make you well. She brought things with her—bottles of red and green that caught the light and glistened, bandages of pure white, as white as thistledown, covers of gold like warm wheat fields, and baskets piled high with fruit and roots and chocolate cookies which she left by The Forest edge. I wonder if she knew that we were here also, waiting and waiting and waiting for you?"

"Our prints are in the streambed!" whispered Opossum, in a surprised voice.

"I think she knew then!" said Moonbeam with wide eyes, and somehow that idea filled him with joy and took away all his worry. Energy raced through his body.

They stayed the next few days with Groundhog in his hole, but only went to the stream for water quickly at mid-morning. They feared being seen by Shadow-Black or leaving a scented trail behind for him to follow at night. Though they no longer feared Eagle, for Moonbeam, from high treetops, had seen him fly powerfully out, up and over, south of the morning sun and disappear. Moonbeam tried to remember the way as well as possible, for he remembered that Owl had said that was where he would find The King of The River. But it was not easy because the sky each day grew more busy. Herons flew east. Geese flocked by calling loudly. Then one evening, when the setting sun had turned the clouds above a shimmering orange, Swans flew over with their long necks stretched before them, their wings curving the sky, or so it seemed. Opossum blinked as he watched. "We should move on!" he said. "At each minute The Five Worlds is becoming Spring! Perhaps Silversheen is changing into Spring. Perhaps The King of The River changes."

"No, I believe not! The King of The River cannot change!" said Moonbeam without looking round and with eyes still staring at the Swans. "In the water on my log, I saw a Swan ahead of me, glistening. She seemed to beckon to me. These seem to do the same. You see where they fly?"

"Not in the way of Eagle!" said Opossum strongly.

"No, in their own way. Another invisible way used time after time by their own kind," said Moonbeam, with his eyes racing across the clouds. "Come! Come, let's go!" he cried. Groundhog smiled. He felt so well now—better than even before. He smelt Spring, excitement and adventure on the breeze, but he also smelt that wonderful smell of Creatures going to their Spring dens and nests at last after a long time! Like the Herons! Like the Swans!

"The world becomes Spring!" he cried, laughing.

And now where is my own Spring den? thought Opossum. The swans fly to theirs this way, and the Herons to the east. Shadow-Black stays here. The Eagle goes to Eagle Bridge. But us! What about us? "Where're our Spring dens?" he called out, not so much expecting an answer as surprised he didn't have one.

Why? His den in The Meadow below the Garden would certainly have been taken by another creature by now—probably a Skunk!

"My own den is in the future!" answered Moonbeam. He had never felt so sure he would stay on this far side of The Forest, never go back to The Garden by The Great House. He thought again of The Girl in Green. Had she really come and healed poor Groundhog, or was that just a dream—a vision of a better world? A dream they all shared. Though he remembered there had been tales about her, even in The Garden, that said she walked The Old Wharf Road and even went as far as The Great Dark Forest Bridge. Perhaps she walked to Dreamer's Elbow, then to this small, silver stream glade. Perhaps she came often to think alone, to watch the Herons fly overhead. Perhaps she walked to the River Silversheen, to Moonlight Inlet, to Eagle Bridge!

Moonbeam scurried around, searching for her footprints. But he couldn't find them. He listened for her voice, for its softness, sweet and light like wings, for her call—"My Moon-Eyes!" But he heard nothing. She had gone.

# Chapter SEVENTEEN
# Gifts of Dawn

**Moonbeam, Opossum,** and Groundhog did not follow any trails after the stream glade but went across The Forest in the direction of The Eagle's flight— South of the sun and South of the moon at sunset. And before long, in fact before a full two days had past, they stepped suddenly, unexpectedly, into a small valley with gently rolling sides and a gurgling stream across its center. At one end marsh grass grew, strong smelling and rustling in the breeze; at the other the water widened out around a narrow island, and there Swans at their journey's end silently floated. Moonbeam tried to talk to them, but they did not understand him and drew back in alarm, circling away to hide in the Bulrushes.

In the streambed were the prints of many animals. They thought they even saw Shadow-Black's print with his long claws. They swam across, this time without even talking about it. The water pulled them downstream into the island, and they had to push our strongly to get across the current. On the other side, wet and cold but lively, they talked about their adventures, and their ideas. Green Water Glade, Green Island, Muskrat, the Great Dark Forest Bridge—all seemed a long way away in another world. And The Green Queen, the Golden One, became more and more unreal—a magic Queen from the lands beyond Silversheen.

A Water Rat splashed his way out of the water onto the bank behind. They called out to him. They asked him about the valley. But he looked startled and sprang back into the water. A Field Mouse raced in front. The lush valley grass parted around him in waves. They cried "Good Evening!" and asked him what he knew about The Forest on this side of the valley. But he spun round and sped away, until all they saw was a dark line opening through the grass.

"What a strange valley!" said Opossum nervously. "No one wants to talk! They seem not to understand a word we say!"

"But any moment it will be Spring," said Groundhog. "Everyone is busy getting ready. There is no time to talk. There is so much to do."

"That is true," Moonbeam nodded seriously, "and the young must be protected from harm. All dens and nests, all tunnels and hollows must be hidden."

"But do they understand what we ask, or do they just not want to answer?" fretted Opossum. He had grown used to friendship and talk and he did not want to go back to his lonely, silent world.

"I do not think they understand any more," said Moonbeam softly. "Everything is separate now, separate and waiting—."

"Will they never understand again?" asked Opossum, unwinding his thin, pink tail.

"In Winter I think they will but not now," said Moonbeam slowly, unsurely. And did they talk in Winter either? Had he really heard their voices, he wondered, or was that all a dream, a Winter-dream?

They walked uphill to The Forest on that side of the valley. The lush grass rippled against their stomachs and sprayed dew on their noses. Lovely yellow and black Butterflies darted upwards, swerving from side to side, murmuring in strange voices. At The Forest edge, Squirrels scurried by busily, with eyes only for their own kind. Moonbeam, Opossum, and Groundhog ducked into the trees. The Forest swelled uphill gently before them. The undergrowth was full and wildflower buds waited everywhere to shake out their heads in rich perfume and colour. Spring would break out at any moment here, gilding everything with glory and freshness. They caught strong whiffs of it on the air and saw it waiting in everything they passed. The Forest had a strange dreamlike look as though time had stood still. They were overwhelmed by a curious inner longing that they even tasted in their mouths. They thought of berries and fruit, of nuts and roots, of green leaves reaching upward to the sun. And Moonbeam thought of fish—every kind of fish, but especially pink Crayfish in clear water—Crayfish as sweet and fresh as meadow grass. He thought too sometimes of magic trees, cascading upward to the silver moon, and the more he thought about them, the more sure he was that they existed somewhere—perhaps across The River where the Deer said the dew was sweeter and the grass greener.

The sky drew darker and darker as they walked. Thick clouds covered the moon and stars. And just before dawn, just after they entered a small, mossy clearing to drink from a small pool, it stormed. Thunder clapped loudly overhead and echoed through the trees. Lightning flashed across the sky, turning everything suddenly white as if in bright moonlight—brighter by far than any moonlight they had ever seen. They hid as best they could under some roots and moss while rain poured down in sheets. They had to shout to hear each other.

Later, when the storm died down, the sky was still covered with a sheet of grey clouds draped over everything, and they found that all The Forest smells, even their own, were washed away. They had no idea where they had entered the clearing or which was the right way out.

They sat glumly around the little pool, chewing their nails and fretting, and Moonbeam though often about Eagle—about the sorrow and pain he had caused them, and about the secret knowledge he had given them, which they had now lost.

"But how long must we wait here?! exclaimed Opossum, "This clearing is so drab and chilly!"

And that was true. The storm had left it very messy, branches and logs were scattered all around them, and a chill wind blew constantly from behind; it had a strange smell, strong and full.

"Is that mud or waterweeds?" asked Groundhog sniffing.

"Smells a little like fish to me!" said Opossum, turning to stare at Moonbeam.

Moonbeam sniffed. There was a slight hint of fish in the air. "I wonder," he said musingly, standing and walking round the clearing, tapping his forehead with a sharp finger. "I wonder—."

But before he had time to say more, Heron, squawking loudly, rose out of The Forest behind them and flew over the clearing on slow, high wings. "So that's it!" cried Moonbeam. "Come, let's follow the Heron east. We can find Eagle Way later when they sky is clear again!"

They ran. They ran and ran and ran; their eyes fixed on the sky overhead; the wind blowing through their fur. They rolled downhill and raced uphill, cartwheeled over dips and leaped out over holes. And the Herons flew on out, dipping and rising, calling and sailing through the air, their huge wings rising and falling like great blue waves.

How long they ran! On and on and on! So fast it seemed to them as if the world turned under their feet, traveling back toward the Garden, toward their past. Then The Forest opened out before them, dipping down and soaring up over a crest and, breathless and excited, they tumbled out into a different world. The air suddenly became warm, sweet and spicy, and blooming wildflowers flashed by beneath their feet—Bluebells, Wild Strawberry, Buttercups, Daisy, Forget-me-nots, Violets—in rich patches of colour circled by the new green of woodland Moss. Birdcalls filled the trees, Insects buzzed, Bees droned lazily, drunk on nectar that they smelt all around them. And then, when they had least expected it, they saw Laurel ridges again running beside them, but this time surrounded by white Lilies on slender stems. The world pulsed, The Forest danced. Energy surged through them, filling every corner of their bodies, making them aware of every sound, every smell, every colour. The stars came back, the moon, and then at dawn a clear, silver sky. The Herons blazed bright blue.

"It's Spring!" cried Groundhog, somersaulting and rolling in the damp grass. "Wonder of wonders! It's Spring! We have raced headlong into Spring!"

Opossum was thrilled and, with his head full of visions of warm nights, clear skies and delicious snacks, whirled round on his thin, pink toes as he ran. And Moonbeam? Well, Moonbeam was speechless with joy—a joy so great that he couldn't stop running and hardly realized that he had turned again into Eagle Way, South of the Sun, South of the Moon. He felt cool and smooth and free. He felt as if he flew over the grass. Spring had become a part of him, filling him with all its energy, all its joy, all its goodness. He had never felt more glad to be a Raccoon. Soon they left the Herons way behind, dipping east over the treetops into the sunrise. And soon Moonbeam had outrun his friends, and they were calling him, begging him to slow down, begging him to wait for them. He ran around the corner, their voices echoing behind him and, unable to believe what he saw before him, stopped suddenly, skidding in the grass.

Groundhog ran up behind, panting loudly with his pink tongue hanging out. "You—run—like—the—wind!" he said between pants. There was a gold gleam of admiration in his eyes.

"Gracious!" called out Opossum in a surprised voice. "I didn't know you could go so fast! How do you expect us to keep up?"

"Look out there!" whispered Moonbeam breathlessly. "Look!"

They followed the line of his finger and stared. Before them, stretching as far as their eyes could see, as silver as a winter moon, was The River.

"Silversheen!" whispered Moonbeam, stunned by its width and beauty, surprised it should be round this corner, surprised it too should be part of Spring—this Spring, his Spring!

Silversheen was bright silver and stretched out before them, on and on as far as the eye could see. Far, far away in the distance they thought they saw parts of a dark shoreline, swelling here and there in black hills, but they were not sure.

A lifetime away! thought Opossum with a gasp.

A dream away! thought Moonbeam sighing and remembering his cascading magic tree. And it seemed to him as if the whole Forest, The Creek, The Meadow, The Garden—The Five Worlds—would fit on the back of that wide River—wider, brighter, smoother and more lovely than he had ever dreamed.

They climbed very slowly down the bank to the beach below and walked very softly to the water's edge as if one noise, one word would cause the River to disappear like magic. Here the water was full of gentle colour, rimmed with silver, and lapped smoothly on a white, sandy shore. Each ripple spread out to catch the light like a transparent Dragonfly wing in the sun. Moonbeam leaned forward and touched the water, half afraid of its beauty and with the same care he touched air bubbles on a creek which would pop unexpectedly beneath his fingers. The water was cold and smooth. It filled his hands with liquid silver.

"How Otter would love this!" exclaimed Groundhog in a whisper.

"And Beaver too, and Muskrat!" added Opossum, placing his front toes in the water and remembering how he never would have done that all that time ago in The Meadow by The Garden.

Soon they were laughing and playing and splashing each other like young Otters on a first swim. Their voices drifted out across the water, mellow and joyful, and the waves they made flashed gold and red in the sunrise and fell into their hands like brilliant gems.

"This is no time for playing; Shadow-Black may come down to drink, Eagle hunts at dawn, Ships set out upriver filling the sky with billowing white sails," a voice called out urgently behind them.

The three travelers turned. At the top of the bank stood a Raccoon. He was no longer young, there was grey in his fur, but his eyes were bright and wide, glittering with the colours of dawn. He looked surprised when he saw their faces and frowned slightly. "I don't think I've seen you before. Are you new to these parts?"

"New! Well, yes!" admitted Moonbeam slowly.

The Raccoon eyed him carefully. "You are not of The Bridge! That I can tell! You look more like—yet no, you wouldn't have come so far!" He climbed down the bank and paced across the sand to them. He was slim and agile, and Moonbeam could tell that this part of The River, this side of The Forest, seemed to him to belong to him.

"We have come a very long way!" said Opossum quickly.

"To see the River?" said the Raccoon softly with understanding. He stared deeply into their dark eyes.

"The River and The King of The River," said Moonbeam in a whisper. He felt somehow as if the Raccoon knew all this already, knew it the moment he looked into their eyes.

The Raccoon nodded slowly. "But for now come with me. There are many dangers in the world. When you leave Home in the evening you have no idea if you will return to the same comfy den next morning, or any morning." He looked up and down the beach. The sun now created a way of pure gold across the water. "But it is a fair enough swap," he added brightly. "The world is beautiful and our joys are great. Gift after gift tumbles around me, especially here by Silversheen."

"But where are you going?" asked Moonbeam anxiously.

"To Moonlight Inlet below Eagle Bridge. I have a den there—you wouldn't believe!"

It was not far to Moonlight Inlet. They ran down the beach and across a part of The Forest that jutted out into The River, and then across a small clearing rich with the smell of new green—new life. Then they scrambled down a sandy cliff full of holes and full of the buzzy voices of Bank Swallows and across a beach and up the other side.

"That's it! That's Moonlight Inlet!" panted the Raccoon, bounding over a hill and down a small, sandy cliff.

Moonlight Inlet swung in below them as smooth and silver as winter ice. A narrow, white beach circled round it. The sand was as soft as powder beneath their feet.

"That's my den!" the Raccoon grinned, pointing to a high cave roofed by deep grass and Buttercups.

It was a long climb up, but once inside they had to admit it was quite the coziest and most gracious den they had ever been in. The rooms were large with high, domed ceilings, the floors deep in green Moss, Thistledown, and flowers, and the walls—well the walls were out of this world. They were covered with hollows and shelves and perches and trinkets of every kind and colour! "Some from The River," the Raccoon exclaimed, pointing at his treasures proudly. "Wonderful things wash up right at my doorstep! In the Fall berries hang over my doorway, nuts and roots gather above on my roof, and in any season I can fish, fish in the night and bring my catch here to eat as I watch the sunrise!" The Raccoon tilted back his head and began to sing. His face was full of joy.

> "I watch the setting sun
> Float like liquid gold
> Among the curves of gentle hills
> And dapple snow-cloaked forests
> Shimmering pink.
> Like a dark Jackdaw I shall swoop down
> To scoop up that gold and store it here.
> I watch the hills
> Turn brown and grey then black
> Like bright-chested birds
> Folding drab wings
> For sleep.
> Like a gatherer of gems I shall dig down
> To scoop up that colour from underneath.
> Who knows how many seeds wait there
> To shake out their heads in rich perfume!
> Who knows how many Butterfly eggs wait there
> In a cool, damp place for another Spring!
> So I watch the blackness of Night descend
> As I leave my House for Silversheen."

And then The Raccoon showered them with tasty tidbits and began to tell them wonderful stories of The Forest and The River—of pirates and massive ships, of fairies and honey mead; of battles between the bears and wolves now long over, and of magic conch shells which gave one the power to see and hear the world on the far shore; of stars that touched the water and winter waves that swept away the beaches, Eagle Bridge and Moonlight Inlet; of the return of the Eagle and of the Arc of Light itself, shining silver and gold, fanning from shore to shore and traveled only by the courageous and adventurous; and of The King of The River flashing through the dawn in his blue robes!

Moonbeam gasped. This was like the banquets in his dream where they drank blackberry wine from fruit-skin cups and sung songs and told tales deep into the morning. "Swiftpaws!" he gasped. "You must be!—You are!"

# Chapter EIGHTEEN
## Beyond the Arc of Light

*It was a dusky evening* when the sky and The River lay back to back like silver twins, and it was a strange night-journey by an even stranger silver moon through a part of The Forest deep in marsh grass and shallow water and full of fiery Swamp Lilies—their flame-coloured heads stood like fairy torches along the waterside, marking their way. They thought they saw Shadow-Black's dark shape against the white sands of the beach. Swiftpaws pressed a finger to his lips and led them swiftly on towards Eagle Bridge. "Tread softly, Bears have sharp ears," he whispered.

"How many of his kind live here?" asked Moonbeam, glancing back.

"No one knows for sure," answered Swiftpaws anxiously. "More than used to be but less than at the beginning of The Five Worlds when The Bears shared The Forest with The Wolf and Wild Boar. They quarrelled all the time, or so stories tell, and they drove the woodland creatures out of Silentvale, though it was not called that then."

"Silentvale?" questioned Opossum, with wide eyes.

"A wide and beautiful valley to the West," Swiftpaws answered, nodding across The Forest behind them. "No one there has forgotten that time. They still live in fear and scurry about in silence, especially in Spring."

Moonbeam, Groundhog, and Opossum stared at each other. "Is that the nest of The Swans?" asked Groundhog surprised.

Swiftpaws turned. "Yes, they have returned I am told, but it is not a safe place for them. There is still danger."

"We came that way," whispered Moonbeam. Swiftpaws stared deep into his eyes, said nothing and hurried on.

"Now we must wade up-water. Bobcats live hereabouts, and Eagles nest the other side of those trees," whispered Swiftpaws, pointing out across the marsh. They followed a shallow channel hidden by tall reeds with blue-green leaves and silver plumes that hung over in an arch above their heads. The water was cold but wonderfully smooth. They sank quickly up to their elbows in soft mud. It squelched around Opossum's thin toes in a way that made him shiver.

The marsh and The Forest on either side were oddly silent and still. "Always a bad sign," whispered Swiftpaws, who knew that such silence surrounded the hunter. He looked about and overhead, lifting his feet high out of the water and placing them down squarely so that he made no noise.

Moonbeam looked around too, searching for those narrow eyes among the reeds and high in the sky. He would not be caught out again!

Then suddenly they heard a loud splash and echoing call. They stopped and stared at each other. Opossum gripped Moonbeam's arm. "It's just Eagle fishing along The River," Swiftpaws nodded. "He's too busy to bother with us now. He won't leave Eagle Bridge for many, many moons. His nest will take all his time to mend after such a long, hard Winter. I am told his eggs are shining white like stars."

Groundhog pulled down, his stomach touched the water. He did not like to talk about Eagle. He did not like to hear Eagle's cackling call.

Swiftpaws did not notice. "From my Home I have seen The Osprey too, with his legs stretched out into The River to catch fish, but he does not fish like The King of The River who dives so deep I believe he must touch the bottom with his crown!" Swiftpaws smiled with wonder.

They moved on slowly. The narrow channel opened out. They pulled themselves up onto the grass. A breeze drifted by full of the smells of flowers, green life, and fish. No night had ever smelt more beautiful. "Now we are the other side of Eagle Bridge," whispered Swiftpaws softly, "and this is the land of The King of The River. His realm stretches as far as your eyes can see."

It did not seem like a part of the real world. It was bright silver and marked here and there with flaming Lilies. Stars reflected in the water as if they had fallen there, fallen and drifted and settled against the shining pebbles like wildflower petals. And all around was peace, so deep and full it seemed like a special mag- ic—a magic that would have the power to protect all things, to create all things. A magic even greater than Spring.

Moonbeam followed Swiftpaws, but he no longer felt as if he followed. He felt rather as if he was being pulled forward by a mysterious force, a force that made him move ahead quickly. He began to almost run. Soon the others were no longer with him. He could not hear their steps on the grass. He could not see their shapes against the moon. Energy filled every limb. Excitement turned into joy. He raced on over the grass. He knew not where. Suddenly night broke, and silver dawn flooded the sky in the East. Silversheen was there again before him and by his side was a small inlet, deep in morning mists that rose and swirled around him, cloaking him in white and separating him from everything. He was completely alone.

And through that mist-made island he came to him. On out-stretched wings of brilliant blue, The King of The River glided and rolled out of the mist, hov- ered and rose high, flamed out and dived deep down into the water. He surfaced, folded and gleaming as if dipped in diamonds. He raised his crown of sapphire and jet, twirled and reeled away. His collar glistened silver-white like smooth crystals in a streambed. Then, whirled forward through the mist, he stopped briefly on a tree limb, dipped forward, spread his wings, glided and dived again. He fell into the water to rise again shining like the dawn. And all the space across the water, and even the water itself, seemed to belong to him, seemed like a place where he alone created beauty and brilliance in his flying. Moonbeam's heart beat fast within him.

And then The Fisher-King turned suddenly, swerved down and in a flash his dark eyes touched Moonbeam's through the swirling mist. They sparked with surprise and joy, but Moonbeam saw deep within the shine of desire, the shine of a future hope. Moonbeam was stunned. He could not believe what he saw. "Of what do you hope?" he cried out without meaning to. The Kingfisher smiled softly. The mist rolled over him. He swerved and sped away so quickly that Moonbeam could not believe he had ever been so close. His tail flared out behind. It was spotted with gems of pure white like falling snow. Moonbeam ran forward to the very edge of the water. He reached out with a dark hand. The peace deepened. The mists parted and lifted. Rain began to fall, filling every niche of the waterside with a strange but soft music. But what adventure could The King of The River hope for? he cried to himself. What could he of all the creatures in The Five Worlds long to discover or create? What adventure was beyond his misty realm of glistening water?

Moonbeam turned. The sky over The River was yellow. The edge of the sun floated on the water like a piece of ripe apple. Day had begun. Moonbeam ran along the bank toward The River, and there he paced up and down waiting and waiting in silence to see The King of The River again. He thought if he could only look just one more time into those dark eyes he would find out the answer—he would know what The King of The River hoped for, why every creature in The Five Worlds seemed to hope. Suddenly a voice called out to him from behind, "Look! See the Arc!"

Moonbeam swung round and stared. An arc of light fanned out across Silversheen in a perfect silver and gold curve The Beavers would have loved. He watched and waited, expected to see the dark shadows of the courageous climbing up and up and over to the magic world on the other side. A hand touched his shoulder. Moonbeam turned and looked into Swiftpaws' face. "I did not hear you come," he said, puzzled that he had known Swiftpaws was there with him.

"No, you seemed a long way off, almost in another world," Swiftpaws said gently, as if waking someone from a deep sleep.

"It seemed like another world. I saw—I saw—," Moonbeam's eyes blazed out. He looked about restlessly, searching for the right words to describe what he had seen.

"Later," said Swiftpaws, taking Moonbeam's hand. "We will talk about it later. It is day now and time to go Home."

Back in Swiftpaws' cozy cave, Opossum sat at the doorway and stared over The River. How he adored Moonlight Inlet! It was to him the most wonderful place he had ever known—surely the most wonderful place in all The Five Worlds! He explored every nook and cranny, every clearing and every tree. He counted out all the bushes that would bear berries, and he gathered flowers to decorate the shelves in Swiftpaws' rooms. And, when he slept, he saw The King of The River swirling toward him again through the mist, and he woke with his heart beating with happiness.

And Groundhog? Well, dear Groundhog rose each morning to greet the sun with somersaults on the beach. Spring swelled within him and surged down into his toes, and he dug tunnels above the cliff—wonderful tunnels, full of grass-soft rooms, with views of The River at dawn and dusk and with a special window looking out on Eagle Bridge. And he thought often of how The King of The River dug tunnels like him and lived like him beside the water. He vowed he would never, ever leave!

Meanwhile Moonbeam, full of joy and energy, explored the new world around him—the beach in front, The Forest behind, that spit of land called Eagle Bridge where he saw an Eagle's nest high above him, swinging in the treetops. Bears, Opossums, Bobcats, Mink, slender Weasels, pure white Ermines and even the Red Fox came by night to The River and then, in the dawn and dusk, he thought he saw Beavers, Muskrats, Deer, and far out, cresting the water, the flash of Otters. Butterflies drifted round Swiftpaws' doorway and high above The River glided Eagles, Ospreys, and Herons. And Swans floated on the back of the mighty Silversheen like Water Lilies in the wind. Then, in the dark before dawn, Moonbeam went often through the mist alone to the realm of The King of The River beyond the marsh. Sometimes he thought he saw him darting toward him and diving down into the water, veering away and calling from a distant bank. Then Moonbeam might wander to Silversheen on that side of Eagle Bridge and stare out to the other shore—dark here and there, swelling up into the dawn. He would close his eyes and imagine his magic tree at the center of that far world, silver and full of ripe fruit, and underneath was the deep grass The Deer longed to touch.

Spring pulsed on into Summer, and the world became full of young—fresh-sprung from their eggs and hollows and dens, to walk on wobbly legs and fly on unsure wings. Flowers bloomed on and on. Later the Laurels burst out in pink and white flowers like fairy goblets, and fiery Wood Lilies shot up through the Moss. Then poor Groundhog huffed and puffed at mid-day and had to sleep because of the heat, a heat so hot that Moonbeam and Swiftpaws found it hard to sleep by day and would sit and talk for ages and ages about everything under the sun, especially about The Garden they had left behind and The King of The River they had come here to see—of his blue beauty and brilliant flight, every pattern of which Moonbeam remembered with fascination and love. Then at night, restless but happy, they collected blue things to fill their shelves—dark blue Day-Flowers, the blue insides of a pebble, a powder-blue Butterfly wing found by chance, a small blue bottle washed up on the beach, and then later dusky Blueberries which Opossum could not help eating. Opossum admired collections now and loved all the colour and glossiness spread about Swiftpaws' rooms, but surely, he thought, they could never hope he would be content to just stare at berries and not eat them, even if they were blue!

"Well they are not magic berries!" Opossum would scorn. "Why shouldn't I eat them whenever I like?"

Moonbeam's mouth fell open. "They're not for eating, Pos! They are for colour—for decorations!"

Opossum sighed deeply and left the room, his pink tail trailing behind and then flicking out at the end as if to say, "I don't care!"

"Are there really magic shells that give you the power to see and hear the other shore?" asked Moonbeam whirling around, remembering Swiftpaws' stories.

"So stories tell. They say there is a magic shell, a special shell that is only where the magic is thick and full in the rivers of the Fisher-King. It gives you the power to see the very center of the world across Silversheen." Swiftpaws continued to rearrange all the blue things on the shelves. He added white flowers and pale shells.

"Where we were that night, you mean?" asked Moonbeam breathlessly.

"Yes, I believe so, but I've never found them," Swiftpaws frowned.

"You've looked!" Moonbeam said quickly.

"Oh yes, and I've dreamed," Swiftpaws left the room hastily, calling back something about supper, something about fish and mushrooms.

Moonbeam only half heard him and ran to the door. The night air was fresh and lovely. He could hear Groundhog snoring above; sound asleep in his new-dug Home. Moonbeam knew the way back to that silver inlet by heart. He crossed the marsh quickly, barely noticing the sounds around him. The night was full of noise—the Hunters were either not up yet or had gone elsewhere. He began to run as he always did once he had scrambled out of the water into the silver world of The King.

He ran and ran and ran headlong into the silver mist. It swirled around him, cloaking him in silver-white. Then silence fell suddenly as it always did, even his own footsteps sounded distant and muffled as if the footsteps of another Raccoon on a far-away hilltop. Moonbeam stopped at the inlet edge. He was panting and yet also full of energy. He searched with shining eyes along the banks for magic shells—shells that would let him see the center of that world on the other side of Silversheen. He ran down the inlet, entered every hollow, looked behind every tree. He found shining Moon shells and yellow Venus shells, Ark shells with their inner curtain of eyes, and glistening Gem shells. Graceful Angel Wing shells, tiny wheat-grain-sized Dove shells and bright Butter shells, long Pea-Pod shells whose creature can even bore into solid rock! But he found nothing he didn't already know, nothing that only lived here in the realm of The King of The River. He sat down, now somewhat tired, on the edge of Silversheen at the mouth of the inlet. The River was smooth, clear as winter ice. He lowered his head and drank. The water was cool and soft. He looked up suddenly, a wide smile on his dark lips. Straight before him on Silversheen he saw a ship. It was slim with white sails spread in the breeze, drifting slowly across the water. He squinted in the moonlight and stared. Suddenly, unexpectedly, he saw The Girl in Green. Her auburn hair streamed out behind her. Her green robes flowed over the bow like waves. She turned. She saw him. Where was she going? Why did she leave him? She waved. Her soft call, "My Moon Eyes?" drifted over the water to him.

"Golden One!" he called out. "Where are you going?" There was no answer; the ship sailed on further and further until just a speck on the horizon—a speck no bigger than a Swan. He stared. Something strange happened—the white speck beckoned to him as the Swan had all that time ago after he left Turtle. A layer of himself seemed to fall away. He jumped up and ran forward. "Wait for me!" he called loudly. "Wait for me!" And he had never been so sure he would cross Silversheen, perhaps not long from now, perhaps even next Spring!

He did not tell Groundhog and Opossum that the Girl had gone. He thought it would upset them. But he returned with a bright light in his eyes, a strange energy as though he was planning something, and a smile that came and went oddly as if he was remembering something quite wonderful. Groundhog thought he must have seen the King of The River again. Opossum thought he had found a cozy den full of trinkets, especially blue ones. But they both could not help noticing the return of Moonbeam's thoughtful stare and odd, distracted ways. Opossum nodded and pursed his lips. "Another adventure!" What kind of adventure, he wondered, and where would it all end this time?

And so Winter came, Winter with its biting cold and snow, its rain and sleet and howling winds. Silversheen crested on the shore in high waves that threw whole trees up on the beach and covered their windows with ice. And Moonbeam would stare through the ice; stare out across The River with eyes full of fire. "Wait for me!" he would whisper, and his breath would steam up the window. He slept much, and when he slept, warm and cozy, cuddled down among his friends, he dreamed of the lands beyond Silversheen—lands under the full moon, overflowing with fruits and nuts and fish and crayfish and, at its center, the Girl in Green sat under his magic tree, calling out to him. She carried creamy chocolate cookies in a gold chest set with jewels like raindrops, and when she opened the lid wider, a bright light sprang forth. It raced across The River and touched Eagle Bridge in an Arc of Light. The Eagle swirled into the air calling loudly. Moonbeam ran up to the light and touched it. Woodland creatures were crossing, crossing to the other side. He raced behind them calling out "Wait! Wait for me!" Owl circled up before him. "Who? Who are you?" he called.

"I'm Moonbeam of Moonlight Inlet!" he answered quickly, running on. "And I want to see the other side of Silversheen!" He jumped up, he woke. The wind howled overhead.

"It is just a dream," said Swiftpaws softly, sitting him back down. "It is a Winter dream."

Moonbeam stood again and paced to the window. He looked out. He felt full of excitement, full of longing, full of joy. He could not wait for Spring. In Spring he would find Her! In Spring he would see that other shore! In Spring he would see his magic tree!

"Wait! Wait for me!"

## *Finis*

ISBN 141202520-6